AVRIL SPENCEI

Searching...

Peace Publisher

ISBN 978-1-7393411-0-7

Printed and Bound by Catford Print Centre.

ACKNOWLEDGEMENTS

First and foremost I would like to thank God for giving me the gift and creativity to write this book.

I thank my husband Dennis who has believed in me and supported me throughout the writing of this book while I spent many hours on it.

I would like to thank my daughter Teresa for her practical suggestions to make improvements and guiding me through the technology to do the cover of the book.

I would also like to thank my sisters Janet and Brenda for reading the book and taking the time to carefully edit it, give feedback and encouragement also.

My thanks goes also to Alison Delaney an accomplished author who kindly gave her valuable time with general advice and guidance about the book publishing process.

I'm thankful to all my family and friends who have shown a genuine interest in my work and encouraged me along the way.

Finally, I thank all the staff from the professional agencies who have given helpful advice and direction to aid in the publication of this book.

Chapter 1

Karen was of mixed heritage. Her father hailed from Jamaica and her mother was native English. She was one of three children and was the middle child. She always felt the effects of 'middle child' syndrome and often felt overlooked by her parents.

Susan her elder sister by two years she always felt was her mother's favourite and Fiona who was three years younger, she believed was her dad's favourite. Where did she fit? She always felt a little left out. She was sure her parents didn't do it deliberately but her placid easy going personality never gave rise to any demands so they always thought that she was just fine. She behaved well and did everything that was expected of her. She knew her parents loved her but Susan shone in every way, bright, organised and focused. Fiona was the 'baby' of the family and she was beautiful, engaging and endearing. She felt she was none of those things but she needed to be loved too for who she was.

When she was fifteen, she met Pete. He took a 'shine to her' and gave her all the attention she needed and craved. It had happened so unexpectedly one day after school in the playground when he started chatting to her and they walked home from school together. That was the start of their friendship and every day they walked home from school together, spent lunch times together and generally hung out together. She was happy. Really happy!

She felt close to him, she could be herself with him, he shared everything with her and together they would make decisions about where to go and where to meet. There were times when she decided where to meet, what to eat and where to go and he was so easy and relaxed with her decisions. She started to grow in confidence and trust her own ability and instincts. He was good for her, she really liked his company. They shared everything, whether it was a sandwich, an ice cream or even helping each other with homework, it was perfect. It didn't matter that she wasn't anybody's favourite at home, she was Pete's favourite. For a whole year and more, they were just good friends and companions in every sense.

Their first kiss happened one afternoon about fifteen months into their friendship while they sat in the park on what had become 'their bench' eating their shared sandwiches and drinking their favourite orange fizzy drink. They were chatting as they usually did about everything and nothing. That's what was so special about their friendship, whether it was recalling something that had happened at school that day, teasing one another or having a serious discussion, there were no boundaries.

Suddenly without warning, Pete leaned forward kissed her gently on her lips and pulled away quickly. Before Karen had a chance to respond or say anything, he apologised and mumbled that he didn't know what had come over him they were good friends, nothing more. She smiled as he awkwardly chewed his lips.

'Do that again,' she said softly.

Chapter 2

'I'm pregnant,' Karen stated.

'What?' Pete replied in shock.

'What are we going do?' Karen asked simply.

'Hold on! Are you sure, how do you know?' Pete responded.

'I missed my period, I've done a test and it was positive. I'm scared Pete. I can't imagine how mum's going to react and my dad is going to kill me! Do you love me Pete?' Her face searching his while she waited for him to answer.

'Baby, of course I do, I just don't know what to say,' he looked away trying to process what he had just heard and trying to digest it all at once, thinking of the right thing to say, 'we're too young to be parents. You're just sixteen and I'm only seventeen. We can't provide for a child.'

'What are you saying Pete? We could get jobs, get a flat maybe...' she trailed off. She shrugged her shoulders unsure of what they could do, 'we would be a family.' She smiled feebly and reached for his hand. He held her hand for a few minutes in silence.

Pete suddenly released her hand and stood up and started to pace back and forth while Karen waited for a reply. He sat back on the bench his head bent low with his hands clenched together, 'c'mon, don't be silly, have you any idea how hard all that is going be?'

'But we love each other, isn't that enough?' Fear etched into her face with the realisation that this wasn't going as she expected.

She thought that Pete loved her, she felt confident of it. It was the hardest thing that she ever had to do, to walk into the chemist and ask for a pregnancy test. When she missed her period, she thought it was just late and never dreamed she could be pregnant. But as the days went by and her period never came, the possibility started to become real. For the first time, she hadn't felt able to share it with Pete straightaway! She wanted to be sure first and there was no one she could even talk to about it, no one even knew that she had a boyfriend.

Karen had briefly wondered whether to tell Susan but something stopped her. Susan just seemed to do everything right and Fiona was too young for all this. No, she had to do this by herself. When the test showed positive, she felt shock, disbelief, how could she have been so stupid to get herself in this situation? Why hadn't they taken precautions? They both knew the consequences, but somehow it never really got discussed. They'd never talked seriously about the future, they were young and enjoyed each other's company and had plenty of fun and laughter. *But she believed he would be there for her.* Pete was always so attentive; he told her how gorgeous her caramel skin and big brown eyes were and he loved the way her hair fell in perfectly formed ringlets. *This was not going well!*

'Karen, think about it, we've got no money, you're at school, I'm in sixth form. We've haven't got a choice, you'll have to get rid of it!' He stated matter of fact.

Karen couldn't believe what she was hearing. All of her senses reeling. *Of course she knew it wouldn't be easy, did he think she was stupid?* This was their baby conceived in love. She couldn't just destroy it like that!

Abortion was wrong! Wasn't it? That's what Grandma Rose always said. Grandma Rose was staunchly religious and attended church regularly. Karen and her sisters along with her parents had always gone to Easter and Christmas Services for Grandma Rose's sake.

Karen recalled some of the stories her dad had told her when he and his brother were little children and the 'look' they would get from Granny Rose if they even fidgeted while in church. Her upbringing, certainly from her father had bought a religious and moral influence and a very strong sense of what was right and wrong. All life was precious, even a spider that happened to find its way into the house had to be caught, quickly trapped in a glass jar with a piece of cardboard covering the top to prevent it escaping and it would be released into the garden. And flies weren't swatted; no, the window was opened until they found their way out. You didn't kill them. All life was important, from an unborn child to an old infirmed person, *right!* She knew from the Bible that one of the Ten Commandments was not to kill, and here was Pete telling her to murder their baby!

How could this be? Karen could not hear anything, she felt like she was in a daze. Her sobbing drowned out everything around her. As they sat on 'their bench' where many happy times had been spent, it seemed as though she was spinning even though she was sitting perfectly still.

She could hear him saying that he loved her but he just wasn't ready for this. If she had the abortion, then they could carry on just as before.   Nothing would change. *Everything had changed!* She screamed inside. That he would go with her for the termination, she wouldn't be alone. But Karen's heart had already started to break, her world was already shattered!

A woman and her baby in a pushchair walked passed. How ironic? Normally, she wouldn't even have noticed a mother and baby. But today she did. She suddenly felt very sad. Where was the Pete she loved and thought she knew? She never dreamt his reaction would be this way. *What a shock?* In that moment she realised, she was alone... Again!

Chapter 3

Karen was in the last stage of labour with her mum beside her. As she held her mum's hand tightly and pushed with all her strength, her baby boy was born.

It was exactly as Karen imagined it would be when she told her parents about her pregnancy. It was shock and disbelief from her mother and the disappointment on her father's face made her want to crawl under a stone. She was disgusted and upset with herself for bringing this situation on them. They had no idea that she even had a boyfriend. Karen had kept him to herself. She hadn't wanted to share him, he was hers and she was his. So this was a bombshell they were not expecting.

After all the tears from everyone, decisions had to be made. The house wasn't big enough for a baby and changes would have to be made. Karen shared a room with Fiona. There was no choice Karen would have to have Susan's room as it was bigger to accommodate her and the baby. Then of course, there was school, what did she want to do? Continue? Or leave? There would be childminding arrangements to make. Her dad Cecil was a lorry driver and her mum Marina also worked full time as a manager of a busy office which she loved. While the children were young, it had been hard but she had always enjoyed working and had been elated when she had got the promotion to office manager that she had always dreamed of. She wasn't ready to give that up and just be a grandmother, besides they still needed her income and even more so now with another mouth to feed. Karen and Marina had long talks over many evenings about what Karen wanted. Cecil was away most of the time with his job and there were times in the past when he wished it could be different. But with this shock news that his sixteen year daughter was pregnant by a boy that he never even knew existed, let alone even met, was hard to process. He was glad to be away.

Her parents were supportive and she loved them for it, but they made it clear that it had to be Karen that had the final say, if she kept the baby then Karen would have the main responsibility for the baby. They would help in the evenings and at weekends, financially there would be no problems, they would support her. If she decided to continue at school and further her education, they would help in finding childcare. All three of the children had been in nursery and Marina never really felt any guilt about that. They were safe and she had no qualms about the same for her grandchild.

Although Karen's parents had given practical solutions and were willing to support her, it was very clear to Karen how discouraged they were.

Karen's head was spinning about the future. Her parents had asked about the 'unknown' father. Who was he? How and where had she met him? Where had it happened? All of these questions, Karen did not want to answer. She had been so confident about Pete and his love for her, she just couldn't forgive him. He had hurt her deeply. *Why did he not understand why she couldn't have an abortion?* He had said repeatedly how much he loved her and if she could just reconsider, they could just get back to how they were. *How could he think that they could ever be the same?* Nothing would ever be the same.

Karen decided very early into her pregnancy that for her sake and the baby's it was best to get it adopted. She was still at school, just sixteen and Pete had disappeared from her life. The house wasn't big enough for an addition. *Was she being selfish?* At least she wasn't going to kill it. She had to be honest and admit she was scared of being a young single mum. The prospect was daunting! It was a massive responsibility and even though she had her family, she would still be alone raising a child. The thought frightened and overwhelmed her. It would be for the best, the baby would provide a childless couple with great happiness. There was no other choice. She comforted herself with that thought.

She told her parents of her decision, and they said they understood. They reasoned with her and reminded her of the possibility of regret in the future. But she had made her mind up.

The adoption process was something she was not prepared for, interviews, meetings and discussions. They had been great and the advice and support she received was incredible but she was struggling with it all. She felt like she was sinking into the depths of despair. Inside was emptiness and sadness beyond description. *How? Why?* Nothing made sense. She felt her head would explode.

She was told that at any time she could change her mind and keep her baby. And change her mind she did, endlessly. She played many scenarios in her head. The one she played the most and always made her cry was the scenario of herself and Pete and their baby living happily together forever. But that was never going to happen. Pete had shattered that dream. So she was left with the single mum scenario juggling a baby with school and college and living with sadness about how things had turned out. She wasn't sure how strong enough she was for that particular scenario. And then there was the adoption scenario where she knew the baby would go to parents that wanted it and she could get on with her life. *Simple!* But she was really not prepared for the rollercoaster of emotions that she would experience.

Going through the pregnancy all alone had been hard, much harder than she could ever have imagined. She was grieving for the child she knew she wasn't strong enough to keep and the man she loved and lost. *What a mess?* Soon it would be over and she could get on with her life. Or so she thought. Lessons learned and all that... She would be fine, that's what everyone kept telling her. Surprisingly, everyone was really kind, Susan was incredibly supportive and a new deeper bond was formed between them.

Pete had tried to ring her several times throughout those lonely months while she was waiting for her baby to be born, but she couldn't speak to him. The hurt and desolation was indescribable,

Karen felt real physical pain in her heart whenever she thought of the times she and Pete had spent locked in each other's arms in his single bed in his bedroom after school when his parents were at work. They had been tender moments that were beautiful and cherished.

She recalled it all: walking through the park, swinging high on the swings, chasing each other until they were out of breath, lying on the grass looking up at the sky, sharing food, telling jokes. So many memories...

If she couldn't keep her baby, then Pete had to go. They came as package or not at all.

Chapter 4

It was three months since she gave up her beautiful baby. Her body and its symptoms a cruel reminder of what she no longer had.

She decided not to go back to school, she just couldn't face it. It wasn't what her parents wanted but there was little resistance, they could see how fragile she was and decided to step back and let her do what she wanted.

Karen had no idea what she wanted to do and didn't much care if she was really honest. A position for a shop assistant came up in a chemist on the other side of the city, it was two buses away but that didn't bother her. Karen applied for it and no one was more surprised than Karen to get it.

She was pleased to be out of the house away from the memories of the past year. She was looking forward to her first day at work and something new to occupy her thoughts. She loved it. It was a busy shop in a vibrant High Street with a constant stream of customers delivering prescriptions and collecting their medicines as well as other purchases. She stocked shelves, worked the till, made the teas and coffees and listened to customers making polite conversation.

Karen got on well with all the staff but she bonded in particular with Lynda, a small pretty bubbly girl who was just twenty. She had been there four years and knew the job inside out and was very willing to share her knowledge and help Karen anytime she needed advice.

Karen felt normal again, but she never shared her story with anyone, not even Lynda who she really liked and got on so well with. Having Lynda definitely helped, she seemed to take Karen under her wing. Karen liked her job it was a welcome distraction from her thoughts and somehow found each day got just a little easier.

It was a wet Saturday in January when Karen left work. The wind and rain beating down with a force that took her breath away. Cold and damp, she made her way along the High Street to the bus stop. Pushing through the crowds of people who just seemed to be dawdling irritated her beyond belief. *Christmas was over, why was there still so many people around?*

As she weaved and squeezed, she caught sight of her bus as she rounded the corner. Karen picked up pace, ran the last few yards and jumped on the bus. She found an unoccupied seat next to a rather tired worn out woman whose eyes were closed and her body slumped as if relieved to have acquired a seat. Karen's stomach growled reminding her how hungry she was, she couldn't wait to get home to the soup that her Grandma cooked for them every week.

As she put her key into the lock and opened the front door, the pleasant aroma of the Kidney Beans soup coming from the kitchen enveloped her.

'Karen, is that you?' her mum shouted from the kitchen.

'Yes,' she replied, 'I'm starving.'

'C'mon then love, the soup's ready, I'll dish you some up.'

When she swallowed that first mouthful, it caressed her tongue and warmed her throat; the heat of pepper took her breath away. Truly delicious! She was glad to be home.

Karen's life was made up of small satisfying moments like a tasty meal, a film on the television or a purchase of yet another pair of shoes. Her obsession with shoes, was even worrying her. She tried to find happiness in small things and tried not to think too deeply about her life and what lay ahead.

She had conversations with her mum about meaningless and inconsequential things, anything other than talk about the elephant in the room, *the baby she had given up*. She regretted that more than anything and she knew although unspoken, her mum did too.

It had been enough in the days, months and first couple of years after giving up her first born child to remain detached emotionally from everything and not engage in anything that required more than an immediate physical response or brief interaction. She did not need any further drama in her life. There had been an abundance of that to last a lifetime. She existed only on small insignificant and mundane pleasures and did not think too deeply about anything.

And then there were her alone times in her bedroom that she cherished. She no longer shared with Fiona as Susan had gone to University as was expected, so Karen had moved into Susan's room and when Susan came home, she would sleep in the single bed in Fiona's room that Karen once occupied. So Karen's peace was guaranteed and she was grateful for the safe space of solitude.

She didn't want to meet another man. It had taken her a long time to stop loving Pete. She wondered if she ever really would but she was surviving without him and that was sufficient. She somehow had managed to bury her feelings for him to the point where she felt no pain.

The baby now, was another thing altogether. She couldn't bear to even allow herself to revisit that period in her life. *Why hadn't her parents persuaded her to keep him? She had been too young to make such a big decision.* Whenever she did reflect however she understood and realised that if her parents had persuaded her to keep him, then it would not have been her decision. They had made it clear to her that it had to be her decision, that they would support her either way. And they had, it was true. At the time, she felt sure it was the right thing to do, but now... she wasn't so sure. She had changed. The old Karen had gone and a new Karen had taken her place.

Chapter 5

Fiona had taken a completely different path to Susan. Where Susan had been studious, hard working and dedicated to her studies with no inclination to party, Fiona seemed to do nothing else. She was happy and carefree, listening to her music and dancing around the house. She was always planning the next night out with her different groups of friends either from school or work. It didn't matter who with as long as she had fun. Karen envied her lightness of spirit, nothing seemed to bother her. Fiona appreciated that Karen had been through a lot but she still never understood why she never went out even occasionally. It had been four years since Karen had Robin. Fiona had never talked to Karen about Robin. In fact Fiona noticed that nobody talked about it. But she remembered it well. She was thirteen at the time and although she didn't fully understand the extent of Karen's pain, she knew it was a big deal because she always saw how sad Karen was and that she cried a lot. When the baby went, Karen seemed to be okay but she was always quiet and didn't go anywhere. She was always in the house, *she needs to go out and have some fun,* Fiona often thought. Fiona loved going out and couldn't comprehend how Karen could spend so much time in the house. So whenever she was going out, she always asked her even though she knew Karen wouldn't come. So when Karen finally agreed to go out one night Fiona was elated.

The atmosphere was light and happy that night as the girls got ready for their night out. Karen must have tried on ten different outfits before deciding on a pair of cream trousers and a dusty pink chiffon blouse that seemed to float as she moved. She carefully applied her makeup which transformed a pretty girl into a stunning woman. Karen started to feel excited surprising even herself. Although nervous, she felt ready to face the world again. It was time. She couldn't bury herself for ever.

Fiona had recently obtained a job after leaving sixth form working for a large Shipping company. She had become friendly with the group of girls in the office and it was to Cheryl's twenty-first birthday party that she had invited Karen. It was being held at the Piano Bar wine bar and promised to be a good night.

She hadn't noticed him at all. However Richard had been staring at the awkward looking girl who seemed so out of place, for quite some time. She was stunning but she seemed completely unaware of it. He could not take his eyes off her. *She was gorgeous! Where did she come from?* He had been standing with his friend Ben, Cheryl's brother. If anybody was going to know who she was, it would be Ben, he knew everyone. So when Richard gave Ben a nudge and inclined his head in Karen's direction and asked if he knew who she was, he was surprised when Ben replied, 'haven't got a clue, mate.'

Richard hesitated only slightly before he sauntered across the room. His tall slim build eased effortlessly through the various groups of people who were laughing and conversing amongst themselves.

Karen had been nursing a brandy and lemonade for the best part of an hour when she heard a voice in her left ear say hello. She turned and looked into the face of a young man and as she studied him, she observed that he wasn't stunningly handsome but he was quite good looking with a warm smile and a pleasant demeanour. She was drawn to him. 'Hello,' she replied.

'I've not seen you before,' Richard stated, 'where have you been hiding?'

Karen smiled nervously and took a sip of her drink, 'I don't go out much.'

Richard noticed that she had a faraway look in her eyes as she answered. There was sadness in her eyes. He liked her though, there seemed to be depth to her. Something that had been missing from most of the girls he'd known. There was something about her that was interesting and sincere.

He had just finished with Candice who had been the latest in a long line of girls that he had dated but he had been bored with her. He had only had a couple of dates with her but he had known quite quickly that she wasn't for him. But this beautiful, mysterious girl with sad eyes had piqued his interest. 'Would you like to dance?' he asked at the start of a slow track.

'Okay,' she swallowed the remnants of her drink in one mouthful and placed the empty glass on the nearest table. With her shoulder bag tightly gripped, they slipped comfortably into step as they danced closely. They danced all evening. Fiona saw her and mouthed from a distance, 'Are you okay?' When she saw the smile on Karen's face along with the slight nod of her head, Fiona disappeared to the other side of the room.

For the first time in years, Karen felt good and was genuinely enjoying herself, much more than she imagined. She actually felt light and carefree. It was so good to feel free even for one evening from the burden she so often felt she was carrying. *Maybe, she could live again.*

Chapter 6

'I love you Karen, do you know that? I've not felt this way about anyone before.'

Karen sat across from Richard at the little round table in the corner of the pub and smiled sincerely.

'This is the moment when you're meant to say it back to me,' Richard said with a smile, as he reached for her hand warmly. Karen could see that he was smitten with her and she was truly flattered. *How confident he is.* She thought. He knew how he felt and wasn't afraid to say it, and hadn't even seemed hurt that she hadn't said it back to him. She really admired him. *How she wished that she had such confidence.*

'You don't really know me Richard, there's so much you don't know,' she said with a serious look on her face. It had been six weeks since they met and they had been inseparable. Karen could not deny that the last few weeks since meeting Richard had been magical. They had been many places even in that short period of time. She liked his self assurance and he seemed really grown up. He enjoyed introducing her to different restaurants to eat at and new places to go to. He was twenty seven and had a very responsible job as Branch Manager of an Estate Agent. He had a level head but he also had a wonderful sense of humour. He loved his job and regaled her with stories that were so witty. There was definitely something very endearing about him. She liked him a lot and enjoyed his company. Love however was another matter altogether.

'C'mon then, spill the beans! You're a bank robber aren't you?' A crooked smile with a little wink accompanied his ludicrous statement.

'If only...' Karen shifted in her chair, 'let's get out of here, I need some air.' And as she jumped up and grabbed his hand, she allowed him a few seconds to down the last of his beer.

Chapter 7

Richard was the only child born to his parents Eva and Greg, but as far back as he could remember it had been just him and his mum. Having lost his dad after a fatal car crash when he was six years old, his recollections and memories of him were few.

Richard and Eva's relationship was incredibly close and very strong. No other person had ever come into their lives. Eva was broken after Greg's death and clung to Richard desperately. He had grown up very fast assuming the role as 'man of the house' and in the early years after his father's death, with Eva's emotions in question a lot of time, Richard became resilient and cool headed in most situations. He took care of her and she took care of him. They were a team. It worked.

He never took any girls home, not because Eva didn't want it, in fact it was the opposite. She was constantly asking him when he was going to settle down. Eva desperately wanted Richard to have what she and his father had had, even though it had only been a precious few years for them. Greg had been her one and only true love. Eva remembered their first meeting often. They had met on a train on her journey back home after staying with her parents one weekend. She recalled how he had smiled at her and started an easy conversation about the weather. He was tall slim and dark haired with the most beautiful green eyes. Yes, she liked the look of him. The conversation flowed from one subject to another: films, music. The hour train journey ended far too quickly. It was no surprise to her when he asked her for a date and there was no hesitation on her part at all to accept. They exchanged numbers.

They were married within 18 months of meeting and enjoyed three magical years of married life before Richard was born and completed their happy family life. Eva felt satisfied and blissfully content now she had her gorgeous baby boy with the man she loved so deeply.

Then that fateful day happened, Eva would never forget it as long as she lived. Greg was seriously injured in a car accident and died three days after that fatal crash when she had to make the heartbreaking decision to switch off his life support.

She was naturally protective of Richard and was aware that there were times when she relied on him too much especially when he was a young boy. It had taken a long time to get over the loss of Greg and she was grateful for the passing of time when she did indeed start to feel that life was worth living again. She recollected the many times, when people had said that time was a great healer and feeling that could never be possible, but they were right and she now felt whole again. And so she wanted Richard to get on with his life. She didn't want to be one of those mothers who robbed her son of his own life because of her, so she encouraged him to go out and make friends and enjoy himself and find a girlfriend. She herself never felt the need for another relationship but she wanted Richard to have one. She felt proud of what he had achieved and was ready to embrace whoever he brought home. But he never took anyone to meet her, until now.

Chapter 8

Eva liked Karen a lot. She was a wonderful addition to their small family unit. She was quiet and good-natured. Karen soon became a growing and important part of their lives. Richard was clearly smitten! He didn't hold back, he had his arm around her at every opportunity and even stroked her face when she spoke. He was incredibly tactile all the time and nothing was too much trouble for him to do for her. She didn't doubt that Karen was very fond of Richard, but Eva observed that she was much less affectionate although very warm and gentle with him. She was young, Eva observed and not as confident as Richard but she could see a closeness between them that was promising.

Eva's relationship with Karen was amiable and friendly. Karen always offered to help with washing the dishes or drying up. Karen even showed an interest in Eva's passion for cake baking and would often join her in the kitchen while Eva baked. Karen was her biggest admirer and didn't hold back with compliments about her creations. It was wonderful to have Karen in their lives, she loved having her around and couldn't have asked for a nicer girl for Richard but there was something about Karen that Eva felt was unknown but she just couldn't 'put her finger on it'. There were times when Karen would arrive and she was happy and warm and then as if a light bulb had been switched off, her mood would change and she would be quiet, sad even. Richard however didn't seem to notice if her mood changed. He was always so preoccupied with the practicalities, planning the entertainment for them both. He would get a movie, usually science fiction which he loved, and Karen would just sit and watch. Eva noticed that she never really challenged him or made many suggestions about how they should spend their time together. She was passive. Eva noticed on one occasion that Karen did say that she wanted to watch a love story and Richard pulled a face and said straightaway that there was no way he could sit through that rubbish. In some ways that troubled Eva, she knew that Richard was a little selfish at times and tended to feed only his desires and interests assuming others wanted it too.

Richard loved to cycle so he bought Karen a bike and they would go out for hours cycling. He loved to take long walks and together they would walk for miles. She appeared to enjoy these shared activities. *But did she really?* Eva observed that Karen seemed to take the easy route and seemed to go along with everything that Richard suggested.

Eva's conclusions were right, even though it was unspoken and no conversation about this had passed between them. Karen was happy she had someone who clearly adored her. Richard's obvious and open love for her had given her confidence to believe that she was someone worth loving. That meant a lot to her and she treasured it. She could see he wanted to look after and protect her and it was a nice place to be. She had started to feel 'normal' again and her sadness was lessening. So much had happened in her life and she had a chance of happiness with Richard. Okay, so she didn't love him in the same way she had loved Pete but it didn't matter, she still loved him very much, just differently. He took care of her and he always planned everything with her in mind. He always wanted to share experiences with her. She wanted to love him in the way he deserved but she knew she couldn't commit to loving him properly until he truly knew who she was. She was aware that he loved a 'veneer', someone he thought he knew but it wasn't the real person. It was time to tell him the truth.

Chapter 9

Richard listened without saying a word as she told him everything right from the beginning. He was totally absorbed in her story. The autumn leaves were dry and crisp underfoot as they walked around the park. Dusk had fallen and they hadn't even noticed.

Tears streamed and stained Karen's face as she remembered and recollected. Richard reached out and put his arm around her shoulder protectively as she talked.

'It's okay, honey don't cry, I'll take care of you. We'll have our own baby that you can take care of,' Richard said softly. How she loved him for saying that, she was determined to love this man with every fibre of her being and make this relationship work. She had a second chance and she wasn't going to screw it up.

'Richard, I really love you.' He squeezed her tight and they carried on walking out of the park gate. And as she said those words, she really meant them. Her love for him from that moment had deepened. She literally felt a burst of love from within for him. It had been liberating to share it with Richard. It was as though a burden had been lifted. She felt free.

'I can't wait to tell your mum now,' Karen said smiling.

'I don't want you to tell mum,' Richard stated.

'Why?' Karen asked surprised.

'Let's just keep it between us eh? Mum doesn't need to know.'

'Okay, I really like your mum though Richard, I'd like to be straight with her.'

'I said no!' Richard said rather sharply. His voice hadn't raised but his tone was even.

Karen was surprised at his response but was left in no doubt how he felt. She was a little baffled but figured he knew his mum better than she did and so she decided not to push it.

As they walked, silence hung like a curtain between them. She was still reflecting on all that had just happened. Of course she wouldn't say anything if that was what he wanted. He'd been amazing and had taken it so much better than she had anticipated. Of course, they would keep it between them if that was what he wanted. *How could she ask for more after he had shown such love and support?* There was plenty of time for his mum to know the truth. It could keep for now. Nevertheless she was doing again what she always hated about herself agreeing and going along with things to keep the peace. *Why did she never feel able to confront or object and simply say what she wanted? Why did she always feel that her thoughts or opinions about things weren't as important as someone else?* Then she reminded herself, it was easier that way, she couldn't possibly do what she wanted. She didn't know how to. It didn't matter whether it was with Richard or anybody she never really did what she wanted. *Why change now?*

Chapter 10

Karen was happy! Yes for the first time in a long time, she felt good and nothing was going to spoil it. Not even those little nagging doubts about Richard. There was something about him that bothered her. She wasn't quite sure what but she knew there was something 'missing' for her. She was aware that she did not feel complete satisfaction or deep fulfilment but was she asking for too much. *Was this the right relationship?* She asked herself. *Of course it was.* He was so very sweet, kind and attentive. So she ignored her instincts and if she was honest she didn't really trust her instincts anymore. After all she had got it all wrong before. She never dreamt that Pete would have let her down so what did she know? Richard was a good and loving man. *Why was she questioning herself, had she forgotten what had happened with Pete?* Richard loved her despite everything and wanted to marry her. *Enjoy it girl!* She told herself. Men like this didn't come along often. It was the chance of a 'normal' life like everyone else. But she couldn't stop thinking about why he was so insistent that his mum shouldn't know about Robin. Something just didn't add up. Eva was such a warm and welcoming person and had shown no sign of having a judgmental attitude ever, Karen felt sure it would not have been an issue. Karen really liked Eva and she felt that Eva liked her. Their relationship seemed genuine. Karen and Eva had had many conversations about different things, and Eva always had an understanding of both sides of any argument or discussion whatever the topic. She was consistently fair in everything. She was incredibly realistic and had a commonsense approach to life. Karen and Eva's relationship was relaxed and there was evidence of mutual affection. Karen would have loved to have been completely honest with Eva. She felt a fraud now. Without realising it Richard was stopping her from being her real authentic self. She had spent the last three years 'acting' at work and that had been hard enough but her colleagues were not a part of her personal life so it didn't matter if they didn't really know her or her story.

The only person at work that she had felt confident to share her 'hidden story' with was Lynda and that had only happened after she had met Richard when she had felt so much happier and self-assured. Lynda liked Karen and had been drawn to her from the first day that Karen started. She observed that Karen was always so quiet and hardworking. She displayed a vulnerability that made Lynda interested to get to know her more. Lynda was intrigued by this naturally beautiful young girl who seemed to have no idea just how pretty she was. She was timid and unassuming with a humility that was quite unusual for someone so stunning. Lynda was a sociable and incredibly compassionate person with a big heart. Karen was aware of the effort Lynda always made to talk to her and include her and she appreciated it so much. Lynda had been an amazing colleague and slowly their friendship grew and she really wanted to tell her about Robin. There had been so many times when she wanted to share her story but couldn't find the words. There had been countless opportunities as they very often had lunch together but whenever she thought about opening up, it was as if she had been struck dumb. Karen wanted an honest friendship with Lynda but to find the courage and the right time had been an issue. So she felt a great sense of relief after pouring out her heart to her one evening after work at the local pub situated just minutes from the chemist. It was a totally unplanned visit following a spontaneous invitation from Lynda to go and relax with a drink with her before going home. It took their friendship to a deeper level because now Lynda fully understood her. She didn't have to put a bright smile on her face when she didn't feel like it or if she was having a bad day, Lynda knew why. It had helped her more than even she realised it would. Lynda was a naturally open person and Karen had wanted to be real with her. She had felt so much happier for sharing it with Lynda. She now at least had one person at work she could be herself with. Lynda had been so kind and inclusive and had displayed a genuine fondness for her and she proved to be trustworthy too.

Karen had no desire to tell any of her other colleagues. She didn't have that close connection with anyone else and that was why telling

Lynda had been so important to her. And she felt the same way about Eva. She had been so warm and kind. She deserved to know the real Karen not a veneer. The 'mask' needed to come off.

Karen had tried one more time to persuade him to tell his mum after his unexpectedly sharp rebuff. She told him how hurt she felt when he had snapped at her and he apologised saying he hadn't realised that his tone had been so sharp. She then tentatively asked him why he felt so strongly about her not knowing. He stated simply and firmly but kindly that he did not want her to know. He gave no explanation and swiftly changed the conversation. *How could she challenge him? What right did she have really?* But she couldn't deny to herself that she was baffled! It didn't make sense, but she had no choice but to leave it. She had to respect his wishes.

There were other things that started to concern her. He seemed to control everything, what they ate, where they went. It was subtle. She hadn't noticed it at first. It was so comforting to be taken care of. He was so protective in every way, kind, caring, loving and generous with his time. *What was there to complain about? Did it really matter that he chose what movies they saw, what restaurant they ate at or what holiday destinations they went to?* After making the biggest decision of her life and messing up, it was easier to let Richard make the decisions for them. So she reasoned that control was too harsh a description. He took charge and that was the sign of a decisive character, surely? *Nothing wrong with that!* She told herself.

He would often say 'I know what's best for you darling,' and he seemed to. It didn't matter that he was making all the decisions. He discussed what plans were being made but somehow, Richard always had the final say and as time went by she got used to it. There were the occasional times when she asked herself if she should question more but somehow she never gained the confidence to ask.

They had lots of fun and plenty of laughter she always felt she was learning something when she was with him. He was so knowledgeable and confident. She liked that about him. She felt loved and valued, there was no doubt about that so she decided to embrace her new life. She was looking forward to the future.

The wedding plans should have set 'alarm bells ringing' loudly but again she chose to ignore them. Richard planned every detail, even her engagement ring wasn't what she really wanted, but it didn't matter because the plans for choosing it had been a wonderful memorable day decided by Richard.

It was one Saturday and Richard had said he would pick her up at 10am. He arrived promptly and they went to one of the most expensive jewellers to choose the ring. Karen couldn't believe it. There were so many styles to choose from. So much variety and she tried many, but her favourite was a single diamond solitaire. Richard however wanted her to have the sapphire flanked with diamonds. She liked it for sure but there was something about the simplicity of the diamond solitaire she liked. She tried them both alternatively.

'Yes, this one!' Karen said, 'I like this one.' She looked at Richard, he was leaning his head to one side and had his lips pursed, 'I'm not sure honey,' he replied, 'I like the sapphire and diamonds it suits your fingers and compliments your skin tone beautifully.' There, he said it, he gave a reason for everything and that was what she admired. She also liked the fact that he loved her mixed heritage and often commented on her beautiful skin tone. He had no problem with her background. She loved him for that. There had been times in her life when she had experienced racism and it had affected her. She and her sisters had talked about it with their parents and how it had made them feel undervalued at times. Cecil and Marina had comforted them and acknowledged that not everyone was appreciative of diversity, and they would have to accept that. But Richard actually embraced her difference.

So Karen walked out of the jewellers with the sapphire and diamonds that had been Richard's choice but it didn't matter. So what if it wasn't what she had initially wanted, the diamond solitaire now forgotten!

They went for lunch to celebrate. It was a Spanish restaurant that Richard loved, they frequented it often. The meal was delicious and they enjoyed it. Afterwards, they drove out into the countryside, parked the car and walked and talked, sitting occasionally on the grass or on a bench. It was the best day, a day devoted to them alone. *What more could she ask for?*

Chapter 11

It was a beautiful day in June. The sun was shining from early dawn and peeped through the slit of where the curtains met. Karen's eyes opened suddenly. She climbed out of bed and pulled the curtains back. Bright daylight flooded her room and she looked out and up at the sky which was already a beautiful blue. The day had arrived. It was her wedding day. She was going to be Mrs Jackman. The house was quiet. She looked at her watch, it was ten past six. Not even her parents were up. Karen opened her bedroom door quietly and took measured steps down the stairs. She wasn't ready to share this time with anyone just yet. She entered the kitchen, tilted the blinds and put the kettle on to boil. She unlocked the back door. It was a little chilly even with the sun shining but Karen pulled her warm fleece dressing gown tightly around her and sat on one of the chairs surrounding the table on the patio with a parasol in the centre. *She would miss this garden.* They had moved here when she was twelve years old from a terraced house with a small backyard. It was one of the reasons her parents had bought this house, the garden was so private and established, matured and well proportioned. Her mum and dad had taken such pride in it and had maintained it well and both were always happy when they were gardening together. The hedge surrounding the garden with its vivid red leaves contrasted well with the large evergreen trees standing tall along with the scent of the lavender shrubs and aroma of different herbs that grew together. The neatly cut lawn complimented everything so well. She felt so peaceful being out there that when the kettle boiled she made her coffee and sat back outside.

Thoughts of her little baby flooded her mind. *How was he? He would be nearly six now. At school, did he have many friends? Was he shy or confident? What did he look like?* All her memories were of him as a baby, with pale skin and light brown eyes. He had looked like Pete. *Why did she give him up? Why didn't she keep him? You know why!* She chided herself. You wanted him to have what you couldn't give him, the love of two parents like you had. *Why are you thinking about this now?* She said to herself out loud! *Today is the start of a new life with Richard, you can have more children. Yes, Pete was your first love and you gave up your first born child, and you're never going to forget them, but this is a fresh start, grab it with both hands.* She told herself. As she sat thinking back over the last six years of her life, she reflected how much had changed in her life. She never dreamt that she could ever dare to be happy again.

'Karen, are you okay? What are you doing out there?' Her mum's familiar voice interrupted her thoughts.

'I'm fine, just enjoying the peace and quiet before all the busyness starts,' Karen replied quietly.

Marina observed that Karen appeared slightly melancholy and guessed why but she didn't have the courage to ask if it was about Robin. She just knew that even if she dared to be bold and mention Robin, today was not the day to do it. She needed Karen to be happy and excited about her big day and to be looking forward to her new life ahead, not sad and reflective about the past. That's for another day Marina thought.

'Shall I do you some breakfast, what do you fancy? Shall I do the works? Eggs, bacon, sausage, beans, mushrooms, it's going to be hours before you eat again.' She didn't wait for Karen to answer before she turned and walked back into the kitchen and went to the fridge for the ingredients to prepare breakfast.

As Karen's mum was chatting from the kitchen partly to herself and partly to Karen, about all the things that they had to do before 1pm, Karen became thoughtful again pondering to herself and thinking; *that's mum always looking after me and feeding me but never asking me how I am.* She knew that her mum felt sadness about Robin and that was why she never ever talked about it. Both felt the pain but never shared it. *Another missed opportunity.* Karen thought.

Chapter 12

As she walked down the aisle on her father's arm, she felt nervous. She didn't dare look around at the crowd of people that filled the church. She just held her head straight measuring every step. She saw the back of Richard's head and for an instant she wasn't sure how she felt. It was the second big decision she had made in her life. *Was it the right one?* Giving up Robin was her first. She was going to marry Richard. It was too late to worry about that now. When she was just a few steps behind him he turned and gave her a dazzling smile that both soothed and warmed her, all doubts left her immediately.

As they left the church as man and wife and the confetti tumbled all around them, she felt happy. Throughout it felt like she was in a dream. She felt like she was observing someone else. She had to pinch herself. She was married now, a new future lay ahead and she told herself that she was determined to enjoy it.

The next morning as they headed to the airport to catch their flight to Brazil, they chatted and reflected on the wedding day and how it had gone. They both agreed that it had gone perfectly. All thanks to Richard, with his attention to every detail.

Two glorious weeks in the sun had done them both well. Karen couldn't fault Richard he had planned every trip and excursion, every meal and pastime with the right amount of rest and relaxation weaved in. He made it a honeymoon to remember and remember it she did, for a long time.

Life was good. Karen and Richard settled into married life very smoothly and enjoyed many evenings of walks and talks, watched movies, planned meals and organised nights out. Their life was calm and ordered. Richard ensured that. Apart from when they were at work, every hour was spent together. They visited their families together, even that had somehow become part of their weekly routine. Every Wednesday they had dinner at Eva's house. She always had a beautiful meal prepared and the three of them enjoyed their time together. Karen really liked Eva who treated her just like a daughter their relationship was easy and warm and had become more so since she and Richard had married.

It was one evening six months after the wedding and they were both in the kitchen, when Eva asked Karen out of the blue when she and Richard were planning to have children. Karen told Eva that it was on their agenda and she hoped it would happen soon. Eva started to recall and tell Karen all about her pregnancy and how she enjoyed it, the first kick and flutter inside her stomach as her baby grew and the excitement that she and Richard's father Greg felt. As Eva talked and shared details of that time, Karen felt sadness flood over her about her beautiful baby boy that she had not felt strong enough to keep.

She desperately wanted to share with Eva what had happened and that she knew all too well about pregnancy and the different stages of it. Only it had been very different. Instead of happiness and excitement, it had been sadness and trepidation. She listened as Eva talked without saying a word. Suddenly Eva said 'Listen to me going on, I've not let you get a word in edgeways,' she smiled.

'It's okay, I enjoy listening,' Karen replied. In her heart wishing that she could share the story of her own pregnancy instead of pretending that she had no idea about it and Eva thinking she was someone she wasn't. What a fraud she felt with this lovely woman who was her mother-in-law, she couldn't have asked for anyone nicer. *Why was life so complicated?* She felt sick inside about her secret.

Saturday afternoons were visits to her family, with her Grandma there too. It was always a lively time especially if her sisters were there as well. Fiona had met Guy recently and he too had become part of the Saturday get together. It was very different to the Wednesday evenings spent with Eva that was very orderly in contrast with her family where it was noisy and animated. Even so she always enjoyed being back with her family partaking of the Kidney Beans soup that her Grandma Rose cooked for them. It was an enduring tradition that always reminded her of childhood. There were lots of joke telling and plenty of laughter. Karen could see that Richard enjoyed being with her family too.

But again for Karen there were times when she was with her own family that she felt she wasn't being herself either but for very different reasons. Everyone in her family knew about Robin but no one talked about him. She knew that her mum had regretted not talking her out of the adoption and offering to help more because they had had a short painful conversation after her baby had gone. It was a very difficult subject for either of them to revisit and so it became the 'elephant in the room' for her and Marina. The rest of family were only too aware of the pain and heartache Karen had been through and so wanted to help put it behind her. They were all so kind and didn't want to upset Karen. She looked happy with Richard who seemed to be taking such good care of her, and was so affectionate and gentle with her. Her life had taken an unexpected turn, living in a lovely house in a good neighbourhood enjoying a comfortable life with no money worries. They could not have hoped for better for Karen, and from their point of view it was time to move on.

But for Karen, as time went by, she seemed to torture herself even more for a whole host of reasons. She couldn't talk to Eva because she didn't know and she couldn't talk to her family because they wanted to forget. She could however talk to Richard and although he was very sympathetic of her feelings the only comfort he could bring was that they would one day have their own baby and then she could forget. *That was the problem, she didn't want to forget!*

Chapter 13

Karen was so excited. She was five days late! She was never late, she must be pregnant. She made the decision to do a pregnancy test at work and then tell Richard later. It turned blue. Yes she was pregnant. She couldn't wait to see Richard's face.

'Sweetheart, that's wonderful,' Richard stated after she told him the news. 'When did you find out?' he asked.

'I did it today at work!' Karen beamed.

'Why didn't you do the test at home this evening while we were together?' Richard probed.

'Because I wanted to be sure before telling you, does it matter?' Karen asked with a puzzled look.

'As it so happens, yes it does, it's my baby too you know,' Richard emphasised.

'And it's my body. Why are we arguing about this? It's good news I really don't understand what the problem is,' Karen said wearily. The despondency showed on her face.

'I just wanted us to do it together honey, don't worry I forgive you. You know I like us to do things together. Next time, just check with me beforehand. Yeah? Agreed?' He looked at her in anticipation wanting an answer.

'Okay agreed,' Karen nodded her head at the same time. Richard smiled happily.

Karen sailed through her pregnancy and felt well all the way through. She was happy and excited at the prospect of having and keeping her baby this time. Richard shared her excitement and he pampered and spoiled her every day. They decorated the small bedroom ready for the baby and shopped for all the necessary items, nothing was left to chance. It was a truly happy time in her life with her mum and Eva being so supportive and helpful throughout, checking up on her almost daily to see how she was doing. Even Susan and Fiona had shown genuine interest and elation too. And of course Lynda knew just how much this pregnancy meant to her. They never discussed Robin again after Karen had confided in Lynda but there was such joy from Lynda for her and Karen knew why. She felt like the luckiest girl alive.

Richard was with her throughout the birth. After going into labour in the early hours of Monday morning, she had a beautiful baby girl at 11.20am, who they named Grace. When Karen came home with baby Grace, the family were all there to meet her. Their house was full and when everyone left after a couple of hours, Richard sat and held Grace with Karen next to him on the sofa. Together they just sat staring at her beautiful face with her heart shaped lips. She was everything they dreamed of and more. Together they cared for Grace making sure her every need was met. It was a wonderful time for Karen and Richard and they grew closer as a couple through this shared experience of parenthood. When Grace was born, they had been married for just under two years, the timing was perfect and they were thrilled to have her. Richard had said that there was no need for Karen to go back to work as he earned more than enough for them to live on. Karen did not argue with that, she wanted to spend every waking moment with her gorgeous daughter. Very often she would visit Eva during the daytime as she didn't work and she had become very friendly with another new mum she met while in hospital. Karen felt happy, gloriously happy! She still thought about her little boy but tried to push thoughts of him to the back of her mind. While she was busy and distracted looking after Grace it was easy to do that but thoughts of Robin would flood her mind whenever Grace was sleeping.

Both Richard and Karen wanted to have another child so that Grace could have a sibling close in age and so they made the decision to try for another child when Grace was eight months old. No one was more surprised than Karen when she missed her period a month later. This time, she told Richard straightaway and together they did the pregnancy test. It was positive. Neither expected it would happen so soon but they were delighted. Nine months later, Grace's sister Amelia was born.

Chapter 14

It had been subtle, so much so that Karen had not really noticed just how much Richard controlled almost everything they did. With two small children to take care of and the house to look after too, she was initially glad for Richard's ordered and organised approach. He had taken two weeks leave when Amelia was born and he had been absolutely brilliant. He fed and bathed Grace, kept her entertained, cooked all the meals, shopped and even changed Amelia's nappies. The list went on. Karen was in awe and was so grateful for his care and she felt so supported and loved. She was able to give Amelia all the attention that a newborn baby needed.

But then when he went back to work, Karen realised that he was still controlling everything that happened at home. He organised the meals for every single day of the week, with the menu pinned to the notice board in the kitchen, Karen had no say in the matter. She couldn't deny it had been incredibly useful in the first few weeks with a new baby and a toddler to care for as it meant that she didn't have to think about what meals to prepare. But it became apparent as time went by that nothing was changing. Karen wasn't naturally a creature of habit when it came to food, she liked variety and she liked to change what she had on any particular day as the fancy took her. There were times, not very often, but now and again she didn't want the same weekly routine of meals. On one occasion she was surprised at his response when she mentioned that she just didn't fancy having salmon on one particular Tuesday.

Richard had fed Grace who was sitting quietly next to Karen while she was breastfeeding Amelia. He had folded the washing and put it in the laundry room ready for ironing and was tidying the living room and conservatory and was putting out the toys for the day for Grace to play with.

'Do you fancy chilli con carne for dinner tonight Richard?'

'No thanks, we're having salmon tonight. It's Tuesday. We always have salmon on a Tuesday. You know that,' Richard replied with a smile.

'Yeah, I know that but I didn't think it was set in stone, I just don't fancy it today,' Karen stated simply.

'You really are awkward sometimes,' Richard said sharply, 'I go to the trouble to organise the meals, so you don't have to think about it, and now you're telling me you don't *'fancy it','* he emphasised.

Karen was stunned into silence. *Where did that come from? She would never have described herself as awkward.* Richard kissed her and left to go to work.

That had been the start of many incidents that started to concern Karen. On the one hand he was caring, loving, thoughtful and helpful but then there was a stern side to him that Karen felt she just couldn't challenge. She was a little annoyed with herself that she didn't have the courage to protest or object but she was determined not to let it get her down but it did disturb her. She was beginning to realise that Richard was not quite the man she thought he was. However having Grace & Amelia had bought so much joy and comfort that she felt so grateful for the life she now had and so for a long time she went along with what Richard wanted to keep the peace.

'Karen, this can't carry on! The house is a mess. I've made a list of things to do. It should not be this hard for you,' Karen stared at Richard as if she didn't understand what he was saying, 'Karen, what's wrong with you? This can't carry on,' he repeated.

Richard walked in to what was becoming a familiar sight every night when he came home from work. Amelia and Grace were playing with the toys on the floor with Karen sitting on the sofa. Nothing had been done. Clothes were strewn everywhere and dirty cups and dishes in the sink. There was no aroma of food cooking or evidence that it would be started. He would have to do the dinner again!

'I don't know Richard. I'm just so tired all the time, the girls run me ragged.'

'But I help you, don't I?' He paused and shook his head, 'I do the shopping and plan the meals for you to cook. Surely it can't be that difficult?' His question was more of a statement rather than a question that he wanted an answer to. He felt exasperated and found it difficult to hide his feelings.

'I'm sorry,' Karen said as she dragged Amelia away who had just at that moment hit Grace over the head with a plastic brick. Grace screamed and Richard immediately went to her and soothed her.

Richard was getting tired of this situation and could see no end in sight. *This isn't right. She must be depressed but why?* He thought.

Grace was three and Amelia was fast approaching 18 months and it was getting worse, not better. He knew it wasn't easy looking after two young children which was why he gave her all the help he could. He had thought that with the children getting older, she would have coped better especially as he had roped in both their mothers to give a helping hand whenever they were free. Marina wasn't free during the day but she would pop in at least once a week after work and help Karen tidy up or occupy the children while Karen prepared the evening meal and Eva would come around a couple times a week to sit with the children while Karen got the chores done. So he was perplexed why Karen seemed to be struggling. She was getting as much help as she needed. It was great that Karen had always got on with his mum and he was pleased about that but he just wished that Karen didn't keep going on about telling Eva about her son. *What purpose would it serve now so many years on?*

Chapter 15

Karen was exhausted but she just couldn't sleep. Her mind was full of everything that she tried to shut out. *How was her little boy? What did he look like? Why wasn't she allowed to talk about him as if he never existed?* With every passing day came a dawning realisation that Richard was killing the love she had for him. He wanted to control everything, even her thoughts. It wasn't fair, she felt helpless? She loved the girls with all her heart but she felt guilty and sad that she had not kept her little boy. *Why had she been so weak? Why did she give up so easily?* She wished she had been stronger. Sleep eventually came that night but it became a reoccurring pattern.

Karen knew that Richard was getting exasperated. She felt it. He hadn't really hidden it. She knew she had to fight her feelings and so she woke one morning with a new determination that today would be different. She was going to show Richard that she could be a good wife and mother. She decided today she would get the children ready and go to the 'Mums and Toddlers' group. Every week she kept promising herself to go and somehow it never happened. It all seemed like too much effort to get the girls washed, fed and clothed as well as getting herself ready. It was easier to stay in her dressing gown until just before Richard got in from work. She always made sure she was dressed by the time he walked in or he would have had a fit! He could be so pedantic about things and Karen knew it would not be worth the earache she knew she would get if he found her in her night clothes.

That day however was different, Karen felt stronger. She wasn't sure why, but she was ready to embrace it. As she walked into the church hall from the side entrance of the church, she saw small groups of mothers and their children. She knew a couple of the mothers, who she had spoken to from previous visits but she hadn't seen or been in contact with them for a while. 'Hey, Karen come and join us,' shouted Joy. Karen made her way to the small group and was introduced to Samantha and Jenny who were sat in a small semi circle with Joy. Karen didn't know Joy terribly well but really like her. She was a big, bubbly girl who was still carrying a lot of her baby weight but was totally comfortable in her own skin, Karen observed.

The four of them chatted and laughed and watched the children as they played and interacted. It was just what Karen needed and she was surprised that a morning at a 'Mums and Toddlers' group had boosted her mood so much. She felt alive and energetic and she hadn't felt like that in a long time. It had been good to get out of the house and socialise and the children seemed happy and relaxed too. The thought of going straight back home was unappealing and she knew she had to get the children their lunch so she decided to drive to the City Centre. She really was feeling brave today. So after parking the car and carefully strapping Grace and Amelia into the double buggy push chair, she headed for the nearest fast food restaurant. She pushed aside her feelings about not giving the children junk food, it was a one off, what did it matter, she reasoned.

She ordered chicken nuggets, fries and drinks for the children, a fish burger and a coffee for herself. Karen settled herself down and opened up the free drawing book and pencils for Grace to occupy herself and Amelia was happy eating her chicken nugget in the highchair provided. *This is nice.* She thought. She felt relaxed as she drank her coffee and ate her meal. She enjoyed watching people walk by and wondering what their lives were like.

At first she wasn't sure, but as she stared out of the window trying hard to focus, she realised it was Pete. He looked exactly the same. He was walking towards the restaurant. She wasn't surprised. He used to love burgers. Karen started to feel hot and bothered. Just seeing him stirred all kinds of emotions that she thought were dead and buried. Memories of their relationship flooded her mind, she remembered the walks in the park, the jokes they shared and the fun they had... before it all went so horribly wrong. She immediately realised that she couldn't cope with seeing him and that she needed to get home with the children. This *is my life now, stop thinking about the past. What's the point?* She asked herself. *Get a grip Karen!* She told herself. As she started to get the children into the double buggy and was strapping them in, she heard a voice above her.

'Karen, I thought it was you. How are you?' Pete said.

'I'm good thanks, how are you?' Karen mumbled.

'I'm not bad. Are these your kids? They're beauties,' Pete remarked, 'not surprising, you're still pretty stunning too!'

'What?' Karen said in disbelief. In her mind, she thought she looked pretty average, today anyway. What Karen didn't realise about herself was that she had naturally good looks whether she had no makeup or a face full of makeup. *She has such a beautiful face.* Pete thought as he stood looking at her.

'You need your eyes testing,' Karen said with a smile, 'thanks anyway.' *This is so strange I'm in a conversation with my ex, the father of my beautiful baby boy as if we were just old friends.*

'Karen you're modest as ever,' Pete said sincerely, 'I'm sorry, really sorry,' he continued, 'I let you down, I know that now.'

Karen stared, unable to speak. Just at that time Grace said 'Mummy, can we go to the park?'

'I'm not sure yet darling, maybe tomorrow now,' she replied as she finally strapped her in.

'I've got to go, bye,' Karen then pushed the double buggy and was already a couple metres away before Pete could utter another word. He stared after her and realised just how much he wanted to say to her. He couldn't let her go. He hadn't seen her in years.

He ran after her and said, 'We need to talk.'

'There's nothing to talk about,' Karen answered.

'There is, and you know there is. Please,' Pete pleaded.

'I need to get the kids home, not now Pete this isn't the time or the place,' she said with emphasis.

He hurriedly took a pen from the inside of his jacket and dug into the front and back pockets of his jeans before he found an old receipt and tore off the bottom and scribbled his number on it. 'Please ring me!' His tone was imploring. Karen took the paper quickly from his hand and pushed it into her coat pocket. She immediately left him standing there without looking back. No goodbye, nothing, her mind a complete whirl. Her heart was beating hard and fast like it would burst out of her chest. Eventually when she knew she was out of sight, she slowed her pace and allowed herself to breathe deeply. *That was so unreal. Who knew that today would have such significance? Why today of all days?* She hadn't been out of the house in weeks, she hadn't wanted to but this morning she had felt differently. She was obviously meant to see Pete today. She couldn't lie to herself, it had really unsettled her. It was going to be hard to act normal tonight when Richard got home, but somehow she told herself, she would have to manage it.

Karen looked at the number on the roughly torn paper every single day for the next three weeks. She really wanted to speak to him but she had been struggling with her feelings ever since that unexpected meeting. She was unsure of how she felt seesawing in a sea of emotions that were all consuming. *Why are you torturing yourself? Why do you keep looking at his number?* She was annoyed with herself for being so weak. She wanted to throw the piece of paper away but something stopped her so she decided to put it in the back of her purse and not look at it. She needed to get strong again and just forget about Pete and get on with her life but seeing him had made it even harder now to get her little boy out of her mind.

Chapter 16

It had been strange seeing Karen, Pete reflected as he walked back to his car. She looked really good and those children of hers were beauties. He felt a tinge of jealousy about that even though he knew he had no right to feel that way. She deserved to be a mum. She had been ready to step up to the plate first time around even though they had been no more than kids themselves. It was unbelievable, in all the years he hadn't seen her and today he ran into her. He hadn't planned to go into town today, but he decided at the last minute to go in his lunch break and collect a book that he had ordered from the bookstore. *Was it luck or fate?* Ever since it had become clear that the longed for child wasn't going to arrive for him and his wife Vanessa, his thoughts had turned to his child that he didn't know. He had wanted to tell Vanessa so many times but somehow the words just couldn't come out. He knew that Vanessa would have been incredibly hurt that he had kept such a big secret from her and now that she had the knowledge that she couldn't have her own children, how would she take that anyway? He just wasn't sure. She had become quite sad and fragile he had observed recently. They had had many conversations about it. She felt that she was denying Pete the right to be a parent so there was a lot of guilt as well as deep sadness. Pete knew this wasn't easy for her but he had mixed emotions himself. He really wanted a child now, he was actually ready to be a dad and financially they were in the best position ever. They'd had all the foreign holidays that they wanted, both had the cars they desired and more clothes than they could ever wear. Inside however he didn't feel worthy to be a dad because of what had happened with Karen and the fact that he had let his first child down. Not being able to have more children had had a humbling effect on him and had made him reflect on his behaviour all those years ago. There had been many times that he wished he could see Karen to say how sorry he was. He was glad that he had seen her and had the opportunity to say it. Now it made him more determined to know what had become of his child. It was a double edged sword.

He needed to share with Karen that he was ready to now acknowledge the child he had wanted to forget eleven years ago. Since bumping into Karen he had gone back many times in his lunch hour to the same burger shop, just in case she was there but no sighting at all. He was desperate to see her or hear from her. *Why hadn't she called him?* He asked himself. *She has two young children and is therefore very busy.* He reminded himself. *Anyway why would she want to ring you?* The voice in his head said loud and clear! *You deserted her when she needed you. She probably threw your number in the nearest bin! Forget it, it's done, it's dusted! Move on...* He told himself.

Chapter 17

Several months went by after Karen's unexpected meeting with Pete but not a day went by that she didn't think about it. Remarkably, since then she had felt better, stronger and more able to cope with the children and life in general. She had seen an improvement with her relationship with Richard too. He was still the same, but somehow she just didn't allow him to get under her skin. Strangely seeing Pete had helped in a way she never thought it would. She had done a lot of soul searching and asked herself many questions about who she was and what she wanted. She loved her girls and was enjoying being their mother each day more and more. She took them out and met with other mothers at the 'Mums and Toddlers' group. She was managing to stay on top of the cooking and the housework. She still saw Eva a couple times a week but their time was spent in leisurely activities together. They loved going to the park and having lovely chats as they watched the girls playing and squealing with delight. She really liked Eva, she always had. She was more like a friend than a mother-in-law and she found it easy to open up to her about Richard and the way he was. She would listen and give advice on how to handle her only son. She admitted that losing his father when he was so young had impacted him because she had relied on him too much. She blamed herself for putting a huge responsibility on young shoulders. Richard never enjoyed the kind of childhood other children did because he had taken on the role of caring for his mum. Eva recalled a time when Richard had been invited to the birthday party of one of his friends from school and how he arranged to leave early so that Eva wouldn't be on her own for too long. After speaking to the mother who had hosted the party, Eva discovered just how much control he had taken of his own time. Apparently Richard had spoken openly about how he needed to be with his mum as much as possible to look after her. He had learned to organise his recreation time to ensure that everything was taken care of at home. He was eight years old at the time. As Karen listened to stories about Richard, she felt sad for a childhood that had been snatched from him when his dad died so suddenly and she tried not to judge him too harshly. He was used to making decisions and taking care of people, that was what he had done from an early age. She soon realised that he wasn't being manipulative in a sinister way, he was just used to taking control of every situation. However, it was an issue that was beginning to affect their marriage as he managed and influenced everything. It dawned on Karen that she didn't actually make any decisions about anything! Without realising it he even tried to tell her how to think.

She had noticed that whenever she tried to talk about Robin, he was, in her opinion, being consigned to history by Richard. Thoughts of her son would suddenly crowd her mind and her emotions were sometimes so overwhelming that she felt sad and melancholy, but he didn't want to discuss it because he believed that she should have come to terms with it and moved on. One day, she was completely taken aback when he said, 'Karen, you need to take control of your emotions. I had to when my father died.' He said it so matter of fact. He really didn't understand at all. She couldn't fully describe the pain she felt from that sentence but it felt like a blow to her heart and she knew right at that moment, her love for Richard had changed. Richard handled things differently and she wasn't like him. Besides, Robin wasn't dead. She couldn't just forget him. Neither did she want to. How she wished she could tell Eva. They had become such good friends, Karen felt sure that Richard had read his mum wrong on this issue. With her mum working full time, Karen just didn't know how she would have gotten through most of her days without Eva.

Chapter 18

Pete felt his phone buzzing in his back pocket and pulled it out quickly. He looked at it and saw that it was a number he didn't recognise and hoped that it would be Karen

'Hello Pete.' It was almost a whisper. She wasn't sure why she was whispering. There was no one else around.

'Karen, is that you? It's so good to hear from you, I'd almost given up hope of ever hearing from you,' Pete gushed, 'I'm coming to the end of my mid morning break so I can't stay long. Can I ring you at lunchtime?'

'Oh okay,' Karen felt deflated. It had taken so much courage to make that call, the girls were playing in the conservatory with their toys and she had decided to 'strike while the iron was hot'. She wasn't sure that lunchtime would suit her. She would be feeding the girls.

'I'm not sure, I shouldn't have rang it was mistake, bye.'

'Karen, wait! Please don't go, I work in a school and I'm covering a class that's due to start. You have no idea how much this means to me, I've got your number now,' he looked at the number displayed on his mobile phone, 'I'll ring you about 12.40.' He was gone!

Karen looked at the phone as though it were some alien object that she didn't know what to do with. She stood for several minutes rooted to the spot holding it in her hand. *What have I just done? This is crazy.* She thought. *What purpose is this going to serve?*

Her thoughts turned to Robin. Her little boy who had gone who wasn't hers anymore. She remembered the day he was born and the six weeks she held him, fed him and cared for him while she made her decision. There were the visits from Social Services and the Adoption agency with everyone around her asking her if she was sure about her decision. Of course, she wasn't sure, but she knew in those few weeks that she wasn't strong enough to do it on her own. But she did love him, her beautiful little boy who deserved so much more than a sixteen year old mum who didn't know her own mind. She had been so undecided about whether to name him and he remained nameless for a few days, but then one morning a red robin appeared on the windowsill and seemed to linger for a while and then he was gone. That little bird was beautiful just like her little baby boy and soon he would be gone too. She named him Robin.

Most of her time with Robin had been spent in a haze of emotions. She had felt love for this vulnerable baby who belonged to her but she hadn't been able to quite believe that he was hers either. She had been extremely overwhelmed and confused. No wonder she had been so unsure. It was the hardest decision of her life and Pete had done that to her, how she loved and hated him all at the same time.

Karen's thoughts came back to the present. *So why was she ringing him now? He was history and needed to remain there.* Yes, he was Robin's father and would always be her first love but the dream had been shattered, it couldn't be mended now. Like a mirror broken in many pieces with no chance of ever putting it back together, there was no hope of getting her little boy back.

It was quarter to eleven, so there was time for Karen to prepare the girls lunch, make sure that they ate it all and then get them involved in some sort of activity so she could be ready for his call. Grace and Amelia were little angels today, she observed. She was glad and it gave her time to wash the potatoes ready to put in the oven, grate the cheese and open the can of beans ready. They loved jacket potatoes with cheese and beans. It was always a joy to watch them eat. She then cut and prepared a variety of fruit ready for them to eat afterwards and got their carton of drinks out of the cupboard. Her aim was to have them sat down ready to eat at 12 noon. She hoped they would be finished by the time he called. She decided to get a film ready for them to watch rather than an activity that they would constantly try and involve her in. She could do no more she thought and silently prayed that all would go according to plan. The time flew by while she tended to the girls and gave them lunch, Grace fed herself really well and Amelia was taking each mouthful too. So far so good! Karen settled the girls ready for the film explaining that mummy would be a few minutes on the phone and Grace put a protective arm around Amelia as they sat together on the sofa. Karen felt a warm glow and reminded herself how blessed she was to have the girls. Her grandma Rose had reminded her of this so many times whenever she seemed sad or mentioned Robin. It was strange because her grandma had been the one person who didn't avoid the subject. She had always said God knows the reason for everything, and to count her blessings for the girls. It had given her the comfort she needed at those times. Oh, how she loved her grandma for a whole host of reasons and she always looked forward to seeing her every Saturday at her parents' house.

The phone rang, the number with no name flashed up on her mobile. She knew it was Pete and suddenly she wasn't sure whether to answer it.

Chapter 19

Karen swiped the screen on her phone and immediately heard his voice. 'Karen, Karen.'

Silence, she couldn't answer. After what seem like an eternity, she found her voice, 'yes, it is Pete,' said Karen.

'Are you ok?' he asked concerned.

'I'm fine, but I can't stay for long. Have you any idea how hard it is to try and occupy two small children? Fortunately, they're watching a film so I'm okay for now, let's see how long eh?' She laughed weakly.

'No, I don't, we don't have any children and it's not likely to happen. Karen I've been so selfish all my life. It's payback time. I walked away from you and our baby because I was a coward. I'm sorry Karen, you didn't deserve it, I'm so sorry,' Pete trailed off.

'We were young none of us knew what to do. I knew I couldn't do the abortion thing, but even I didn't keep him, did I?' She asked rhetorically, 'I was selfish too, we both abandoned him. Poor soul didn't deserve it, I've regretted it ever since. Even having my beautiful girls hasn't helped. In fact my pain has intensified.' Karen's eyes filled with tears that threatened to spill as she spoke deeply for the first time about Robin in a very long time to anyone.

'Karen, please don't blame yourself, it was all me. It was my fault. All mine. I really need to see you again, speaking on the phone isn't ideal. When can we meet? I think we both need closure, I've been struggling too. Oh Karen, I'm so sorry.'

'It's too late for sorry Pete, way too late. It's done! We both made our decisions eleven years ago, what is there to be gained now? All it's going to do is re-open wounds, not sure I can go there.' Karen was sobbing now. She was standing in the hallway looking beyond the lounge and into the conservatory where the girls were sitting watching their film. She noticed that Amelia had fallen asleep with her head leaning to one side. She didn't want Grace to see her upset but she knew she needed to move Amelia and lay her down into a more comfortable position. She wiped her tears away.

It had taken her a long time to get to a place where she had some kind of routine with the girls. Richard had been pleased with her progress. He still organised everything but she accepted that now and appreciated that it did actually make life easier for her. So on the whole, life had improved but she was slightly irritated with herself that she seemed unable to make even simple decisions. She didn't feel confident to trust her own judgment. Even when they were planning to move the girls into the bigger bedroom so they could be together, she couldn't decide what colour to paint the girls bedroom, what carpet to get, and even choosing bedding and curtains were hard. That should have been easy. *What was wrong with her?* Well, deep down, she knew why. Richard felt that every decision should be discussed. He always had to have input. *So what was the point in even trying to think about it?* The chances were he wouldn't want what she chose so it was pointless but she was aware that she was losing the skill of making even small choices. He always said that he had an eye for detail, he prided himself on knowing quality and he needed to feel totally satisfied with anything that was bought. Richard had a real aversion to the colour green, he just didn't like it. So it was never an option, not clothes for her or the kids, not carpet, not curtains, nothing! She actually liked the colour green but that didn't matter. With Richard there was no compromise, if he didn't like something then it couldn't happen. She knew how committed he was to her and the kids so how could she complain. It was very hard to argue against either something he wanted or something he didn't want. He didn't impose things in a contentious way it was so much more subtle than that. He would just give a very reasoned argument that was so persuasive it would leave her feeling unqualified to dispute it. He was truly confident in his opinions in a way that she envied and wished she could be like that. It was quite admirable in some ways and so in spite of his need to control and be a part of every plan they needed to make, she felt she had to overlook the effect it had on her as it was only one aspect of his personality and he had so many qualities. He was incredibly loving and caring, an amazingly 'hands on' dad too. So it seemed churlish to challenge him when essentially he was a kind person.

'I don't know Pete, let me think about it. I'll get back to you,' Karen replied.

It was more than Pete expected or thought he deserved. He was just happy it wasn't an outright refusal. 'Okay,' Pete said. He felt grateful, 'I'll wait to hear from you, then. I'm so sorry. You'll never know how much. It's not too late, you know. Maybe we can find him together?'

'I've got to go now Pete.' The phone went dead.

Karen went into the conservatory, picked up a sleeping Amelia and cradled her close to her chest and sat down next to Grace encircling her. Her precious children were a real comfort right now.

Chapter 20

Richard walked in that evening to find Karen where she had been several months earlier. Nothing had been done in the house and the girls were practically fending for themselves. On top of that there was not even any aroma that dinner had been started. *What had gone wrong?* He wondered. Karen looked upset, like she had been crying. Richard knew what was planned for dinner as it was on the rota. That was one of the reasons he liked a rota, he could just get on with it without having to think about what to eat from scratch. Thursday night was always pasta. Simple enough!

Richard tried to talk to Karen but all he got was literally one word answers from her. He reasoned that she was clearly not in a good way so he was just wasting his time. So he proceeded with what needed to be done. He prepared dinner. Fed and bathed the girls and got them ready for bed. He decided that he would try and talk to Karen later.

It had been a difficult evening. Richard was a naturally loving person and he knew from when they met that she struggled to show the level of affection he needed. However over the years, he could see that she had improved a lot but tonight there was a clear distance between them. There seemed to be a gulf that appeared impossible for him to cross. After the girls had gone to bed, he suggested they watch a movie together and although she said yes and dutifully sat next to him, he knew that she wasn't in the room; physically yes, mentally no. *Something had changed!*

Karen sat next to Richard not watching the film at all. If someone had asked her what had been said in any of the dialogue even minutes after hearing it, she would not have been able to recount it.

Damn Pete, she thought. *Why did that man cause her so much pain and why did he still have an effect on her that Richard never could. Poor Richard, he meant well. But she couldn't talk to him, she couldn't tell him that she missed her son and that she wanted to feel normal and not live life in a bubble that wasn't real. She felt a fake!*

Why didn't he see that it wasn't fair for him to expect her to forget her past like it didn't exist. It was what made her the person she was now.

The phone call with Pete earlier had transported her back in time to when she was sixteen and all those memories flooded her mind and she was back to that sad teenager again, alone and hurt. She really needed to talk to someone and she immediately wished it could be Eva. She couldn't talk to her own mum. She knew how hard it had been for Marina, it was just too close to home. She could however talk to Grandma Rose about her feelings because she was so sweet and compassionate and always listened intently to how she felt and Grandma always reminded her that she should pray and believe that God was looking after Robin and that he was happy. It was lovely that Grandma talked so easily and freely about Robin. It did help her. And of course Grandma would remind Karen how blessed she was now to have the girls and would offer to pray for her to find inner peace. Karen did appreciate it and she definitely felt a degree of comfort from prayer but because there were still so many emotions that were so painful and intense, it provided only partial comfort. There was still a lot that troubled her deeply. Robin was an important part of her past and had had a life changing impact on her. She didn't want to forget him. The more she thought about it, the more she realised that what she struggled with the most was Richard not allowing her to talk about him. *If he didn't want her to talk to him about Robin, she understood that, but why not Eva?* Karen was sure it would help her. She wanted to be honest with her. It had begun to eat away at her. Round and round, her thoughts went. Karen felt like her head would explode. That night, she tossed and turned while Richard slept beside her. *Would she ever find any peace in this situation? Maybe she should just try to forget Robin and endeavour to live her life fully present with Richard and the girls.* Robin was from another lifetime. He had new parents now, he was happy and settled. But the same questions obsessively occupied her thoughts.

Why had she been so weak at the time? Why had she been so short sighted? If only she had kept him, there would be no secret, no shame, no sadness and no part of her past that haunted her. Why oh why did it have to happen? But if she had kept Robin, maybe Grace and Amelia wouldn't be here. If buts and maybe's? Why was she torturing herself? Stop it! Stop it!

Richard slept soundly and how she envied that. Karen pulled the covers back and proceeded out of bed. She shivered slightly at the coolness of the night atmosphere. She placed her feet quietly onto the carpeted floor of their bedroom. It was warm underfoot and beautifully soft. She grabbed her dressing gown hanging on the bedroom door and slipped her arms easily and swiftly into it. The kitchen was strangely comforting as she put the kettle to boil. She opened the blinds and stood perfectly still as she looked through the window at the night sky hoping for some tranquillity and peace. It never came. The boiled kettle clicked off! She sat at the kitchen table and drank her tea with a million thoughts running through her mind. She had no idea how long she had been there but as daylight streamed in through the window, she was glad to have made it through another troubled night.

The following weeks saw a gradual and very apparent decline in Karen's behaviour. Almost every evening, Richard came home to what could only be described as chaos. Things had been going so well in recent months. She seemed to be coping and doing everything with ease. *What had happened to bring this recent change? She hadn't mentioned her first child in a long time, so it couldn't be that!* He felt that he had finally got through to her. He had said on many occasions that she couldn't change the past so there was no use dwelling on it. Besides, she should be grateful for the girls that he had given her and the life he had created for them. He was getting very irritated with her obsession to talk. The thing that baffled him the most was the need to share it with his mum. *Why?* It was unnecessary. The many conversations about it had tested his patience.

He never dreamt for one minute that Robin could have ever become a problem between them. *How had that happened?* It had started to annoy him and that was why he had made it clear to Karen that it had to stop before it got out of hand. And it had and she seemed so much better. Her mood, her appearance, the children's behaviour had all improved. They had enjoyed some really good times that had grown them closer with each other and the girls. This was the wife and mother he had wanted. Okay, he understood that she had been through a lot and her confidence wasn't great but was it too much to expect her to look after the house and the children like other women did, he didn't think so. He knew he had some shaping to do and felt confident that he could achieve it. And he had! Or so he thought, until that Thursday when everything just seemed to change and had gone back downhill.

He tried everything, even decided to raise the subject of Robin to see if that was bothering her again. But she had been emphatic, there was nothing wrong. She was fine. *But she wasn't 'fine'. She was far from 'fine'.* Everything about her behaviour was worrying. She would go from compliant to defiant, from chatty to withdrawn and from happy to sad in an instant. She was totally unpredictable. He knew she had not been sleeping well, he had lost track of the nights he would find her 'gone' from their bed only to find her in the kitchen. There had been times when she would come back to bed without resistance and other times when he had to practically fight with her. He wasn't sure how much more he could take and the girls had started to become affected too.

Chapter 21

Eva had been sat reading in bed in the early morning as was her usual practice. She had found recently that she didn't seem to need as much sleep anymore and usually around 5am most mornings her eyes would pop open which she found most annoying. Occasionally she would manage to drop back off to sleep again for another hour or so. But this particular morning, try as she might, she couldn't get back to sleep no matter how many times she turned from her left side to her right side. She then lay on her back for a while staring at the ceiling. Nope! Sleep had flown. She went down to the kitchen and brought her freshly made coffee back to bed and settled into the book she was currently reading. She loved crime thrillers. The suspense and anticipation kept her gripped and engrossed. She was completely lost in her book when the phone rang. It was 7.40am.

'Hi mum, it's Richard.'

'Are you okay love? To what do I owe this early call?' she queried.

'I'm worried about Karen, she's acting strangely!' Richard responded immediately without his usual question of asking how she was. Eva sat up straight moving from her relaxed position.

'What do you mean, strangely?' Eva asked with real interest and concern. *What could he possibly mean?* She pondered and waited for him to carry on. Richard paused. 'Richard, c'mon love, you're worrying me now. What do you mean?' Richard knew that he was only giving his mum half a story but hoped that she could help anyway. Knowing how much Karen liked his mum he thought maybe Eva could help her to get organised. He hoped that if his mum could provide some advice about developing a routine of some kind, Karen might just take it on board, anything to break the habit of disarray.

'Well, I came home last night to find the house upside down. Grace and Amelia running riot and Karen sitting like a zombie. When I asked her what was wrong, she just stared at me,' Richard paused while Eva sat digesting the information, 'it's not the first time that I've got home and had to cook the dinner, bathe the kids and put them to bed.'

'Is there anything you want me to do to help? Have you considered taking her to the doctor Richard?' Eva was really concerned now.

'I'm not sure that's the answer just yet!' Richard knew that he was probably putting off the inevitable but wanted to see what else could be done. 'Mum, can you go and see her today? Don't tell her that I asked you to come, just pop in and see how she is. Just be casual about it and see how you can help.'

'Of course love, no problem,' Eva said.

'I've got to go now mum,' Richard was gone.

Eva stared at the phone slightly baffled for what seemed like forever but it was actually only a few seconds. Eva liked Karen and hoped that she could help. *Karen is something of an enigma. S*he thought. She had always got on really well with her but there was something she couldn't quite put her finger on.

It was 10.30am when Karen answered the door to her mother-in-law. 'Eva, I didn't expect it to be you, what a lovely surprise!' Karen looked unkempt, Eva observed.

'I was passing, are you ok my love? Where are my beautiful girls?' Eva said as she leaned in to hug her.

'They're playing in the lounge.' Eva could see from the hallway that they were playing with their multi-coloured plastic bricks and were engrossed in trying to fit them together. She decided not to disturb them just yet and see how Karen was.

Karen asked her if she wanted a drink and led her into the kitchen. While the kettle boiled, they chatted easily as always but Karen did seem a bit remote, Eva noticed. She couldn't quite figure it out but there was something different about her. 'What are your plans today Karen, can I help at all? I've got a few hours free.'

Karen had no plans at all that day. It was too much effort as it had been yesterday and the day before that. 'Nothing planned at all,' Karen replied flatly.

'I know, why don't you take some time out for yourself? I'll watch the girls for you,' Eva suggested.

After some consideration and a furrowed brow, Karen said, 'Actually, I do need a new coat. I could go and have a look around the shops,' she paused before continuing, 'Richard normally likes to go shopping with me but I can always take it back if I find one that he doesn't like I suppose. Okay I'll do that, thanks Eva. I'll go and get ready.'

Eva wandered into the lounge where the girls were playing. 'Nanny,' they said in unison and flung themselves around her.

'Look at my castle nanny,' Grace said.

'Look at mine,' Amelia added, both competing for Eva's attention. Eva lowered herself to the floor and helped them finish their plastic castles while Karen showered and changed.

As Karen walked down the stairs, she started to feel quite excited at the prospect of some time for herself. She didn't get it often and was looking forward to shopping on her own without Richard and the girls in tow. She hugged and kissed the girls and thanked Eva once more as she closed the front door behind her.

Karen headed straight to her favourite Department store and walked out of the shop with her new coat in record time. She tried it on and knew instantly that the camel coloured coat with a soft brown fur collar and a tie belt that flattered her frame was the one she wanted. She really liked it. She hoped Richard would too. *What should she do now?* She thought. *It's way too soon to go home.*

She walked into the coffee shop, ordered a latte and made her way to small round table in the corner. It was quiet. She looked at her phone and was going to phone Eva but decided against it as she knew the girls would be fine. *What could she do next?* She wondered. Karen was surprised at how lost she felt. *Who could she contact that would be free now?* No one, she reasoned. It wasn't as though she could meet anyone as everyone was at work and there was no point in contacting any of the mothers from the 'Mums and Toddlers' group, as they would have their children. *What would be the point of spending time with other people's children when she was free of her own?* She sat staring into space with her thoughts. Things had improved slightly with Richard but he still wielded a degree of control and power over her that made her feel uncomfortable. She recalled the events of the previous weekend when his behaviour had really affected her. All she asked was to sit and watch a film that was her choice for a change. Yes, she enjoyed a good adventure film and there had been many that had offered good entertainment but she had definitely had her fill of science fiction films. But no, it was another science fiction and she was just not in the mood. She'd spotted a romantic comedy on the other channel starting at the same time. 'What about that Rom Com on the other side? That would make a nice change from science fiction all the time,' Karen said casually.

'When are you going to come on board with me on this?' He replied with a smile but through gritted teeth.

'But I don't enjoy them as much as you.'

'Don't whine Karen, it's irritating. I'm trying to organise some 'us' time while the kids are in bed and you're just so ungrateful,' he spat out.

'Richard, where's this come from? It's just a film.'

'You can watch your films anytime when I'm not here, I can't watch that rubbish.'

'It would just be nice to watch my choice of film with you for a change. That's all...' she trailed off.

That was it she felt herself conceding as she always did. It just wasn't worth the hassle. She would sit through the film he wanted as always. She was annoyed with herself for being compliant Karen again and as she sat and watched the film with Richard, she felt sadness creeping over her. She had to fight the feeling of hopelessness. She had lost her confidence and decision-making ability. *What kind of mother was she? How could she help them when she couldn't help herself? What did the future hold for her and Richard? Did she love him? Had she ever really loved him?* He was her 'knight in shining armour' her 'saviour' from her 'old life' that she had wanted to escape from so much. Yet had she rushed it and just grabbed at the first opportunity to be 'normal' in her eyes. She loved her girls with all her heart but she knew she wasn't enjoying them in the way she wanted. She just didn't feel capable, and even doing simple tasks seemed like hard work. Richard was such a perfectionist and criticised her at every turn. Granted he said it nicely most of the time but he never just ignored something or let it go. Nothing was good enough it had to be done his way. *Why was she so pathetic?* She wanted so much to feel good about herself. What *a mess she had made of her life!* Immediately her thoughts turned to Robin. She thought she was going mad. *She had let Robin go! She couldn't let her girls go too! She was more than capable but she had to start believing in herself.* She picked up her phone and dialled the number in her contacts.

Chapter 22

'Hi Pete it's me Karen. I'm not even sure why I'm ringing you to be honest,' She sighed.

'I'm glad you rang, it's good to hear from you. It's perfect timing too. Where are you?' Pete asked.

'I'm in the coffee shop on the ground floor of the Shopping Centre,' Karen told him.

'Give me twenty minutes and I'll be there,' there was a pause before Pete continued, 'Karen, thank you, I'll see you in a bit.'

What had she done? Her thoughts were a jumbled mess. *What good would this do?*

Pete walked in the door, searched the room and headed towards her once his eyes found hers. He bent down to hug her while Karen sat rooted to her chair, 'how long have you got?' Pete said as he sat down opposite, 'do you want another one?' He was pointing to the second half full cup of latte sitting in front of Karen. 'No, I'm good thanks,' she said.

He returned with his espresso and looked at Karen. Small talk followed about the weather, the traffic and even Karen's purchase. Then without warning Pete blurted out, 'It's so good to see you. What a fool I was Karen, seeing you today has made me realise that I still love you. I was so selfish.'

Maybe it was how she was feeling but hearing that reminded Karen of the young girl of sixteen madly in love with the handsome boy of seventeen who had been her world. 'I still love you, never stopped if I'm honest,' she said with sadness, 'why did you let it go Pete? It's too late now, I'm married to Richard and I've got my beautiful daughters.'

'Karen, I was an idiot and I've paid the price.' Karen sat and listened while he told her all about his life with Vanessa and their inability to produce a child. She sat absorbed without interruption nodding in all the right places. She watched as the tears flowed freely down his face and she knew in her heart that he was truly sorry for what he had done. He told her that he loved Vanessa too, poor sweet Vanessa but he knew deep down that Karen was still his real true love and knowing that she had had his child and that he let them both go caused him more anguish than he could describe. She didn't enjoy seeing him in so much pain but it helped her in a strange way. She had suffered so much and was still suffering in many ways but it felt like some of the weight had shifted. She could share it and for the first time in years, she could talk about Robin. She didn't have to bottle it up or pretend it hadn't happened.

An hour had passed as if it were only five minutes, Karen looked at her watch and realised the time. She couldn't take advantage of Eva's kindness any longer, she had to go home. Pete understood. They parted and promised to be in touch again. Today had been healing and truly cathartic for both of them.

Talking to Pete about his life and seeing the pain etched in his face and hearing the sorrow he felt had really impacted her in a way she had not expected. They both felt sadness for letting go of their little boy knowing they would never share in his childhood. Robin had new parents now but Karen felt that at least she and Pete could share with each other how they felt, they could grieve together and even dream together. *What did he look like? What was his favourite food? Did he like sport?* So many unanswered questions about the son she gave birth to but knew nothing about. *But it was good that Pete wanted to know too!* She felt strangely lifted, somehow she could face the future there was hope. For a long time, she had spent so much energy trying to forget, trying to move on but she decided she wasn't going to bury her past anymore. She wanted to confront it and understand where to go with the pain. She felt stronger for the first time in years. It was time to regain control, for too long she had relied on Richard and it wasn't healthy. As she walked to the car park, with a spring in her step, she was happy that finally something could change, and that she could make it happen.

Chapter 23

As Karen put her key in the door, she looked at her watch and realised she had been out for just over three hours. She had never done that before. On the drive home, Karen reflected on her time with Pete. How easy it had been, how relaxed she felt. It seemed so natural. In comparison, it never really felt like that with Richard, she always felt like she was acting, being what he wanted her to be instead of who she really was. That was the problem with their relationship it was about what Richard wanted so that was what was played out. He was good to her and she didn't want to crucify him but that was the difference between the two men, in the short time spent with Pete, she felt like she could be Karen, she knew he loved her for who she was as he had all those years ago. There was no thinking about how to behave or what to say, she could be herself and he seemed pretty relaxed too. She couldn't believe how he poured his heart out to her, the tears streaming down his face. This was something she was not expecting at all. And then to tell her that he still loved her. Wow!

For many years, Karen had felt a phony. With everyone she was just acting, even with her own family and certainly with poor sweet Eva, whom she adored. But in a few short hours, she felt real again like she could be in touch with who she was and understand and enjoy that. Richard had robbed her of it. *Where did she go from here?* She loved her girls with all her heart but then it became evident to her that she hadn't fallen in love Richard. She loved him because he was good to her and he had accepted her history without judgement. She would always respect him for that. It was a different type of love but it had never been that 'heart stopping, butterfly feeling in the stomach' kind of love. *Would and could it be enough to last a lifetime?* The meeting with Pete had made her ask herself questions now.

And then there was Robin, her son who she didn't know. She could talk about him to Pete, someone who wanted to talk about him too, someone who had regrets like herself, someone who was feeling the loss of a child, and for Pete he had the unexpected pain of childlessness. Before returning home she had parked up for a while on a nearby street and sat with her thoughts.

When Karen walked into the lounge with Grace and Amelia sitting on either side of their grandmother with her arms around each of them watching their favourite cartoon, she felt a sudden rush of guilt. While she had been out with Pete, her wonderful mother-in-law had been looking after her children. She knew Eva loved the girls dearly and thoroughly enjoyed her time with them. She was a natural nurturing person and Grace and Amelia were very comfortable with her. *What was she doing?* She was keeping this wonderful woman in the dark about who she really was. It just wasn't fair she had a right to know. Karen couldn't get past the feeling that she just wasn't being authentic with her. It was time whether Richard wanted it or not, whatever the fallout to tell Eva the whole truth. She needed to share it.

Karen sat and watched the last ten minutes of the show with them and it was apparent as the credits rolled that Amelia was ready for a nap, her eyes were slowly closing. She put her down to sleep. Grace wanted to dress her dolls up in their various outfits which could occupy her for hours so Karen left her to play. Karen put the kettle on and she and Eva sat and chatted. Richard wasn't due home until about 6.30pm and so Karen asked Eva if she wanted to stay a bit longer. Eva was happy to. It was time. It could not be put off any longer. As Grace played happily in the conservatory, Karen plucked up the courage.

'Eva, I've got something to tell you. Something I wanted to tell you a long time ago actually and I can't leave it any longer,' Karen hesitated. Eva looked at Karen intently and waited for her to continue. That was exactly what Karen liked about Eva, she always remained calm, and right now she allowed Karen the time she needed to get her words out, 'I've got a son,' Karen stated. Eva waited for her to finish, 'his name's Robin. I was sixteen when I had him. He was adopted.' The tears started to flow down Karen's face, hot silent tears that flowed unchecked down the sides of her nose and onto her lips. She could taste the saltiness coming from them.

Eva rose from the armchair that she occupied and went over to Karen who was sitting on the sofa opposite and put her arms right around her. It was too much, such kindness broke her even more and her body racked with sobs. It was heartbreaking for Eva to witness. Fortunately, Karen was out of view of the glass door which led from the lounge to the conservatory and it was closed so Eva knew that Grace couldn't hear her mum crying. Eva grabbed some tissues from the box nearby and gently wiped Karen's face. Karen felt relief flood her body. *Finally, it had been said, it couldn't be unsaid.*

Eva listened as Karen gave a brief outline of the events of her former life. Eva's face and body language showed compassion and empathy. There was no hint of judgement at all.

'You poor love,' she soothed, 'why didn't you tell me before?' she asked.

'Richard told me not to,' Karen replied through sniffs.

Eva looked incredulous and said, 'That doesn't surprise me. Richard's always trying to protect me. He's been doing that all his life,' she had a faraway look in her eyes, 'maybe I'm to blame for that, I relied on him too much when his dad died. I went to pieces and he watched me, poor boy,' she paused, 'he has always treated me like I'm made of glass,' she shook her head slowly, 'anyway, that's enough about me, you poor girl.'

'So, you don't mind that I'm not who you thought I was?' Karen asked.

'Of course not, why would I?' she replied, 'it makes no difference to me, I have always loved you and hearing this changes nothing,' she paused, 'actually I'm lying,' Karen looked worried. Eva continued, 'if anything, I love you more.' Eva said quietly and smiled. Karen couldn't believe what she was hearing. What a beautiful person Eva truly was.

Chapter 24

Eva and Karen decided after much discussion and deliberation that it was best that Richard did not know that Karen had told her about Robin. Karen was really worried about his reaction and going against his wishes. Eva knew Richard and the way he could be and she understood why he behaved the way he did sometimes. She didn't always like it but she felt a tremendous guilt about the heavy burden placed on him when his father died because of her inability to cope at that time. It immediately changed their roles and he became her protector and Eva had noticed over the years as he grew from boy to man that there were times when she couldn't reason with him. He did things his way and would not change even with gentle persuasion. She had learnt over time not to challenge him, he would become stern and defensive. He would make it clear that he had made his decision and that was that. She recalled a time when Richard still lived at home and the lounge needed decorating. Richard had got a decorator in and chose the colour scheme without any discussion with her. Eva loved her floral designs on soft furnishings, but Richard had decided 'that look' had to go and in came what he described as a more classic design in curtains and cushions. When Eva tried to re-introduce her florals, Richard told her that he didn't like it and didn't want it. It had taken her by surprise because it was the evenness in his voice and the deliberateness in his delivery that told her this was not a battle worth fighting. She had to admit that he did have good taste and so she did in the end come to like the new decor. She understood what Karen was dealing with as he genuinely seemed to believe that whatever he did was for that person's benefit, even if they couldn't initially see it. He was such a good son, who cared and protected her in every way and they got on so well but she knew that if he had knowledge that Karen had broken her promise to him; he would feel betrayed. It was best that he didn't know. Nothing would be gained. He had been acting in her best interests, she understood that. Eva noticed that

Karen seemed really fearful and was adamant that she didn't want Richard to know she had told her. Eva reassured her that it was their secret.

It had been such a weight off Karen's shoulder to eventually be able to share it with Eva. It had deepened their friendship. After that day of unburdening, Eva spent many days listening to Karen helping her to deal with her emotions. She found herself spending more and more time with Karen and the girls. Talking to Eva had really helped Karen. She felt able to think about Robin now without guilt but the more she thought about him the more her curiosity about him grew into an obsession. She needed to speak to Pete.

Karen and Pete spoke at every opportunity about Robin. They wondered what he looked like and hoped that he was happy, truly happy. They both dreamt about a day when they could meet him. Karen walked into the coffee bar. Pete was sat with her latte waiting for her. They smiled at each other. It was good to recall the good times that they had and to think of Robin who had been the result of their love. Karen felt relaxed and happy. She could remember Robin freely and dream of a day when she would meet him. At times they became sad when they talked about him but it was as if they both needed to do it anyway. And so it was the start of many meetings in the coffee shop; an hour here and an hour there, but it was just what Karen needed.

Six months had passed since her first meeting with Pete and Karen wondered how she had survived without him. It was as though a part of her that had been lost had been returned to her. It felt so natural, it didn't feel wrong. Yes, she felt guilty about Richard because despite everything he was good to her and he was the father of her beautiful girls. He was the provider and took full responsibility for all of them. *He is a good man.* She kept telling herself. *So why do I feel the need to keep meeting Pete?* She asked herself. He had let her down, caused her untold pain and the reason she gave up her first child. It was his selfishness. But Karen could see he had changed, he was deeply sorry about his actions back then and his humility was evident. She understood that they were the reactions of a boy, not the man he was now. She forgave him, he had cried openly on more than one occasion. His sadness about Robin was visible. Karen asked herself if he would have felt the same had he and Vanessa managed to have a child of their own. Of course, it was impossible to know the answer to that but she reasoned that she had her girls but still missed her son, so maybe it would have been the same for him. Of course, having the girls had helped her enormously but then there were times when she found the loss of Robin and the memory of the pain around his birth hard to bear; knowing that her first born child had been adopted and wasn't a part of her life. She knew it was something that she had to come to terms with. Ironically being able to talk to Pete was helping her even though he had been a part of the problem. It didn't make any sense to her. Over and over again, she questioned what she was doing, risking her marriage and her new life for snatched conversations about the past and contemplative musings about a future with Robin that was unrealistic. Her head was all over the place.

Eva had been amazing she would allow her to just talk whenever she felt sad. She would simply listen with an expression of sheer compassion and even shed tears with Karen as she cried. They spent more and more time together, they were not just mother-in-law and daughter-in-law but friends too. Some of their conversations were about Richard and both acknowledged with each passing year, he seemed a little more controlling and that it was hard to reason with him at times.

Eva had a very strong sense of guilt about her only son and blamed herself for the person he had become. She felt so sorry for Karen who had been left with the task of dealing with him. It was a load too much to bear at times for a fragile young woman with already enough to cope with. Eva knew that she had to support them both as much as she could. She didn't want Karen to break emotionally. She could see that she was just about coping. She loved her granddaughters so much and was growing ever closer to them the more time she spent. It was a joy to play games with them; read books, watch films and see the pure pleasure on their faces while they ran around the garden. She'd noticed that Richard was happier too, he was always pleased to see her if she stayed for dinner.

Meanwhile Richard had observed that Karen was more relaxed and seemed more organised and in control. He wasn't having to remind her of the things that he liked, or how he wanted things to be done. Yes, life had started to improve and finally felt like things were moving in the right direction. Maybe now, he thought Karen would start to show some interest in sex again. She just seemed to make excuse after excuse to get out of it but now that he had seen an improvement he hoped with time and a little bit of coaxing, things would happen naturally. Karen however had no such inclination. She had struggled for a long time with being intimate with Richard. Not being able to talk to him about her feelings had pushed her further and further from him. *How could she give him her body when he didn't want her mind?*

It was hard to believe that it had been over a year since Pete and Karen had met up again. It had flown, Grace was now four and Amelia was coming up for three in a few weeks time. Karen felt freer, happier and in control; more able to handle the girls and had developed a routine.

Karen and Richard had been busy trying to decide which school Grace should go to and they had done the customary rounds of visiting various schools, reading the Ofsted reports online and generally researching it all. Richard had been his usual self and he, not unsurprisingly, decided on the school. Karen didn't have any reason to object. She knew that he had Grace's best interests at heart so she just went along with him. Things had improved between them but only because Karen felt guilty about her meetings with Pete even though she had nothing to feel ashamed of as it was only coffee and a chat.

Sometimes a couple of months would go by before she and Pete met up but Karen felt now that Pete was back in her life, she couldn't let him go. They talked and recalled everything that had happened all those years ago, it was as if they were back in time. They laughed as they remembered the good times and cried together when they thought of Robin who was a part of them but was apart from them. How they wished it could have been different.

Life was bearable with Pete back in her life. Somehow she could function normally. She had learned to compartmentalise her thoughts and her life. When she was with Pete, she could forget her current life and when she was with Richard and the girls, she could forget about Pete.

She had developed enormous coping strategies and was somehow able to behave and act in the moment. She couldn't explain it even if she wanted to and she didn't want to. There was no one that would understand what she was doing. She had thought about telling Fiona as she knew that she could trust her and that she wouldn't judge her, but decided against it. Fiona was happy and settled in her relationship with her partner, they had moved into together two months ago. Somehow it didn't seem like the right time. And she never even contemplated telling Susan, *perfect Susan.* *She just seemed to get everything right!* She had got her degree and had a good job. Mum and dad were so proud of Susan and although they never made her feel like a failure, Karen felt that way anyway. They had tried to reassure her many times, that she was doing well, married to Richard with two beautiful children living in a good neighbourhood. They never ever mentioned her beautiful son. Tears filled her eyes as she remembered him. They didn't want to upset her. She didn't blame them, it had been her decision and they had supported her. She always remembered the many conversations she'd had with them and the message that they gave was loud and clear, they didn't want Karen to say that they had made her do something she didn't want to do. But how she wished, they had insisted she keep him, she wouldn't be where she is today but deep down her logical head understood why they had left the decision with her.   She did ask herself time and time again why she didn't keep him but then she remembered how she felt back then and the thought of being a single mum frightened her to death and she was so hurt and fragile.

No one would understand or even begin to understand why she was seeing Pete so she was happy to keep it to herself. It was what she had done most of her life anyway, she had never felt the need to share every bit of her life with anybody not even her family. Karen knew she was complex and at times she didn't even understand herself. She just knew that she was able to function and somehow felt closer to Robin now that she was able to talk about him even if she could never see him.

Eva decided to take the girls out one day. She had been promising the girls that she would take them shopping to treat them to some clothes and then to the cinema to see the latest animation film that had been advertised. She told Karen that she would take them out for lunch too, and just make a day of it. Both of the girls were so excited. It was during August and Grace was due to start school in September so Eva knew it would be her last chance to do this. Karen looked at the door as it closed in front of her and felt the emptiness of the house. She hadn't planned it, but she picked up the phone and rang Pete.

Chapter 25

Pete arrived looking distracted. He wasn't his usual self, Karen observed, 'coffee?' she asked as she made her way to the counter to order their drinks.

'Yeah please. How are you? You look great by the way.' Karen smiled slightly embarrassed. She had been making more and more of an effort whenever she saw him. The close fitting jeans and figure hugging top really accentuated her shape. 'Thanks, you don't look so bad yourself mister.' Their eyes met and connected. The banter continued flirtatiously while they were seated which they both seemed to enjoy. Pete tried to be light and conversational but she knew it was an act. She had really come to know him again.

'What's up?' She asked seeing some sadness in his eyes.

'It's Ness, she's depressed again. Always the same in the summer holidays away from the kids. She's okay during term time but the minute the holidays come, BANG it hits her again,' he said with emphasis, 'the whole baby thing; I can't do it anymore, it's coming between us.' Karen sat and listened as he continued, 'how can I help her when I'm a screwed up mess myself?' The tears flowed down his cheeks, 'I let you down because of my selfishness and now I'm letting Vanessa down. She needs my reassurance that I still love her even though she can't have a baby.' His head bent low as he finished.

'Oh Pete,' Karen said as she got up and went round to his side of the table to give him a hug.

'How can I tell her I love her when I still love you?' He stated, to Karen's surprise. Karen was stunned, they had acknowledged that they still loved one another but they were each married to other people so there was nowhere for it to go. *Why make that statement now? What was he trying to say? It was wonderful to hear him say it but nothing could be gained!* She consoled him as he was obviously racked with guilt.

'Of course you can tell her you love her. She's your wife,' Karen replied.

'Karen, I need you. I've made a mess of everything. I can't believe after everything that's happened that you forgave me. I love you so much more because of that.' Karen's eyes misted over. It was what she needed to hear, she was loved just as she was and for who she was and she didn't have to work at it. They stood and held each other close for what seemed like an eternity. While Pete held her, he asked her if she wanted to go to a hotel for the afternoon.

'Yes,' she said without hesitation.

As they lay in each other's arms in the hotel room, Karen and Pete felt complete. They talked for a long time. *It hadn't been planned! It had just happened! It didn't feel wrong! It had been beautiful and it felt right!* They talked some more. *But it wasn't right! What had they done? It must not happen again. It was madness! This had to be a one-off!* She had Richard and the girls. He had Vanessa. They were both risking their marriages. It didn't matter how they felt, it would be misguided to continue. There were too many people that they could hurt. They decided it had to be goodbye for both their sakes as well as for their families.

Karen drove around quiet streets and country lanes with only her thoughts for company. *What had just happened?* She asked herself over and over. *How could she possibly go home and act as though nothing had happened?* She felt slightly panicky about what they had done but strangely content at the same time. It was that realisation that she still loved Pete deeply. There was something about him that captivated her in a way that Richard never had. She pulled over into a quiet lay-by and listened to the radio playing soothing love songs and she sobbed quietly. *Why was she complicating her life?* She asked herself over and over again. *Why wasn't she making the most of what she had?* Instead she always seemed to be searching. She couldn't bring herself to think about what her parents would think if they knew what she had just done. She could hear them in her head saying, '*you had a second chance to be happy, what's wrong with you? Why are you self destructing?'* Even she couldn't answer that question.

The ringtone from her mobile broke her thoughts and jolted her back to reality. Eva's name flashed up on the phone screen, she knew she had to take it. A feeling of dread gripped her and she wondered if there was something wrong with the girls.

'Hi Eva, is everything ok?' Karen asked tentatively.

'Yes, fine my darling, I wouldn't normally ask at such short notice but is it okay if the girls stay with me tonight?' Karen breathed a sigh of relief, 'only they look so settled, I don't want to disrupt them. It's not as if they've got school or anything is it?'

'It's okay Eva you don't have to make a case for it. I'm happy with that,' Karen said with a smile and lightness in her voice.

'That's settled then, I'll see you in the morning,' Eva said.

Karen returned home with her thoughts a jumbled mess but she knew she had to act normally. Whatever normal was these days! Richard was already home. She saw his car on drive. *Damn it!* She thought. She just wanted to get in the shower and have some time to herself.

As she put the key in the door and walked into the hallway, Richard came out of the kitchen swinging the empty kettle in his hand, 'hi love, I was just about to have a cuppa, do you want one?'

'You're home early!' It was a statement rather than a question but he answered it anyway.

'Mum rang and told me she had the girls and to make sure I got home early so you and I could spend some quality time together. I thought why not, I'm the boss, go for it! They were all surprised when I said I was off early,' Richard said with a smile that showed he was pleased with himself.

'Oh, right,' Karen replied.

'Don't I get a kiss then?' Richard started to walk towards her with outstretched arms. Karen felt like she was rooted to the spot.

'Yeah, of course,' she said as she leaned into his embrace, 'I'm just going to get a shower, I feel hot and sticky after being out all day.' She then retreated from his hug and quickly ran up the stairs.

'You didn't say if you want tea or not?' Richard shouted up the stairs.

'No thanks,' Karen hurriedly replied. *Leave me alone. Why are you being so nice to me? I don't deserve it. You have no idea what I've just done!* Her thoughts crowded her mind as she peeled off all her clothes and threw them in the dirty linen basket. As the hot shower poured onto her skin, she wanted to wash away what had happened. She scrubbed every inch of her body over and over. She had to wash Pete away and forget that today had ever happened. It was doable she told herself. After all she had been acting 'normal' for months now. She would just continue as before.

Her wet hair hung in beautiful ringlets and her brown skin glistened with dampness. She was about to grab her towel to dry herself and lost in her thoughts, Karen did not hear Richard come up the stairs. She was surprised to see Richard holding her towel out in front of her ready to dry her back as he always offered to do. *He really is sweet. S*he thought. *But so controlling at the same time, he always has to be involved in everything.* She chided herself for being ungrateful. 'Turn around love so I can dry your back.' Karen turned around and knew exactly what he had in mind. After he finished drying her, he leaned into her and hugged her from behind. She froze. 'What's up with you, don't you want me to touch you?' Richard said angrily, 'you're as rigid as a stone. We haven't had sex in months. You just keep me at arm's length all the time. Why?'

Why? She thought. *I could answer that, but it's not what you'll want to hear. What a difference between Richard and Pete?* Richard was so demanding and controlling while Pete was so relaxed, warm and vulnerable all wrapped up in one. She really liked that about him. He had been so incredibly honest about everything that had happened and the part he had played. He knew the hurt and pain he had caused and he had found it hard to forgive himself. Karen knew in that moment that she didn't love Richard in the same way she loved Pete but what could she do. She was married to him now and she had the girls to think about, it wasn't just about her anymore. Richard was a great dad and a good provider. He worked hard and he loved her and wanted nothing more than to be loved back. But she couldn't love him in the way he wanted.

The evening was ruined before it started and Richard was hurt and had taken himself off downstairs to watch TV, while Karen stayed upstairs in the bedroom just sitting on their bed replaying her whole afternoon with Pete. It had been beautiful and she shouldn't have enjoyed it but she had. She never realised just how much she had missed him and more importantly loved him. The house was so quiet without the girls and she realised that without them, Richard was not enough and this marriage was not satisfying to her at all.

Chapter 26

Richard sat at work the next morning, a mountain of emails and paperwork to get through but he just couldn't focus. Karen was on his mind. *What had gone wrong?* He thought. She was different, distant.

Richard picked up the phone, 'Hi Mum, how are the girls?'

'They're absolutely fine darling I've just got them ready to take them home. I've really enjoyed having them.'

'That's good. Mum I'm worried about Karen. I don't think she loves me anymore,' Eva listened with interest.

'Why do you say that son?' she replied.

'Well,' Richard hesitated. He didn't find it easy to talk about his problems because he always tried to find his own solutions, 'she won't let me anywhere near her.'

'I can't talk now, I'm just about to drop the girls off to Karen, meet me for lunch and we'll talk then. I'll meet you at the Italian restaurant in the Square at one.'

'Okay mum, see you later.'

Richard contemplated for a while after he put the phone down. This was not good, nothing interfered with his work, no matter what was going on, he was always able to switch off and focus. Not today for some reason. He was even irritated with himself that he felt the need to talk to his mum about it but she had been spending a lot of time with Karen so hopefully she could shed some light. He briefly thought about talking to Ben but something stopped him. Ben had been there the night he met Karen and was a good friend but for some reason he never found it easy to share his feelings with him or anyone really. He sighed and looked at his watch. It was 10.50am he needed to get some work done.

Eva dropped the girls' home to Karen and waved as she drove off. She had been in two minds, whether to say anything to Karen. She now knew about Robin, but Richard didn't know that she knew. She knew the pain that Karen was feeling because she had shared it with her. She decided to wait until she heard what Richard had to say

Eva listened while Richard told her how worried he was about his marriage and how he was feeling. She could see that he was genuinely puzzled by Karen's behaviour. She longed to tell him that she knew all about Robin and the affect it had had on Karen; how much she missed him and the guilt she felt for giving him up, not being able to talk about him and forbidden to tell her too. *If only I could tell him that I know!* Eva thought. She was torn. She felt so sorry for Karen and could only imagine her pain and trauma from that period in her life but she felt so sad for Richard her only son sitting right there in front of her. She felt terribly disloyal knowing that she was keeping him in the dark but she simply didn't know how to play this. She had promised Karen faithfully that she would not let Richard know that she knew about Robin. Karen was fearful of Richard's reaction as he had made it clear that Eva was not to know. *Oh dear!* Eva thought as she listened and made soothing noises to him about giving Karen time and just to spoil her a little. She found herself saying that she would have the girls whenever she could to give them time together to work out their marriage and he seemed happier by the time their lunch had finished. As Richard walked off in the direction of his office and she made her way back to her car, Eva pondered what to do. She drove home with thoughts of Richard and Karen heavily on her mind trying to figure out what she could do to help them both. It was so hard trying to be loyal to Karen because it meant that she was being disloyal to Richard. She deliberated whether to speak to Karen about how Richard was feeling. Eva reminded herself that Karen had been honest with her and had told her about how she had bumped into Pete one day and that they occasionally met up as it helped her to have someone to talk to who fully understood how she felt as he was struggling too. Eva had been uneasy about the fact that Karen was in touch with her ex but as he too was married, she put all doubts out of her mind about anything happening or starting up between them. Karen had shared openly with Eva how it was helping her to come to terms with losing Robin and was moving her to a better place emotionally. Eva knew she had been through a lot and that Richard lacked understanding sometimes. *If seeing her baby's father helped Karen then what right did she have to judge her?* She loved Karen and wanted her to be happy. However there had been times when Eva wondered at the wisdom of them seeing one another but Karen was delicate and needed to heal. After much thought, Eva then changed her mind and decided it was too soon to speak to Karen about Richard's feelings. That conversation could wait until another day. She decided she would keep a close eye on both Richard and Karen.

Chapter 27

In the following weeks, Karen was so caught up in the activities of preparing Grace for school that she was able to put what 'had happened' to the back of her mind. Her thoughts were preoccupied with last minute tasks and she seemed able to cope. Richard was happier and appeared to have forgiven her rejection and she was surprised at their outward normality. She was relieved. With Grace starting school, it had been a distraction from their own issues. She and Richard focused on Grace and they enjoyed this milestone in her life. It was good to hear about her days at school and the friends she was making. Karen had found herself softening towards Richard as they shared and enjoyed their oldest child's new adventure together. She started to feel appreciative of what she had with Richard. It wasn't perfect but he was there supporting her as he always did. She did love him, how deeply, she wasn't sure. She still struggled to be intimate with him but he hadn't pushed it and that had suited her. She had felt too guilty about that afternoon with Pete. *How could she give herself to Richard knowing what she had done? She had been unfaithful and she felt deeply ashamed!* She knew she couldn't sleep with Richard so soon after that indiscretion. She was aware that she was denying him but she reasoned that by putting off intimacy for as long as possible, it was helping her to handle the guilt of her infidelity. It had been at least two months, prior to her afternoon with Pete, since she and Richard had slept together so she appreciated that he was being incredibly patient. When a reasonable amount of time had passed she told herself she would make it up to Richard. In the meantime she decided she would be as sweet and caring as she possibly could be and it seemed to work. They were getting on better and she hoped it would be a matter of time before things got back to normal.

She hadn't seen or spoken to Pete since and neither did she want to. That would have been dangerous, she knew how much she loved him and how hard it had been to resist. She had not wanted what happened to happen; meeting up with Pete was meant to be about Robin, not them. She knew Robin was no longer hers but it had been cathartic and healing to talk to Pete about him. As much as they wanted to see Robin, they knew they couldn't. He belonged to another family. He had new parents who loved him. The sense of loss and grief they both felt bonded them closer and that afternoon spent together had been a source of comfort but it was a mistake and should never have happened! It was a 'one off' and should never be repeated! Yes, she loved Pete but she had to compartmentalise her feelings and carry on as before. It was best for them not to see each other again. Obviously he had felt the same, as she had not heard from him either.

Karen woke several weeks later feeling nausea, and flew to the bathroom just in time to get her head into the toilet bowl before throwing up the contents of her stomach. For several minutes, she hung her head in the bowl until she gradually started to feel better. As she washed her hands and face and brushed her teeth, she realised what was happening. She knew with absolute certainty that she was pregnant and that it was Pete's. Slowly, she got dressed and went downstairs to have a drink. She usually had coffee but couldn't face it that morning so she decided to have a cup of mint tea instead.

While she drank it, Richard walked in the kitchen. Karen couldn't look at him. *What had she done? How was she going to solve this?* He was in a surprisingly talkative mood and didn't seem to notice her preoccupation of thoughts. Somehow, Karen managed to get through the next couple of hours of breakfasting and sorting out the girls ready for school and nursery. Richard had left earlier than usual as he needed to get into the office for a meeting which needed some prep beforehand. Karen was relieved. The last thing she needed was him hanging around; today of all days! Her thoughts were an absolute jumbled mess. But, she needed to remain calm and assess the situation. First and foremost she needed to take a pregnancy test.

Even though she was in no doubt, she needed to see it in black and white.

Karen walked out the chemist and headed straight back home. *Positive!* That blue line had just changed her life! She looked around the room of her lounge and in the direction of the conservatory and the garden beyond and suddenly realised what she had and what she stood to lose. Thoughts of how to deal with this started to hit her. She even thought about letting Richard sleep with her that night when he came home and then she could pretend it was his baby but that would be too cruel and deceitful. She could not play that kind of trick on him! She reasoned that she didn't actually have to do anything right away, not that day anyway. She needed time to get her head around it and of course, Pete needed to know. *Why did she always complicate her life?* She didn't even want to think about what her mum and dad would make of it all. They'd seen what Pete had done to their daughter all those years ago and they would think that she had lost her mind. And of course there was Eva, sweet Eva who had been so good to her all these years. *Would she ever forgive Karen for the hurt she would inevitably cause Richard?* And there was Vanessa, poor Vanessa who couldn't have any children of her own. *How would she cope knowing that Pete had fathered a child to someone else within their marriage? So many people to consider but what about her, what did she want?* The easiest way to deal with this would be to have an abortion, but she reminded herself that she had been there before and it was not an option she was prepared to consider.

She knew however that she had to tell Pete. *How would he take it? What would he do? What did she want him to do?* So many questions that needed answers but all Karen knew was she was sick and tired of being what everyone else wanted her to be. She wanted to live her life making the choices that were right for her. Karen also knew that Richard would have to know soon and that it would be the end of her marriage. For now, however, it could wait.

Chapter 28

'Pete,' Karen said nervously.

'Karen, it's so good to hear from you,' Pete exclaimed, 'can we meet?' She continued without acknowledging or responding to what he said. 'Are you free to meet today, about 1pm at the coffee shop?'

'Yeah, of course I am. Karen, I've missed you so much but I wanted to give you some space and if I'm honest, I felt so guilty about Ness. My head's been all over the place.'

'I'll see you later Pete, we'll talk then,' Karen ended the call. She stared into space transfixed for a minute knowing that her future was uncertain but she had to be strong. This was no time to fall apart. She wasn't that naive sixteen year old girl anymore. She was twenty eight years old and knew the consequences of everything. She also knew that she couldn't depend on anyone other than herself. She had her two beautiful girls and even though she knew she would lose Richard, at least she would have her girls. She had lost Robin and she vowed she would never lose anymore of her children including the one that was growing inside her.

Pete smiled as she walked into the coffee shop. He had ordered their drinks which were ready and waiting. He stood up and gave her a hug before sitting back down. Karen took her seat opposite and smiled. He took her hand, 'It's so great to see you. I've really missed you. I know it was wrong what we did,' his eyes misted over, 'I thought I could keep it as a beautiful memory and not see you again, but seeing you now, I'm not sure I can live without you. We're not doing any harm if we make sure that Richard and Vanessa don't find out, are we? Shall we go to the hotel now? I could ring and book a room?' Pete suggested.

'No, that's not why I came. I do love you and always will. I would love nothing more than to spend time with you,' she hesitated, 'but I can't see you again. I need to be strong for what lies ahead,' she started to falter. 'I can't and won't depend on anyone anymore. So much has happened in my life and I need to know who I am and where I want to go, I need to find myself.' The tears flowed down her face unchecked. She made no move to wipe them away.

'I'm pregnant Pete and it's yours. Richard and I haven't slept together for a while now. So I can say with absolutely certainty that it's yours, but this time don't worry I don't expect you to do anything. It's an even bigger mess than last time. I've got Richard and the girls to think of and you've got Vanessa,' she stated flatly.

'My sweet Karen, I can't believe it,' his face was incredulous, 'I love you and will support you in any way I can. I can't let you go through this alone. I'll be there for you this time, every step of the way, no matter what.' His eyes were full of tears threatening to spill.

Karen couldn't believe what she was hearing. 'Pete, what are you saying? What about Vanessa?'

'I'll tell her, I know this will hurt her more than anything. She wants a child so badly, but I'm not going to walk away from my own flesh and blood again, and more importantly, I'm not going to walk away from you again either. I love you Karen,' he paused, 'yes, I do love Vanessa too and the last thing I want to do is hurt her and it bothers me but I'll have to deal with it.' He had bent his head low and shook it slowly from side to side as he said those words. He then looked up and stared directly into Karen's eyes. 'I never really got over the fact that I hurt you and I don't want to do that again. Thank you for giving me a second chance. I don't deserve it. I was a boy when this happened before but I'm a man now and I have to face up to my actions and responsibilities. Don't worry my love, we'll face this together.'

Chapter 29

Karen sat engrossed in her thoughts. She knew she had to tell Richard and she knew that it would be the hardest thing she would ever do. But she had to decide when to do it. There was never going to be a good time to tell your husband that you were pregnant with another man's child. That was going to hurt him beyond measure. What she couldn't predict was how he would take it. Karen knew she would have to leave but where would she go, back to her mum and dad? And of course there was Grace and Amelia to think of. She had no income. She had long given up her job when she had Grace. Richard had been adamant that she stay at home and she'd been happy with that. She wanted to spend time with her children. Giving Robin up had left her with such guilt, she never wanted to feel that way again. But it meant that she was totally reliant on Richard and over the years it had cost Karen her identity. She had been aware of it but just not known what to do about it.

But no more, this was time for Karen to decide what she wanted and how she was going to do it. It had been a long time since she had really talked to her mum it had been difficult for both of them. Something had shifted between them ever since Robin was given up. She always got on well with her mum but she had never been overly close to her mum, when she reflected upon it. She was always aware that her mum and Susan were especially close. They shared the same interests, both avid readers and loved theatre, whereas Karen's ability to concentrate on reading a magazine or newspaper never lasted more than a few minutes. And the theatre just didn't excite her. Karen loved music and could listen for hours with her headphones on to all the soul classics and she always enjoyed her own company. Even though she and Marina had little in common, they did have a fairly easy relationship. There was never any tension or angst between them and Karen never forgot the support her mum gave her throughout her pregnancy with Robin and they did become closer during that period. After getting married and having the girls and with Marina working, it meant that their time together was limited. The times when Marina visited had been enjoyable and although they never talked about Robin, Karen knew that Marina was sad too. It was just too painful to talk about. Karen decided that although she should really tell Richard first, she wanted to talk to her mum beforehand. It didn't feel like the first time when she was that young frightened girl, she had become a more confident woman who had started to realise what she wanted and wasn't going to be intimidated by her circumstances. Although she cared what her mum thought she was determined to be unconcerned about her mum's reaction. She simply wanted to be honest about who she really was for the first time in her life.

'Hi mum, it's Karen,' she said over the phone.

'Hi love, how are you?' Marina asked, 'and how are the girls?'

'They're fine mum, and I'm okay too,' Karen replied.

'I need to talk to you mum, can I come over later?' Karen asked.

'Yes, of course you can. It'll be nice to have some company you're dad's working away for the next two days. Are you bringing the girls with you? Do you want me to do you something to eat? I could put some jacket potatoes in the oven I know how much they love them.'

'No mum, it'll be just me. I'll give the girls their dinner and get them bathed and leave them with Richard so he can spend some time with them before they go to bed. I'll be over about quarter to seven. See you later mum,' she was gone. Marina held the phone in her hand and pondered. *Karen hadn't even said goodbye. That girl, she really was a mystery sometimes!* She returned to her desk observing that her lunch break had ended.

Karen arrived at her mum's to find a cup of tea and a large slice of chocolate cake waiting for her. Marina had stopped off at the supermarket remembering how much Karen liked that particular brand. They sat and enjoyed the tea and cake with small talk about insignificant things mainly to do with the girls. It was relaxed and Marina enjoyed having Karen to chat to. Then she dropped the bombshell! She had not seen that coming, Karen told her everything. Marina could not believe what she was hearing. *Pete was back in Karen's life again with another pregnancy to face! But Karen seemed unfazed by everything that was happening. Marina wondered if she was really in touch in reality and did she have any idea what she was going to do?* Marina listened surprisingly without judgement. What she felt was sadness for her beautiful middle child who just seemed to be searching for something but she wasn't sure what.

When Karen left, Marina went to the window of the lounge and watched as she drove off. Karen turned and waved to her mum just before turning the corner. Karen knew that she had sent her mum's head into a spin, but she had been supportive and non judgemental, which Karen was grateful for. Marina had told her that her room was still there and she and the girls could come and stay anytime and for as long as they needed. Karen felt better for talking to Marina and she had endorsed all that Karen knew she had to do. Of course, she had to be honest with Richard about everything, no matter how much hurt and upset she caused. Karen stopped the car a few streets from where she lived and let the engine run and turned off the radio while she thought carefully how to tell Richard that she was pregnant with Pete's child. No matter how she rehearsed in her head how to use the right words, it would be like dropping a grenade. She would just have to face the fallout! The thought terrified her.

She put her key in the door, her heart beating so fast and so loudly that she thought it would beat out of her chest. *C'mon girl.* She said to herself. *You've been here before! You can handle it. You're stronger now. You're not that frightened teenager anymore.* Richard turned as she walked into the lounge and smiled. *Oh no!* She thought. *Why couldn't he be in a bad mood? It would have made it easier to tell him why she cheated on him, why she wasn't sure she that she loved him and that she was pregnant with another man's child.* Karen gave a weak smile back.

Karen had lain next to Richard that night and watched him sleep. She hadn't been able to tell him. She'd lost her nerve. The words just couldn't come out. She'd tried, she really had but every time she opened her mouth to say it, something else came out instead. He had immediately engaged with her when she walked in the room sharing some information about something he had just heard on the news. Karen could barely hear what he was saying, her own thoughts crowding her mind. He was telling her about a burglary in their local area and how glad he was that he had made their house so secure. He was praising himself for the sophisticated alarm system that he had extensively researched before arranging for it to be installed. He'd smiled proudly like a small child. Karen couldn't burst his bubble, it seemed cruel. He slept soundly as she continued to watch him in the semi darkness of their room. The street lighting from outside had cast enough light into the room which enabled her to see his face. *It can wait, there's always tomorrow.* She thought.

Chapter 30

Karen sat at the kitchen table looking out of the window. It was peaceful. With Richard at work and the girls at school and nursery, she had a few hours at least to think. She picked up the phone. 'Hi Eva, it's me Karen, how are you?'

'I'm okay love,' Eva replied, 'and you?' she asked.

'I'm not too bad thanks. I need a favour can you pick up the girls today and keep them for a few hours? I really need to talk to Richard and it's impossible with the girls around,' Karen stated.

'Of course love, no problem,' Eva said. *Something's wrong.* She thought.

Karen thanked Eva and put the phone down, relieved that she had at least sorted out the girls. It was one less thing to worry about and she knew that she couldn't put it off again. She decided that neutral ground was probably the best way to tell him. It was still their home and she didn't want the memory of this day to spoil that. The peace of the home somehow had to be preserved for as long as possible.

She had booked a table at a restaurant within walking distance from where Richard worked so that he wouldn't have to drive and he could leave his car on the car park where he worked. She also thought that he would probably not want to drive home with her afterwards so at least he would have his own car nearby.

Karen parked her car in the restaurant car park and went inside. She was early but she needed some time to herself. She ordered a mineral water and sat drinking it while she waited. Richard walked in and sat down. They'd been to this restaurant many times before and were known by the staff. They didn't even need the menu. Richard was a man of routine. Karen knew exactly what he would order it was the same every time they came. Salmon fillet with pasta in a creamy tarragon sauce and garlic bread. Karen on the other hand, always tried something different. Today, she had no idea and didn't really feel like eating anything. Her appetite had been slowly going all day and the dread that filled her stomach was starting to make her feel sick. She looked at the menu and decided to go with the chicken in a Mediterranean   tomato herb sauce. She closed her menu and handed both menus back to the smiling waitress.

'Well,' Richard said, 'this is nice, just the two of us, no kids. As much as I love those little angels of ours, it's good for the two of us have some quality time.'

Karen was staring down at the placemat feeling that any minute she would throw up. 'Richard, I have something to tell you and you're not going to be happy but I want to be honest with you right from the start,' Karen paused and took a deep breath, 'I'm leaving.' Karen heard herself saying. She hadn't planned exactly what she was going to say so even she was surprised. Richard opened his mouth to speak but before the words came out, Karen started talking again. 'I've been unhappy for a long time now. I don't know who I am any more. You know exactly who you are. You're never in any doubt about what you want. Even with your food, you always know. Me...' she paused before continuing. 'I never know.'

'Why Karen?' he asked simply, 'why are you blaming me for your indecisiveness? Is that my fault? You're making it sound like being decisive is a bad thing.'

'I didn't mean it the way it came out, I'm sorry. This is not about you, this is about me. I've never been happy, not really, I'm not whole. A part of me is missing,' tears welled up in Karen's eyes.

'I think I know where this is going. Robin, isn't it? You told me about him and I understood how you felt. I promised that I would give you more children to fill the space and haven't I done that?' Richard asked quietly.

'Yes, the girls mean everything to me but I missed Robin and you wouldn't let me talk about him, you wouldn't even let me tell your mum. I felt a fake, like I was pretending to be something I'm not.'

'Not that again!' Richard said impatiently.

'Yes that again,' Karen snapped back.

Just at that moment the waitress came with their food and placed them in front of them, said the usual line about hoping that they would enjoy it and then turned and walked off. None of them said anything for about a minute. Then Richard said 'C'mon, let's eat.' Karen picked up her cutlery and put a small piece of chicken in her mouth and chewed very slowly.

'I know I've lost Robin, I can't have him. He's not mine anymore. I can't see him until and if he wants to see me. But I should have been allowed to talk about him. He was mine, a part of me. I was a coward, too afraid to keep my baby. It's the biggest regret of my life.'

'I don't understand what this has to do with our marriage?' Richard looked confused.

'It has everything to do with us, you want me to be something I'm not, I can't pretend anymore. I'm tired of not being me. You don't really like me, you like the veneer but not me,' she poked her finger into her own chest several times as she said it, 'you've been kind to me and I know you mean well but you decide everything that happens, everything we do, everything we buy, even what I wear. I have no idea what I like anymore, where I'm going in life and who I am. I need to be free to find out. I know that I relied on you in the beginning and I allowed you to decide everything and it suited me, I had no confidence. You were everything I wasn't and what I needed then but now I feel like I'm slowing dying inside,' Karen finished.

Richard sat silently for a few minutes before saying 'Are you saying we can't work this out?'

'It's too late!'

'Why, damn it?' he started to get angry. It just didn't make any sense to him. *Where was all this coming from?* It just seemed to be out of the blue. Although if he was honest, he had noticed that she didn't want to be intimate with him making every excuse as soon as he touched her.

'Because I'm pregnant and it's not yours!' That was it, it had been said.

'What?' Richard's voice was full of incredulity. He was not expecting this. This was too much to take in. He got up and went to the toilet. He walked past the urinals and straight into one of only two cubicles and leaned his head against the door in distress. *What the hell was going on? What had he just heard? This wasn't real. This could not be happening. His whole life was crumbling before him.* Richard was reeling. His thoughts were all jumbled.

Karen sat rooted to her chair waiting for him to come back. He was only gone for about five minutes but it seemed liked hours. If he didn't come out soon, she would go in there to find him.

Richard walked back out composed and sat rigid in his chair and demanded to know everything. Karen told him about how she accidently bumped into Pete, their subsequent coffee meetings, their chats about Robin, their inevitable afternoon when they slept together and now the unplanned pregnancy. She knew that she owed it to him to be completely honest no matter how much it hurt him. He sat broken. She was not enjoying watching the pain on his face and for all her desire to 'find herself' she hadn't wanted it at the expense of so much hurt to Richard.

Chapter 31

Karen put her key in the door knowing that this was no longer her home. She went upstairs to pack some clothes for herself and the girls, who were still with Eva. She replayed the conversation earlier in her mind with Richard. He had been surprisingly calm, but she knew it wouldn't remain that way. Richard could be as hard as steel. She was well aware of the other side of him. He was hurting right now, she knew that. He had not said one word but simply got up and walked out of the restaurant leaving some cash on the table for Karen to pay the bill. She had no idea what he wanted her to do but she had deceived him and ultimately humiliated him.

Karen gathered a few items for herself and the girls. She decided that she could come back for more things another time. She just needed to put some space between herself and Richard. Just as she was walking down the stairs, she heard Richard's key in the door. She froze. Fear gripped her. He walked in and stared coldly at her and honed in on Amelia's doll held between Karen's arm and chest. 'Where are you taking that?' Richard asked.

'I'm going to take the girls and stay at my mum and dad's until I get myself sorted out. I know I can't stay now not after what's happened,' Karen replied.

'You're right about you not staying Karen, but the girls are going nowhere, I don't want their lives disrupted.'

'But, you can't do this, I've already lost my son, I'm not going to lose my girls,' Karen said fearfully.

'Tough, you should have thought about that before you slept with your ex,' he spat the words out, 'you've got another child coming, let's see if you can hold onto that one,' Richard strode off into the kitchen and leaned against the kitchen cupboard.

Karen chased after him pleading, 'Please Richard don't do this to me,' tears started to flow down her cheeks and she sobbed uncontrollably, 'they need me Richard, you're at work, how can you look after them? There's the school run to do and Amelia is only going to nursery part time.' Her voice was jerky with emotion. She had to fight for her girls. For too long, she had done what was expected or what Richard wanted, but no more. Yes, she knew she had done wrong, she hadn't planned it and yes it was a mess but she was not going to be the loser again! If Richard had been willing to let her talk about Robin or even allowed her to be honest with Eva, it would have helped. She was sick and tired of being a fraud. It was time to be real and true to herself for the first time in her life.

'They're going NOWHERE,' Richard shouted, 'right now they're with mum and that's where they are staying, for tonight anyway,' his voice was even, 'between me and mum, we'll look after them. She already spends a lot of time with them so they'll be fine.'

'Richard, this doesn't make sense, punish me yes but not the girls, they need me,' Karen sighed, 'this is not fair on your mum. She's in her sixties now. She can't look after two young children every day. Have you any idea what a burden you would be placing on her?' Karen continued, 'let me take them, you can see them every day I'll make sure of it,' Karen pleaded.

'No, this isn't fair, damn it!' He banged the kitchen worktop so hard he winced as the pain shot through his hand. 'You sleep with your boyfriend and destroy our family and I'm the one that loses my kids. Does that seem fair to you?'

'Life's not fair! I found that out a long time ago,' Karen replied with resignation, 'everything can't always be on your terms,' she gave him no time to answer, 'all these years I've done what you wanted, I couldn't talk about my first child, I couldn't tell your mum. I was never allowed to be me. It was always about you!' She pointed at him.

'All I ever did was look after you and do what I thought was best for you. Well, I'm sorry for caring,' he replied sarcastically.

'It was never what was best for me. If it was, you would have allowed me to deal with things my own way, but you wouldn't let me. I was dying inside, every day, a bit of me was slowing dying. I didn't know who I was anymore.' Karen slumped onto the dining chair and bent her head low. There was silence, deathly silence for a few minutes. 'Richard, I know that I've hurt you and God knows it was not planned, but I will fight you for my kids. You can't have it all your way. You've managed to do what you thought was best for me over the years, but you failed. I'm not going to let you do 'what's best' for the girls, and get that wrong too.'

'What did I get so wrong Karen? All I ever did was love you all. I'm the man of the family. It's my role to protect and look after my family. I was doing my best but you make it sound so sinister and controlling,' he felt deflated.

'I know you meant well Richard but we all have the right to live our lives the way we want, to be true to ourselves. I don't want the girls to be like me. I want them to know who they are and where they're going in life. It's not your job Richard to control someone's emotions. We feel what we feel and we have to listen to ourselves.' Karen placed her hand on her chest to emphasise her words. Karen suddenly felt very tired. She thought it probably was a good idea for the girls to stay with Eva that night anyway.

Karen opened her eyes after an exhausted sleep. She picked up her mobile phone to check the time and it was 4.20am. She had slept in the spare room, after making the decision that she was going nowhere. The conversation between her and Richard had been emotionally draining. The shouting had stopped and then deep searching questions began that left them both feeling sad and wondering how it had come to this. She asked if he minded if she stayed in the spare room for that night at least. He nodded his head to say yes as if all fight had gone out of him. She suddenly felt very sorry for him. *Why did he always bring out those emotions in her? Why did she feel like the 'bad guy'?*

Yes she had done wrong and she would always be sad about hurting Richard in this way. *But what about her pain, she mattered too.* She pondered that she somehow always seemed to create turmoil. Other people seemed able to get things right and make decisions and live ordered lives. *Why did she find it so difficult?*

Her thoughts turned to Pete and the baby she was carrying. How different things were this time, Pete was so excited and happy despite the circumstances. He was willing to tell Vanessa everything. This time he was prepared to face up to his responsibilities and had promised never to let Karen down again. *But how was that even possible? He was married. Would he leave Vanessa for her?* Then there was Grace and Amelia. *What a disruption this would be for them.* She knew she had to keep things as normal as possible for the girls. *Whatever normal was?* She wasn't sure anymore. Today was a new day and life as she knew it would never be the same but she was ready to face what was ahead. She knew it was not going to be easy. The hardest thing after telling Richard would be telling Eva.

Chapter 32

Richard went to work without saying a word. He had nothing more to say to Karen and needed to get out of the house where he felt he had lost complete control of his life. At least at work, he still had decisions to make and was needed. Routine and normality in at least one area needed to be maintained. He was not going to let every area of his life go to pieces. He was always better at coping when he was busy, the last thing he needed was time to think about the almighty mess that had just become his life. He felt like he had been hit by a sledgehammer.

As he drove through the traffic navigating his way to work, he thought about all the things that Karen had said to him. He didn't recognise himself in the things that she said. She had said that he was controlling and always wanted things his way. *Wow!* He thought he was just caring and providing for his family. *He loved them! How had he got it so wrong?* Karen had felt stifled and not able to be herself. She said that he had done that to her. *Yes, he knew that he had not encouraged her to talk about Robin but what good would it have done?* Talking about something you can't change just depressed you, he rationalised. For him, talking about something was pointless if it didn't change anything, so he had tried to help Karen do the same. *Clearly, it hadn't worked and had made her more depressed. How different they were?* If he had known just how deeply it had affected her then maybe he would have allowed her to talk. But he felt he knew what was good for her. In the beginning, she seemed happy with the way things were, she trusted and believed that he knew what was best for her. He reasoned that having the girls would have helped her get over Robin, but he'd got that wrong too. And this obsession she had with wanting to tell his mum about Robin had annoyed him completely. *What would have been the point?* He never understood the need to outpour everything. He'd always tried to deal with things in his own head. Yes, there had been the odd occasions he had spoken to his mum about things that bothered him, but mostly he dealt with it. Like he had dealt with everything since his dad died when he was six years old.

He recalled the effect his dad's death had on his mum and how he knew even then that he had to be strong. No one told him, he just knew and he had been managing his emotions ever since. Logic and action was needed, emotions got in the way. Looking back, that's probably why it took him so long to settle down. He had played the field for so long with so many girls. No emotional attachments. Life was easier that way. Karen however had been so different to all his other girlfriends, he remembered the night they met and how beautiful and fragile she looked. She had made an impression on him in a way that no one else ever had. He really loved her and now he felt that his heart would break. *But she had made a fool of him. He couldn't forgive that!*

When he pulled into the car park at work, his thoughts switched to his job and all the things he had to do. He had an important meeting that afternoon with other branch managers and executives, he needed a clear head. *Damn Karen!* He would think about this situation later.

Chapter 33

Karen looked around the room as she sat drinking her cup of coffee. Richard had made it clear that she would have to tell Eva about the chaos she had created in their lives. *'You've whinged on enough about wanting to be honest with Mum, well here's your chance to tell all.'* He had said it sarcastically. He was right, she had to do it but she wasn't looking forward to it. She reasoned that telling Richard had been the hardest part, it surely couldn't be any harder to tell Eva but she was nervous about what her reaction would be. Eva had been a solid rock for her and such a help with the girls and if there was one person, she would have liked to spare any pain, it was Eva. She had always been so sweet and welcoming from the day that Richard had bought her to meet her. In all of the talking that had been done the night before, Karen hadn't actually told Richard that Eva already knew about Robin. She felt that would have been a betrayal too far. He would have been even more hurt if he knew that his own mum had known and didn't tell him.

Karen arrived at Eva's house just after 10.am. Eva had taken Grace to school and Amelia to nursery just as she said she would when Richard asked her to keep the girls overnight. She opened the door to Karen with a smile and started regaling her with tales about the girls and the time spent with them. She was beaming and didn't look at all tired after having had the girls overnight. She went straight into the kitchen and put the kettle on while Karen sat in the living room listening to the radio that was down low. Eva always had the radio on in the background as she loved the mix of chat and music from her favourite station. She could hear Eva humming in the kitchen while she made their cups of tea and Karen suddenly felt very sad knowing that what she was about to tell her would change all their lives.

As she placed Karen's drink in front of her and took the chair opposite, she asked if she and Richard had enjoyed their evening together.

Karen sighed, 'no, it was awful Eva and it's my fault.' Karen's body racked with sobs.

'My poor love,' Eva said, 'whatever is the matter? It can't be that bad, whatever it is?'

She didn't know where to start. She wiped her eyes and blew her nose with the tissue that Eva gave to her. *This kind woman, she doesn't deserve this. Why oh why do I always do this?* The tears started to flow down Karen's cheeks again. Eva sat waiting for Karen to compose herself.

'Please don't hate me for what I'm about to tell you. I didn't mean for it to happen, it just did. I know that things will never be the same from here on in but I just want you to know that I will never forget your kindness,' Karen rambled at speed, 'I'm pregnant Eva and it's not Richard's baby.' Karen said the words so quickly that Eva had to ask her to repeat it.

'What?' Eva said in disbelief.

'I'm so sorry Eva I wouldn't blame you if you hate me. Richard's your son,' Karen replied.

'I will never hate you Karen, but I'm struggling to take this in.' Eva suddenly looked and felt very weary. She sighed and said, 'tell me the whole story. Tell me everything.'

Eva sat and listened without saying a word. She actually didn't know what to say. She knew that Richard must be hurting to the core. Had this been someone else's story and not her son, she would probably have felt total sympathy for Karen because she knew that she had not been in a good place for a long time. Eva needed to speak to Richard. 'I need to make sure Richard is okay.' Eva rose from her chair.

'Do you want me to go?' Karen asked.

'No,' she replied, 'stay there.' She left the room.

After Eva had spoken to Richard, she came back in and sat back down. Karen told her how she felt about everything that had happened in her life, and all the emotions she had lived with. Giving up her son, her struggle with guilt, her compliancy with Richard, her meeting with Pete again, their dream to see their son Robin again one day and then that 'afternoon' which resulted in her current pregnancy.

She told Eva about how her marriage to Richard had made her feel incapable as the years went by and how she never felt good enough or equal. In the beginning she acknowledged that she had allowed him to take charge and control of everything because she didn't have the confidence to make decisions and she loved and admired his self assurance. He showered her with love and even after she told him about Robin it didn't alter how he felt. She couldn't believe her luck! But then he made it clear from the outset that he didn't want his mum to know. She couldn't understand why. She had asked him many times if she could tell Eva but it had always been a flat no. Then she noticed if she tried to talk about Robin he would change the subject. It became harder and harder to deal with but he just didn't seem to get it. However meeting Pete again and knowing he understood because he was going through the same emotions was a relief and it felt good to be able to talk about Robin.

Every emotion, every feeling was shared with Eva. She held nothing back. The tears were streaming as she unburdened years of self denial to Eva. Eva knew she should feel anger and disgust if only for Richard's sake, but she didn't feel any of those things, only anguish for a girl that was clearly broken, who had never really been whole. And sadness for a marriage that would inevitably come to an end and two beautiful children's lives would change forever. She knew that Richard would feel humiliated beyond measure and there would be no coming back from this; after all she was pregnant with another man's child. What Eva couldn't work out was what Karen wanted for the future. She hadn't really expressed any expectations; just that she accepted that she had ruined all their lives. Although another child under those circumstances was going to be challenging, she was sure of one thing; that she would never be parted from her child.

Karen felt lighter as she left Eva's house, nothing had changed or been resolved. Her life was still full of uncertainty but at least Eva knew now. She felt she could breathe again. She literally had been waiting to exhale. She got in the car and headed home to gather a few items for herself and the girls. She decided to stay with her parents while she contemplated her future.

Chapter 34

Karen and Amelia stood waiting in front of the school gates to pick up Grace from school. She felt surprisingly relaxed. It had been a lovely couple of hours with Amelia who was in good spirits after her morning at nursery school. She ran out eagerly to a waiting Karen waving a picture excitedly that she had drawn. They had eaten their packed lunch in the local park and Amelia wanted to go on every single apparatus, running around enthusiastically, asking to be pushed and spun. It was a mild dry day and the fresh air had tired her out. Grace walked towards them with a smile on her face and Karen bent forward and hugged her middle child. *She would never forget that Robin was her first child, even if she had to live without him.* She pulled her youngest child in too and squeezed them both tightly. She was happy at that moment with her children, even though her life was in turmoil. She even felt joyful about the child growing inside her which was crazy. She didn't want to think too much about all the changes to their lives that were inevitably ahead of them.

Karen arrived with the children to her old family home where she was welcomed with open arms despite the situation. Karen didn't feel judged by her parents. Her dad was there and he gave her the biggest hug that almost squeezed all the air out of her lungs. He said she could stay for as long as she needed to after all there were now two spare rooms. Fiona had moved in with her boyfriend Guy and Susan had never come back home after leaving university. She had initially shared a rented house with two friends from university until deciding to buy herself a one bed flat just on the cultural outskirts of the city centre with the theatre not far away and lots of trendy bars and plenty of places to eat out.

Cecil and Marina had felt pleased that all the girls were settled in their own lives and unashamedly they were enjoying their time together now that the nest was empty. However Karen had certainly put a spanner in the works. When Marina told Cecil all that had happened they both felt sad that somehow, out of all their children, they had let Karen down. On reflection she had been the most fragile, but in the distractions of life with both of them working full time, they had been guilty of just not realising it. And of course there was Robin, their flesh and blood living with strangers. *How could they have let that happen and why didn't they insist that Karen keep him? Why did they leave the final decision with a young girl who was hurting, frightened and alone in her pregnancy?* They had had many years to reflect and had come to truly comprehend that everything Karen had done since was to try and live a so called 'normal' life to fit in with society's expectations and theirs to some extent. They had been guilty of encouraging her to grasp this 'normal' life too but she had never really dealt with her trauma and loss. She was still carrying it! Cecil and Marina had talked about Robin many times to each other but never to Karen. Now they had grasped that had been a big mistake on their part because she had carried it all alone. They had been more than happy to have Karen back home with her children. Karen had taken the smaller room while the girls were sharing the larger room. Whatever the future held, they wanted their 'searching' middle child to be happy and content. Worrying what people thought and keeping up appearances were long gone.

The following weeks for Karen were the most difficult emotionally since giving up Robin. The change of surroundings for her and the girls had been more testing than even she had imagined. She had taken for granted the home she had shared with Richard and the girls for the last few years. They had much more space with a considerable kitchen diner and a big and bright conservatory at the end of a generous sized lounge, whereas her parents' home in comparison was average sized. She felt as if she and the girls were in the way even though everything about her parents' behaviour and body language confirmed that they were absolutely happy to have Karen and the girls with them.

Pete rang several times to see how Karen was and although she knew that he meant it with her best interests in mind, she didn't want or need the distraction. Her children were her top priority. There had been enough upheaval for them. *How different it had been the last time when he wanted her to get rid of their baby; now he desperately wanted this baby.* Karen wondered if he really did love her or was it just the excitement that he was going to be a father after all the years of thinking that he would never have any more children. The last thing Karen needed was more emotional complications. She had to keep a clear head. He was married and his poor wife couldn't have children of her own. This bombshell would surely break her. Karen had no desire to hurt her, she didn't know her. She would never have planned what happened, but now that it had, she had no regrets about the life growing inside her. However, she did regret hurting Richard, he had loved her and given her two beautiful children, he would always remain special to her. The reality however was that she didn't love him, not in the way she loved Pete. How she wished she didn't love Pete. She just couldn't help how she felt about him but she wasn't going to let that love determine her actions. She was not going to get hurt again. Space was what she needed until she decided what she wanted.

Richard had become so cold ever since that first evening and had not said another word. In fact he had very little to say to her apart from when it was about the children. He would text about the arrangements but nothing more. She knew then that she had hurt and wounded him more than words could ever describe. He despised her and she could feel it. She felt worthless the way that he looked at her but she decided that she would not let those feelings of worthlessness define her. She was starting to understand who she was and what she wanted and how she wanted to be treated. She knew it would take a long time but she was on her way to ensuring that she valued herself. She could and would be happy despite her circumstances.

Chapter 35

The weeks flew into months and Karen buried herself in her parents' home. The children went to Richard every weekend and a routine developed that became a 'new kind of normal' for the girls. He insisted on picking the girls up and dropping them back. He made it clear that he did not want her to come to the house. She understood how he felt and was happy to do things on his terms.

Karen looked at herself in the mirror one Friday evening after the girls had gone to Richard and realised that her stomach was starting to noticeably swell with the new life growing inside. She felt excited about her new baby even though the future was still so uncertain. She had managed to keep Pete at bay; but she had received so many text messages from him asking how she was and saying how much he wanted to see her. It had been just over three months since they had seen each other. She decided that maybe she needed to see Pete and at least tell him how things were going and let him know her due date. She had been given her appointment date with the hospital for her twenty week scan. *Did she want him to be a part of it or did she want to do it alone?* She wasn't sure.

'How are you? It's so good to hear from you. What's happening? Why aren't you returning my calls?' Pete said without taking breath, he had been so relieved to see her name on his mobile.

'I'm fine, really. Please don't worry. I know we need to talk. If you're free we could meet tomorrow?' Karen suggested.

'Yes, I'll see you at the coffee shop at midday,' Pete replied.

'Bye, see you tomorrow,' Karen rang off.

Karen walked into the coffee shop to find Pete already seated at a small round table with a latte waiting for her. She took the seat opposite him and he immediately took her hand.

'Karen, I've missed you so much. Why have you been ignoring me?' He asked intently, his eyes searching for an answer.

'I didn't do it deliberately Pete, but you have to understand that my life has changed, turned upside down. Yours hasn't. I've still got my children to consider and their happiness and wellbeing is my number one priority. This is not just about you Pete. I've got a lot to consider.' Karen looked into space thoughtfully as she replied.

'I'm sorry,' Pete said quickly, 'I'm doing it again, not thinking, I understand.'

Karen smiled, 'It's okay.'

'I love you Karen and I want to be with you. I've made my decision. I'm going to tell Vanessa. I can't live a lie. It's been so hard, I just want to be with you and raise our child together. I'm leaving her!'

'Pete, are you crazy? Do you realise the full extent of what you've just said?' Karen replied wide eyed, 'from what you've told me about her, this could break her. I would love nothing more than for you to be with me but it has to be handled sensitively.'

'Karen, I do love you. You could make all sorts of demands without thought for anyone, yet you're thinking about Vanessa. I'm learning so much from you my darling,' Pete took her hand.

'She does need to know, of course she does and soon before she finds out from anyone else, but you can't just drop this bombshell and leave her to just deal with it. She's going to be hurt Pete. Believe me if I could have done it any other way to soften the blow for Richard, I would have but I really didn't have a choice.' Karen touched her stomach to make her point.

'So how do I do this?' Pete's brow was furrowed with anxiety.

'I can't tell you how to handle this Pete I've got my own problems to deal with. You know Vanessa better than anyone. You're going to have to work this one out yourself.' Karen smiled softly.

'I make a mess of everything Karen. I let you down with Robin and it's only now that I can see the enormity of it all. I don't want to let you down again.' Pete's eyes misted over, 'I'll work out the best way of telling Vanessa, but I want to be there for you every step of the way this time,' he stated emphatically.

'I know,' Karen replied quietly.

Conversation turned to the baby. Pete wanted every bit of detail about how she was feeling, the first kick and the upcoming scan. He wanted to be there, he needed to be there to see his baby. He had seen so many pictures over the years from their friends who had had babies and the excitement of seeing their baby in the womb. How he had envied them. The pain he felt had been deep! He never thought it would happen and it hadn't, not with Vanessa anyway. When month after month, disappointment became despair, they stopped talking about it. Now he had the chance to feel that excitement about becoming a dad and seeing the growing foetus on screen; but it was bittersweet and at the expense of Vanessa's sadness and his marriage. Not forgetting Karen's marriage too and her two small children caught up in tangled web of selfishness, guilt and hurt. He had caused it all, he blamed himself entirely. His actions going back all those years had impacted everyone around him. How he despised himself at times. Karen didn't deserve a coward like him, she was strong. 'Karen, I want to be there for the scan.' She gave him the details of the date and time. Karen stood and he held her tightly and whispered in her ear that he loved her. He didn't wait to hear it back. He was gone. He had promised to break it to Vanessa gently. *How was that even possible?* Karen stared after him and sat back down. She needed a few more minutes to herself.

Chapter 36

Karen opened the letter that Marina handed to her that had just dropped through the letterbox. Richard had more or less stopped speaking to her altogether unless it was absolutely necessary. Then he had dropped a grenade she was not expecting. It was from his solicitor. Richard wanted the girls' to live with him and he was going to fight for full custody. Karen sat down, reading the letter over and over again.

Marina looked at her and asked, 'What's wrong love?'

'Richard wants to take my children mum.' Karen's body racked with sobs as Marina sat down beside her. She pulled her daughter to her breast and stroked her hair.

'My poor love, don't distress yourself think of the baby,' Marina said soothingly.

'I knew it was too good to be true, he seemed to accept things so well. I know I've hurt him mum and I don't expect him to talk to me and exchange pleasantries; but to try and take the girls from me after what happened with Robin is just plain cruel. He knows how much it affected me,' Karen blew her nose, 'well, he's not going to win I'm going to fight him on this. I'm not losing my girls. I'm not a bad mum, am I?' She looked pleadingly at Marina.

'Of course not, me and your dad will do everything we can to help you sweetheart,' Marina replied, 'let me put the kettle on. A nice cup of sweet tea will help the shock.' Marina walked into the kitchen and gave a backward glance at Karen sitting on the settee looking completely broken. If she was honest, she was worried that this wasn't looking good for Karen based on her history with Robin and now her affair within her marriage resulting in an unplanned pregnancy with no job or home to provide for them. Marina did not mind admitting to herself that Karen definitely had a fight on her hands. *Was she strong enough?* Marina certainly hoped she was. Marina had taken the week off work to catch up on some chores around the house. She was glad that she would be home to keep an eye on Karen. Perfect timing she reflected.

Once Karen had composed herself, she rang Richard but it was as she had expected, he didn't want to discuss anything with her. She had made her bed and she could lie in it as far as he was concerned; she had brought it all on herself. Karen knew that she would get nowhere with Richard, he was as cold as ice. Trying to reason with him was impossible but she wasn't going to just sit back and let him win. She had to do everything in her power to keep Grace and Amelia. After fetching the girls from school, she gave them their dinner and left them with Marina. She decided to visit Eva.

When the doorbell rang, Eva guessed it would be Karen and was not surprised to see her standing on the doorstep. Eva stood with outstretched arms and hugged Karen who cried openly. *How could this woman whose son she had hurt so badly be kind to her?* Eva shut the door behind them and told Karen to take a seat while she made them a drink. Karen sat looking around the cosy room that she had spent so much time in before and within her marriage to Richard. This room and her relationship with Eva meant so much to her. It represented and reminded her of the new start in her life after the pain of losing Robin, a time when she was genuinely happy. Eva had always been so warm and welcoming; even now, when so much had happened. She just didn't feel worthy of her love.

Richard had told Eva of his plans to get full custody of the girls. She had tried to dissuade him but he was adamant. She understood his hurt and betrayal and the need to keep his family, even without Karen. His pride had been deeply wounded and he was angry, but she was aware that his anger had manifested itself in a cold hardness determined to prove a point. He had asked if Eva could help with the girls when he got them back, convinced that he would win. Of course she would do anything to help her only son, it had always been her and Richard against the world until Karen came along. She was not about to let him down now when he needed her. He had always been there for her but she just didn't agree with what he was doing. Yes, she had been disappointed with Karen but she had observed a very vulnerable young lady long before she knew her back story. Eva found it hard not to feel sorry for her even though it was her son she was hurting. Eva had never felt so torn in all her life. Grace and Amelia needed their mum to pick them up from school each day not their grandmother or a childminder. Karen was a good mum. She loved them and the children loved her. She could see that Richard had a close bond with the girls and they adored him, but he was at work all day and depending on the demands of his job, he could be delayed home. She knew he was organised and would stay up late to get their clothes and lunch boxes ready for the following day and would get up at the crack of dawn to make breakfast and prep dinner for later, so the children would have routine she was absolutely sure of that. But they needed something much more valuable than routine; they needed their mother.

Eva placed Karen's drink on the little trestle table beside her and sat in the chair opposite holding her own cup with both her hands wrapped around it. Eva didn't know what to say or where to start. There was silence for a while.

'I know why you're here, Richard has already told me of his plans for custody. I want you to know that I don't agree with it. I don't think it will benefit the girls to be away from you but trying to make him see that at the moment is hard. He doesn't want to discuss it. I'm at my wits end.' Eva shook her head. 'You have really hurt him Karen. He loved you. Correction! Still loves you!' she said with emphasis, 'he's not acknowledging his emotions. He's doing what he always does. He goes into this place where he wants to control the situation by practical solutions.' Eva took a sip of her tea and placed it on the coffee table in front of her. Karen sat and listened. For the first time she realised that she had spent so much time throughout their marriage focused on the loss of Robin and the hurt she had been through; that she hadn't recognized that her strong confident husband had his own vulnerabilities.

So many times, Eva had blamed herself for leaning on Richard emotionally when his father died; he had not had the arena to grieve because he had had to remain strong for her. He learnt to do all the things that would help his mum and she recalled how he had been so helpful with day to day things like washing the dishes, learning how to use the washing machine, making his bed. As he grew older, he became self sufficient to the point where he practically made all the decisions on the running of the house. They weren't mother and son, they were partners in everything. Many years had gone by before Eva realised just how much of his childhood had been robbed because of her. She felt incredible guilty.

Eva saw herself in Karen and understood what it was like to be weak. She didn't blame her. Karen had been through a terrible time and even though she knew it had been Karen's decision to give Robin up for adoption, she identified with her loss. Poor Richard, he had had to be strong for his mum and then for Karen. He handled things in the only way he knew, which was to take control. It had been too stifling for Karen and she had sought solace in the wrong place. The problem was how to resolve things as they stood now. Eva wanted to be there for Richard and she would be. She knew he was going to need her help; he couldn't raise the girls alone without her support but she didn't agree that this was the way to go. The girls needed their mother, they were close to her. Eva knew that Richard was relying on her and telling him what she felt was not going to be easy, but somehow she needed to get through to him.

Eva and Karen sat and talked about so many things and tried to find different solutions so that everyone could be happy. Try as she might, Eva could not hate Karen even though every fibre of her being was shouting out for her to do just that. Eva felt weary with it all and she knew that this was going to be a long road. There was still the new baby to come that would be a sibling to her grandchildren but would not be her grandchild.   After almost three hours of heart wrenching conversation,   tears and sadness about the situation, Karen stood up and said she needed to go. Eva agreed that they had talked enough for one evening and they both needed to rest. Eva assured Karen that she would try and talk to Richard again but she couldn't promise anything.

Chapter 37

Pete sat with his head buried in his hands. He had told Vanessa everything and it had not gone well. *What did he expect?* He had decided that he needed to be completely honest. He had spent most of his adult life not facing up to things and he vowed to himself that he had to start now. He loved Vanessa but he loved Karen too. *How did this happen? How had he managed to complicate his life to this extent? If only he had faced up to his responsibility when Karen became pregnant with Robin?* He recalled vividly the conversation that he and Karen had had when she told him she was pregnant. She was so sure that they could have made it work. *Why had he been so selfish back then?* He had thought he could pick and choose when he wanted things to happen in his life. *Boy, had he learnt lessons the hard way!* Now he had two vulnerable women to deal with it.

Vanessa had sat and listened with the hurt and shock on her face so palpable, she looked almost distorted. She had had no idea about his infidelity. She had sensed nothing. That was bad enough but to then hear that he had a child previously that he had never told her about and on top of that to then learn he was having another child with the same woman was just too much to bear. Her pain further deepened by her inability to produce a child of her own. It had been a difficult conversation and he did not expect her reaction. Instead of Vanessa rejecting him like he thought she would, she begged and pleaded with him not to leave her. This was a twist he could not have predicted. She said that she couldn't cope without him. All pride had gone and she was practically on her knees. *What had he reduced his wife to? Where had the confident woman that he met all those years ago gone?* He felt ashamed for what he had done to Vanessa. He owed it to her to listen to what she had to say and it had been excruciatingly painful to witness. She talked and talked and talked. She cried and apologised for not giving him the child they both wanted and for losing a part of herself and letting their marriage lose its flavour. That it was her fault and she wanted a chance to make it up to him, she didn't mind about the baby, she would allow him to be a part of the child's life. Just don't leave her! He was now faced with a dilemma that he could never have foreseen. Stay with his childless wife and leave Karen to go through another pregnancy on her own or go to Karen and leave Vanessa who was showing clear signs of instability. There had been so many times in his life that he hadn't done the right thing. He needed to do the right thing now. *What was the right thing though?* That was the burning question he asked himself.

Chapter 38

Karen woke up with so many things on her mind. She had nowhere of her own to live. Yes she had two bedrooms in her parents' home and they had been great considering the headache she had caused them, but she needed her own place. She had no job and a new baby due in two months and the possibility of losing her girls unless Eva could talk some sense into Richard. And then of course there was Pete, determined to be with her and to leave Vanessa, but Karen wasn't even sure that it was the right thing for him to do. Yes she loved Pete, she always had and despite everything, she was glad to be having his baby again. But it was different this time; she had the girls to think about. *How would Richard feel about Pete being around the girls as a full time stepdad?* She doubted that he would be pleased about that and would probably only strengthen his resolve to take the girls to live with him. Karen knew that for her and Pete to raise their child together would be a dream come true, and would make up for losing Robin; but it wasn't that simple. She was worried about Vanessa. She didn't know her but from what Pete had told her, she sounded pretty unstable. *How could she hurt this poor woman who was already mourning ever becoming a mother herself and then take her husband away?* She reminded herself that it wasn't her decision to make, it was Pete's. She was also painfully aware that a lot of people had been impacted by what she and Pete had done. Pete had promised that he would be there for her this time and she did want to fight to keep her family together. *Why couldn't she have Pete and keep her girls and the new baby? Why couldn't she dare to dream?* Yes, it was a mess and not text book at all but as she lay in bed in the early hours of the morning, she told herself that she had to remain confident that she could make it happen. Last time they had seen each other, she and Pete had dreamed of getting a place together and were looking forward to a future that they could finally have. Just at that time, her baby moved within her and she felt joy as she rubbed her swollen stomach. *Maybe it could happen!*

It was time to get up and get the girls ready for school. It was another day. After Karen dropped the children off, she came back to an empty house as both her parents were at work. She rang her solicitor for an update who advised that they were building her case but Richard was in a very good position financially which would obviously help his case. The solicitor reminded her that it didn't necessarily mean he would win as the courts always consider the happiness and needs and wants of the children and ultimately their wellbeing currently and for the future. She came off the phone hopeful but not optimistic. She knew it would be a battle. And then of course there were legal costs still to consider. *How would she pay for it? Would she be entitled to legal aid?* Her parents had told her not to worry about the costs as they had savings that they would be willing to use. *How sweet and kind they had been to her, she could never repay them. Not in the foreseeable future anyway.* They had told her to think of it as a long term loan that she could pay back whenever she was in a position to do so. These were hurdles she knew she had to cross but she was determined to do all she could. After losing Robin, losing the girls was not an option.

The following weeks for Karen were a blur of appointments and discussions with her mum, Eva and a very reluctant Richard. Pete had said that he wanted to see her but she just wanted to focus on the girls particularly after the upheaval of moving them from their home and all that they knew; and especially before the baby came along.

They had spoken many times on the phone and she could hear the desperation in his voice about how he just needed to see her and hold her and he kept telling her how much he loved her. He still hadn't told Karen about Vanessa not wanting him to leave because it made no difference as far as he was concerned; he was leaving anyway. He wasn't going to let Karen down again. He wanted to be a part of his child's life this time. He was not going to allow Vanessa to prevent that. But it had been hard, he could not deny that. To watch Vanessa literally falling apart before his very eyes was heartbreaking. *What kind of a monster was he?* He had broken Karen's heart all those years ago and now he was breaking Vanessa's heart. Over and over in his head, he questioned himself about what he was doing to both women. He wanted to be with Karen more than anything. She was so special to him for so many reasons; she was his first love, she had his first child, she forgave him and still loved him. It made him love her all the more. He loved Vanessa too but it was different; the intensity wasn't quite there. He reasoned that maybe the years of trying and failing to produce a child between them had taken its toll on their relationship and it had become worn down and joyless. Vanessa had changed. He knew how much she wanted a baby and how important it was to her and to see the gradual change over the years had been so very sad. She was a very different person to one he had met and loved all those years ago.

If he hadn't met Karen again, he wondered what would have happened. They had talked about their options. Should they try IVF? That was going to be costly? Should they foster? There were certainly plenty of children who needed short term stability which they could definitely provide. Or should they adopt a child that they could love to fill their void of childlessness? *How ironic would that be?* His own child had been given for adoption many years previously and yet he had considered the possibility of adopting a child. Maybe that's what he needed to do to put right the wrong he had told himself many times he had done. Vanessa to be fair had been open to all those possibilities. She loved children. He'd seen her at school with the children, she was really good with kids of all ages and she had a genuine love for children, he could see that. They had been a couple years into trying and they were still hoping that one day it would happen naturally. He'd heard many stories of couples trying for years and years and finally after deciding other options had gotten pregnant. They had been comforted with those stories and all the options available. They had planned to do some research before going down the road of any of them, but then he met Karen again and took all of Vanessa's hopes and dreams and shattered them into pieces. He felt so cruel.

His head was constantly spinning and he wondered how he managed to get on with his job. He couldn't deny it, he found it hard, but somehow when he was at work with the demands and distractions, he was able to forget; temporarily anyway. It was when he was at home every evening that he had to face his predicament. After that first conversation when Vanessa had asked him to stay, he had been shocked and surprised by her reaction and he hoped that maybe she would change her mind, but she hadn't. She had even said that when the baby was born, she would accept the baby! *What?* This was not what he wanted. *What about his commitment to Karen?* He knew that Karen was fighting her custody battle and going through another pregnancy on her own, he couldn't believe that it was happening again! Yet it was! The sadness and confusion he felt was beyond description. There were a few weeks left before the baby would come and they were still not together. He needed to sort out a place for them to live. She couldn't stay at her parents indefinitely with three children. Financially however he couldn't do anything to help unless Vanessa was willing to agree to split up and sell their house so he could start afresh with Karen.

He knew that he needed to see Karen to tell her his position but every time he spoke to her she was distressed about what Richard was doing. It seemed that nothing or no one was going to change Richard's mind. He wanted full custody of his children and Karen was beside herself and rightly so. *How could he then tell her what he was going through with Vanessa?* The only thing he could do was reassure her that he loved her and that they would be together one day.

And he was right because knowing that Pete loved her was enough for Karen, she had been happy to hold onto that and not think about their future at that time. She had been so consumed and preoccupied about the girls that she had not given much thought to Pete's situation. She knew that he had said he was going to tell Vanessa and that he would be leaving her, but she was very aware that that wasn't going to be an easy conversation to have so she had put no pressure on him to have it. The times that they had spoken, Pete had simply said that he was sorting things out. He didn't want to burden her with his problems, as Karen had her own to deal with. She never doubted his love for a second and when he couldn't call, he would text and keep in touch every single day. *What more could she ask for in this situation where their love for each other had broken other peoples' lives?* She had no expectations of an easy journey but she felt hopeful of the future they could possibly have together.

Chapter 39

It had been a busy day at school and Pete was exhausted as he put his key in the door. It was another late finish with after school activities and meetings. His mind was in turmoil and there were periods during the day when he was thinking about how to be with Karen and not hurt Vanessa who seemed to be in denial. He knew he wasn't giving his best but at least he was going to work. Unlike Vanessa who had not gone to work for the past three weeks. He'd managed the first few days of her absence with changing timetables for the some of the other teachers, but in the end he had to ring the agency and get a supply teacher in. It was his fault that her depression had come back. *How could he blame her for causing him extra problems at work?* As he got into his car to head home, he was not looking forward to another evening of seeing what he was doing to Vanessa. *Oh how he wished that she was stronger, like Karen!* She seemed so pathetic and it only added to his guilt. He opened the door and lingered in the hallway, hanging his coat on the hook, his head bent low. *What was happening to his life?* He asked himself as he slowly walked into the lounge.

'Vanessa!' he shouted with panic rising within him. She was slumped in the chair, an empty paracetamol bottle lying on the floor. Pete went over to her and started to shake her, then slapped her face but she was out cold. 'Ness, oh Ness, what have you done?' He quickly grabbed his phone and dialled 999. 'Ambulance please, quick it's my wife, she taken an overdose.'

There were so many questions from the operator. He knew they needed as much information as possible, but he just wanted the ambulance to come. Pete cradled her in his arms, while tears fell down his cheeks. Thankfully it seemed like only a few minutes had passed when the ambulance crew arrived. He watched as they took charge of the situation feeling completely helpless but relieved. It had been a long evening and he couldn't describe how he felt. The hospital staff had been great, they had pumped her stomach and she was out of danger, however she needed to stay overnight in hospital.

He poured himself a drink as soon as he got home. He didn't normally drink during the working week, but this was exceptional circumstances. How he needed that glass of brandy as he sat and replayed the events of the evening in his head. *Well, this was certainly going to change his plans. How could he leave Vanessa now?* She was clearly unwell and he knew he was to blame along with the last couple years of bitter disappointment of not being able to get pregnant. And then there was Karen, carrying his baby and going through it all alone. Again! After drinking another glass of brandy, he suddenly realised how hungry he was. He had not eaten all evening.

Chapter 40

Karen opened the letter. The date that was set for the first custody hearing was in three months time. She hoped that she could try and forget about it for the time being. *Oh why had it come to this?* She felt terribly sad.

Another three weeks and the baby will be here, she thought. She had been fortunate that she had been well throughout her pregnancy but she hadn't had the luxury of really enjoying it with so many external factors to consider. She sat down suddenly feeling very weary. There was still so much to do and so much to think about. She put the letter on the sofa next to her. With her head in her hands, the full weight of her situation hit her like a sledge hammer and she cried. Tears for Robin, her beautiful boy who she had far too young while she was still a child herself. Poor innocent Robin, he deserved so much more. She hadn't known who she was back then and had nothing to offer a helpless baby. And more tears for her sweet little girls Grace and Amelia who had bought her so much joy but did she really know what to do for them? She felt guilty for the disruption to their lives. She loved her girls more than anybody or anything in the world, and she could actually lose them. 'My God,' she cried out, 'what have I done?' *Did she really deserve them? Was she a good mother? Was her love enough? Maybe they would be better off with Richard?* She wanted them to grow to be kind individuals who would be strong and know their capabilities. *But how could she teach them something she didn't know how to achieve herself? And worst still, Richard knew it too!* And yet more tears continued to flow for her unborn baby. She had decided that she didn't want to know the sex of the life growing inside her. Boy or Girl? It didn't matter. It would be loved regardless. *Maybe this child would get the real Karen?* She wanted to be authentic and true to herself, not the person that everyone else wanted or expected. So many times she had asked herself questions. *Who was she? What did she want? Why was it always about what other people wanted or needed?* She mattered too! She never really took her own feelings or needs into account. She always felt like she wasn't important enough. There was always a desire to please everyone else, to be liked, to fit in! *But who was the real Karen? Deep down what purpose, what dreams did she have? She knew she was searching for something, but what? And could she ever find the peace and satisfaction that she yearned for so badly? Did it even exist? How could she raise her children without knowing who Karen was and what she wanted? How could she teach them to fly if she hadn't learned to fly herself?* She needed to grow as a person and gain confidence within. There was one thing however she was sure of; she wanted to protect this anticipated precious child with every fibre of her being. She was so grateful for the support from her mum and dad. She really had no idea what would have become of her and her unborn child without them. Everything was so uncertain but there was one certainty that she had determined in her mind; she wasn't going to rely on Pete. As much as he wanted to be there, he was married with still so much that he had to sort out himself.

She could see that Pete just wanted to please her and do all he could, despite his situation. He had been happy to go along with her wishes about not knowing the baby's sex. She recalled the joy on his face when he went with her for the scan and saw the baby on the monitor. He couldn't believe that he was actually going to be a dad again. He kept gently squeezing her hand to remind her that he was there at her side with tears flowing down his face. 'Karen my darling, I'm the luckiest man alive.' He cried a lot and easily, she noticed. Karen had remained quiet, enjoying this special time together as they saw their second child growing inside her. When the midwife asked if they wanted to know the sex, they both shook their head in unison, having discussed it beforehand.

Karen thought she would never stop crying as she sat on the sofa almost rooted to the spot, the tears just kept on flowing. She felt completely overwhelmed. She felt defeated! It was like she was sinking. *Where did she go from here?* She thought her head would explode... There were so many decisions to make and so much was unknown.

Chapter 41

'Listen Ness, we need to talk, you know that I have to go and be with Karen, don't you?' Pete said gently, knowing that he had to be careful not to push Vanessa over the edge again.

'But I forgive you Pete, don't go. I know we can work it out.'

The television was on but neither of them was watching it. Vanessa was lying on the sofa while Pete sat opposite in the single armchair. They had the same conversation that evening that they had had several times before. Whenever he plucked up the courage to remind Vanessa that he had to leave to be with Karen, the tears would start and she would beg him not to leave. She was prepared to accept the baby. She forgave his infidelity and acknowledged that life had not been easy for them over the last few years. It was hard to watch Vanessa lose her pride. *Why wasn't she angry with him?* It would have made it easier for him if she had thrown him out along with his belongings, he would have at least felt that he got what he deserved. But her reaction had really saddened him. He felt so responsible. *How could he then hurt her again when she had forgiven the hurt that he had previously inflicted?* He wanted to be with Karen and the baby when it came; yet Vanessa was making it incredibly hard for him to go. He just didn't know what to do. Karen needed him. She was carrying his second child. And for the second time... alone! *He had to be there this time! He had promised her that he would. How had his life come to this?* He had asked himself that question so many times even though he knew the answer. *If only he had stayed with Karen the first time, he wouldn't be in this position now! He had an obligation to Karen; he couldn't let her down again! He owed it to her. Her marriage was over because of him.* Vanessa kept reminding him however that he was married to her and what about his obligation to her? And she was right. He had obligations to both. The guilt that consumed him was too much to bear. He had caused pain and heartache to two people who didn't deserve it. He was thoroughly disappointed with himself. He always considered himself to be an intelligent person who made sensible choices and in his working life he had always done that. *So why have I created such chaos in my personal life?*

Pete walked to the local pub which was a welcome sight. As he entered, he saw Sam and Adam who motioned for him to join them. They both lived in the area and Pete had gotten to know them both well and would often meet up with them usually on a Saturday afternoon for a game of snooker. After ordering his drink, he sat down and drank his bottle of beer in one go.

'It looks like you needed that,' Adam remarked.

'Yeah, I really did, are you both ready for another?' Pete asked already on his feet ready to go to the bar to get another drink. Sam and Adam watched as Pete drank one drink after another and another. They pleaded with him to slow down. What they didn't realise was that Pete needed to make what he was feeling go away. He was self medicating. He had hoped that drinking would help, but it hadn't. He just couldn't shift the weight of the guilt knowing the untold pain he had caused to two women who did not deserve it. Both women needed him. *How was he going to fix this?* Karen was carrying his child alone again! She was a beautiful person with a caring and wonderful heart. A forgiving heart! He didn't merit that level of love. He had been a coward all those years ago and he was still a coward. How he despised and hated himself. He wanted to be with Karen and be part of his new child's life. He wanted it more than anything he had ever wanted. It was his to take and yet he couldn't because of Vanessa. Poor sweet Vanessa who was really suffering and he was responsible for a large part of it, although he knew he wasn't to blame for all of her pain. She was hurting for the children she desperately wanted and couldn't have but what he had done was pile the pain even higher. She now had the knowledge of his previous child Robin and the new baby that was to come. *Could I have twisted the knife anymore? If only I had been honest with her all those years ago about Robin?* He reasoned that had she known then maybe Vanessa would not have felt as though she had let him down and would have possibly coped better with their childless state. And although she would still be saddened about not having her own biological child she wouldn't have carried the additional guilt of not being able to give him a child. Had she known about Robin, possibly her mental health would not have suffered quite as much. She had been carrying an extra burden that she had had no need to bear. That sudden awareness really hit home. *How could he walk away from Vanessa knowing just how vulnerable she was?* He did have an obligation to her, she was his wife and he loved her. Yes, it was different to the love he had for Karen. Nothing came close to that! It had taken him many years to recognise that too. The love that he and Karen shared was incredibly special. It was hard to even put into words. Every fibre of his being loved Karen, no question at all. But with Vanessa, he loved her because she was a very sweet soul. *What was there not to love?* Had Karen not come back into his life and reawakened everything that he had buried, the love he had for Vanessa would have been enough. Sure the years of trying for a baby had taken its' toll, but he remembered the many years beforehand when they had enjoyed each other's company. They had much in common; their careers, holidays enjoyed and adventures shared. *If only life could have stayed at that point in time? If only they hadn't decided to try for a baby? Their love would possibly have sustained but did that mean that their relationship had been superficial? Did it only work while life was good?* He didn't know if he was being unfair or even cruel to think that way.

Through tears and drunkenness, Pete shared his dilemma with Adam and Sam. He needed to release it. He felt like he was going mad. He couldn't cope anymore and he really didn't know what to do. He felt tortured because whatever he did would cause pain to one or the other. It was a situation where there would be one loser. Both deserved better and both needed his commitment. *But how could he solve this? Could he ever be completely happy? Whoever he chose, would he always be thinking of the other one he let down? How could he let Karen down again? How could he walk away from Vanessa who was clearly unstable?*

'You have to do what's right for you mate,' Sam said quietly.

'Yes, it's a hard decision but Sam's right you need to do what you think you can live with otherwise you'll make yourself ill,' Adam continued, 'and that won't benefit any of them or the baby.'

Pete listened as they continued to give wise words of advice about the effects it could have on his mental health having watched him trying to drink himself into oblivion. As far as he was concerned however, it was too late. There was no light in sight in this very long tunnel. He felt like he was in quicksand and he was sinking fast.

Chapter 42

It was Saturday afternoon at Cecil and Marina's house. And everyone was there including Susan, Fiona and Guy and Grandma Rose. The only people missing were Grace and Amelia who were with Richard as always every weekend. How she missed them and wished that they could be here some weekends to see the extended family but she knew that to start making demands from Richard about that would not go down well. It meant that the children spent very little quality time with their aunties and great-grandma and she felt a little sad about that.

However, Karen always enjoyed seeing her family and there was always plenty of fun and laughter, which was a welcome relief from her problems. Karen had been immensely grateful to her family for the support they had all given and if there had been disappointment, disapproval or even judgment they certainly hadn't shown it and for that she was grateful.

Her dad Cecil always enjoyed having everyone there on a Saturday afternoon. There were many weekends that he was away, so whenever he was home, he was very much the life and soul. He was a man who left the running of the home to Marina. He had never got involved in any day to day decisions with the children when they were little. He trusted Marina to just get on with things. He worked hard and provided well and seemed happy with his role within the family and was certainly a warm and approachable father. He was a strong self assured man but he wasn't overbearing in anyway. If required he would confidently share his views and opinions, but he was always measured and kind. He was a wonderful storyteller and held court well in a group. He shared many stories that were captivating and interesting especially when he was a young man that would have Grandma Rose rolling her eyes with a wry smile and feigning disapproval when certain tales were told. And even when retelling events and situations of his time on the road currently, he always managed to hold everyone's interest. He was a charismatic man. Karen was in no doubt why her mum fell in love with her dad. And Karen was incredibly proud of her mixed heritage. She loved that she was both English and Caribbean. She loved the diversity in the family. It made it interesting and fascinating, and especially when Grandma Rose chipped in with more stories of life in Jamaica when she was growing up.

Karen had much admiration for her mum and dad for making their marriage work against all the odds. Marina was five when her mum died and she was the youngest of a family of four children. Her sister Marjorie was fifteen at the time and her brothers Martin and Matthew were eighteen and nineteen when their mother died of a sudden heart attack. So as the youngest, memories of her mum were very vague but her father spoiled her and gave her lots of love and attention. Her physical needs however were met by her sister Marjorie who became like a mum to her. She used to bath her, dress her, prepare her food and even walked her to and from school each day. Marina loved Marjorie and their relationship grew stronger and closer as they grew older. But Marina's relationship with her dad broke down when she met and started dating Cecil. Her father did not approve. He did not believe in the races mixing. 'I've got nothing against black people, but each should stick to their own, it's not right to mix the two,' he said to Marina when she told him about Cecil. Try as she might, he would not alter his position and said that he wanted no part of it. So their relationship became distant for many years. She also never managed to persuade her brothers Martin and Matthew either who took their dad's stance. However, she remained incredibly close to her sister Marjorie who never gave up trying to convince her dad that Marina and Cecil were made for each other. So apart from their Auntie Marjorie and her husband Frank and her first cousins Charles and Adrian, Karen and her sisters never knew their mum's family. Her mum and Marjorie saw a lot of each other, but Marjorie's health had deteriorated over the last few years due to severe rheumatoid arthritis so she couldn't get out as much as she used to, so Marina would visit her. Karen knew Marina was really sad about the change in the relationship that she had previously enjoyed with her own dad. Marina had kept loose ties with her dad by sending Christmas cards but nothing much improved between them until just before he died, when Marina and Cecil went to see him in the nursing home. In the weeks before he died, her mum re-established her relationship with him where they were able to talk and put the past behind them. Marina had never really felt any bitterness towards her dad as she knew he was of a certain generation who held prejudices that was borne out of ignorance and fear. He apologised for not being a part of their lives and he thanked Cecil for coming to see a dying man who didn't deserve such kindness. Karen had a lot of admiration for her dad Cecil.

So as everyone arrived and settled down together, Karen felt happy and enjoyed the dynamics and interactions of her family. There were always jokes and noisy exchanges of conversation that made the atmosphere so energetic. She particularly loved seeing Fiona and Guy who were always incredibly warm and protective towards her. She observed that they had a really easy relationship. They laughed a lot and gave each other lots of eye contact when they spoke to each other. They appeared really relaxed whether in engaged in private conversation with each other or in company with others. Karen was pleased that Fiona had clearly met someone that she had an obvious connection with. Guy was someone that was so easy going and relaxed most of the time. He seemed to just go with the flow whatever the situation, whether it was choosing a takeaway meal or deciding what time they were going home. Karen had seen Fiona drag Guy away within seconds of eating dinner because she had arranged for them to meet up with friends for a drink; without informing him beforehand. He had simply shrugged his shoulders with a smile and complied. Equally she had seen him sit for hours with Fiona at their parents' house looking perfectly happy. *How she admired Guy*. She reflected how different Richard was, he wanted every detail planned to the minute and how moody and awkward he became if things changed unexpectedly. It was always evident to everyone around when things didn't go according to Richard's plan. *How she wished that she hadn't pandered to him quite so much?* The problem was that he always made her feel ashamed if she showed irritation because it made her seem ungrateful; as he always said that everything he did was for her and the girls. She was reminded of that often.

Karen's thoughts then remained on Richard and she felt sad about how much she had hurt him. Yes, he had tried to control her but he had loved her, she knew that. *What she couldn't work out was why he loved her? She was only too aware of her own complexity. But then she reasoned, maybe Richard needed someone to fix, maybe it gave him purpose.* He certainly seemed to thrive and almost grow in confidence when his plans were executed well for Karen and the girls.

Karen drifted off into her own world, as she sat on the sofa next to Grandma Rose opposite Fiona and Guy who were on the other two-seater sofa. Susan and Marina were chatting about a book that they were both reading with Susan perched on the edge of the single sofa that Marina occupied. They both loved their books and often discussed and debated them. It was as if they were in their own private book club of two. Mum and Susan have always been close she thought, they seemed to have so much in common. She envied their relationship, it was uncomplicated. Susan had done everything right so it just seemed to sail along easily. She had asked herself many times if she was jealous of Susan. She had come to the conclusion that she wasn't jealous but she did feel woefully inadequate around her, even though Susan could not have been sweeter if she tried. The problem was that they had absolutely nothing in common, their attempts at conversation was just so superficial. Karen would ask Susan her about her job but if she was really honest she wasn't that interested. Susan would always enquire about the children and she certainly displayed a genuine fondness for Grace and Amelia and gave them lots of love and cuddles, gifts and treats whenever she saw them. That aside she and Susan seemed to be poles apart.

When Karen compared her relationship with Susan to her relationship with Fiona, she realised why it was so different and why she felt so much more comfortable around Fiona. Susan was quieter and much more closed about her life. It was hard to know what she was thinking. She never talked about wanting children for example whereas Fiona talked about having them as a matter of fact. If Fiona was happy you knew it and if something was bothering Fiona, you knew it. She pretty much talked about her feelings or emotions as a matter of course. If she was annoyed or bored or just miffed about something, she would share. If she'd been shopping and bought new clothes, she would parade in front of the family to get their opinion or approval. She was an open book and everyone who met her liked her. Yes, she was very likeable. Susan on the other hand was much harder to get to know and understand. She had always been studious and loved books and didn't converse much. She had been completely focused at school, college and university. And now she was fully committed to her job. She worked many late nights and the company was pleased with her performance and dedication.

Mum must be so disappointed with me! Karen thought. She felt sad that she had let her parents down. She was the only one who had constantly brought major problems to them. Yes, there had been times when Susan and Fiona had needed Marina's help and advice. Susan had achieved a good grade in her degree at University and she was really pleased to land an immediate graduate placement as an HR Business Partner within a large company with plenty of opportunity for progression. Most of the time she was fine but occasionally she had issues at work where there was rivalry and backstabbing and along with a heavy workload, it really affected her at times. It was then that she would go and pour her heart out to Marina who would listen and give all the comfort and advice she could. That was usually the extent of any drama from Susan. Fiona would mainly ring Marina if there was something bothering her in the moment. She ráng about everything and anything, however small. Again Marina would listen and make soothing noises in all the right places. Both Susan and Fiona would always be fine after a chat and their normal lives would resume. Karen felt that Marina was never burdened by Susan or Fiona but not so with her; she had two unplanned pregnancies, a failed marriage, two small children to care for with no home and no job. When she compared herself to Susan and Fiona, she was a walking disaster! *Mum's been great but how much easier her life would have been if she had only had Susan and Fiona? Poor mum! And dad for that matter!* Karen sighed. Her thoughts overwhelmed her and caused her brow to furrow. Grandma Rose had been watching her granddaughter who seemed completely lost in her thoughts and she felt the need to talk with her privately to make sure she was okay.

'Karen, do you want to come with me in the kitchen and keep me company while I finish the soup?' Grandma Rose touched her shoulder with a firmness which told Karen it wasn't a choice even though a question had been posed. She smiled and gently raised herself out of the chair and followed her grandma into the kitchen and sat at the table. 'Are you okay my child?' Karen loved the way Grandma always used that endearment. It was so comforting and always made her open up. 'You looked a thousand miles away,' Grandma Rose continued, 'tell me what's troubling you right now. I know the situation you're in is not ideal but it's not good for the baby for you to look so sad.'

She always had really heartfelt conversations with her grandma who although in her eighties was still very agile and her mind very sharp. There had been many times when she had given her some real words of encouragement and comfort. Today was no exception, as the two of them sat in the kitchen while Grandma tended to the Kidney

Bean soup that everyone always looked forward to, Karen talked of her situation.

'I've made a mess of my life grandma and caused mum and dad so much headache and disruption. I must be a big disappointment to them.'

'No child, they love you but I won't deny that they are worried about you,' Grandma sighed.

'I'm worried about me,' Karen smiled as she said it. She talked of Robin and the great loss she felt daily and how it had changed her forever. She hadn't been the same person from the day he went. She had become someone else but she still didn't quite know this new person that well and it was quite a journey trying to work her out. This new person could be okay one minute getting on with life, and then a thought could come or a word from someone could bring her crashing down to the depths of despair. She wasn't even sure she liked this new person. Where did she fit with anyone? This new person was complicated. She wondered if she would ever really know her. She had thought, maybe she didn't need to; she could ignore her and carry on and be normal. Whatever 'normal' was? But it didn't work because she felt a fake and there was only so much acting she could do. She needed to be true to herself. But being real and true to herself, had caused deep pain to Richard, disappointment to Eva, disruption to Grace and Amelia, burden to Cecil and Marina, dilemma for Pete and devastation to Vanessa. So many people had been affected by one afternoon of abandonment. It was hard not to feel pitied or judged by her family. She didn't know which was worse.

'My dear child, you cannot take the whole blame for this situation, there were many factors and you couldn't control them all.'

'If only I had kept Robin, things would have been different, why did I think that giving him away would make the situation go away? It actually made it worse because ironically he never really went because he's stayed in my heart and in my mind,' she sighed deeply.

'And now I'm actually in danger of losing my girls,' Karen's voice trailed off in despair.

'Now you listen to me,' there was now sternness in Grandma's voice, 'you will not lose the girls. They know you and love you and even if Richard wins the case and I don't believe he will, you will still see them and be a part of their lives.'

Karen was sobbing, 'I don't want them to live with Richard. I want them with me. It's not fair, why can't he just leave the children with me? I can't lose them Grandma. My heart will break all over again.'

'I'm praying for you my child. Don't upset yourself, remember the baby growing inside you.' With her arms around Karen's shoulders, Rose cradled her and prayed silently.

'Grandma, I don't know what I would do without you,' Karen said quietly.

Chapter 43

'Nanny, this one doesn't fit,' Amelia sighed.

'That's because it's the wrong way up my darling,' Eva took the puzzle piece that Amelia was holding, turned it the right way up and put it in the puzzle, 'there you go, it's all done now. Well done.' Eva clapped her hands at the same time. Amelia's face immediately broke into a big smile. Eva impulsively hugged her youngest granddaughter. *How she loved her?* She looked across at Grace who was engrossed in her favourite cartoon that she had watched many times before. She was laid back on the sofa with the cushion behind her head looking very comfortable indeed. Eva thought her heart would burst with love for these two little people.

It was Saturday afternoon and ever since the split, Eva would spend that time with Richard and the girls. Richard either came to visit her with the children or she visited him. They tended to alternate. On this occasion, Eva had come to them. Richard was in the kitchen preparing lunch. There was tension between them because she had tried to talk to him earlier when the girls were playing with their toys in the conservatory, about the custody situation. She didn't feel it was necessary for him to try and take the girls from Karen and have them live with him full-time. The current arrangement was working well she thought. Yes the girls loved their dad but they loved their mum too. Eva had observed that the girls seemed relatively unaffected by the separation. They had adapted well to the change of circumstances much better than she had foreseen. She was grateful that because they were in contact with both parents they were thankfully too young to fully understand the breakup. But Richard was adamant that he didn't want the girls living with Karen and her new baby. Eva had tried to tell him that the new baby would be their sibling whether he liked it or not and he would have to accept that the girls would have some kind of relationship with the new baby whatever the circumstances. He then accused her of not understanding how he felt and taking Karen's side. And this was where she and Richard had reached an impasse. She wasn't taking Karen's side but she was aware that for the sake of her grandchildren, she would have to accept Karen's new baby too; to an extent. It was a dilemma and it did bother her about how to treat the new baby that would be her grandchildren's sibling, but not her grandchild. Richard was hurt and she knew it but pursuing custody in her view would only bring more pain for all concerned but she just couldn't seem to get through to him.

'Have you any idea how humiliated I feel, do you?' Eva could see how angry Richard was as he had asked her that question earlier. It was clear that he didn't really want an answer it was just the opening line to a tirade of insults about Karen that Eva found painful to hear.

'Richard, please she will always be Grace and Amelia's mother. It serves no purpose to talk about her so disrespectfully.'

'So, I'm supposed to just sit back and let her walk all over me. Whose side are you on?' He raised his arms and held them midway waiting for an answer.

'Yours of course, you're my son, but that doesn't mean that I can't sympathise with the fact that she hadn't dealt with giving up her son. That was a massive thing for a young girl to go through. I can't begin to imagine the effect it would have had on her and then not being able to talk about it.'

'So all of a sudden, she's the victim and I'm to blame. Great!' He rolled his eyes.

'Why didn't you want her to tell me about Robin? She told me everything the night she came and told me about the pregnancy.' Eva felt bad lying to Richard pretending that she hadn't known about Robin until Karen told her about this pregnancy. She hadn't found the courage to tell him. What made it worse was that she had also been aware of Karen's meetings with Pete. She had to admit, that she hadn't felt comfortable about Karen seeing Pete but remembering how fragile and broken Karen was at that time, she simply wanted to help. That was a mistake, she knew that now. But she couldn't tell Richard, he would feel totally betrayed.

'I couldn't see the point of you knowing,' he shrugged his shoulder.

'But if she wanted to share something with me that was important to her, you should not have stopped that!' Eva stated, 'that is a form of control Richard,' she then paused before continuing, 'and that is a trait I'm sad to say I have noticed in you for some time.' She finished off the sentence in a quieter tone of voice and a look of sadness fell across her face.

Richard remained silent for a few minutes and then said, 'I was just trying to look after her and protect her.'

'Did she need protecting from me?' Eva's voice rose, 'No!' She said emphatically, 'I'm not criticising you Richard and I know that you loved her and it was coming from a good place, but it didn't help her.'

It had been a difficult conversation which left both of them reflective. Eva's heart was breaking for her son and the pain he was clearly experiencing. She knew what Richard was like and how he took of control of situations, which was admirable but he didn't seem to realise that he couldn't control people. He had done it with her and there had been times when she didn't like it, but it had been with fairly minor things that didn't really matter, but she was painfully aware that on a daily basis, Karen would have been worn down by it. She felt responsible for the way Richard was because she continually blamed herself for falling apart after his father died, relying on him for support, subconsciously giving him a responsibility that he should not have had to deal with and for which he didn't have the emotional maturity for. *She was the reason he was the way he was, how could she be hard on him now?*

He needed her right now, as she had needed him all those years ago when Greg died. *So why did she feel so torn? Why was she not angry with Karen?* She had slept with her ex-lover and was now pregnant with his child causing the immediate breakdown of the family. That was serious but there was a part of her that understood how Karen must have felt and why she needed to escape the suffocation that she was experiencing in her marriage. Coupled with not being able to discuss her feelings and sadness, it was inevitable that what was bubbling under the surface would rise to the top. She had always liked Karen and knew in her heart that she was not a bad person who had deliberately set out to hurt her son. She was a victim dealing with loss and separation. Eva was only too aware of those feelings. Fortunately Eva had been allowed to express how she felt at the time. Although her parents lived in another city, they were always on the other end of the phone line. Eva would spend hours talking to her mum on the phone during the week and at the weekends her parents came to visit. This continued for many years and even her sister in America phoned and wrote regularly. Talking and sharing helped her to heal, Eva was convinced of that. Eva looked back with gratitude for all the people who just allowed her to talk because without realising it, they had helped her cope with her grief. Whenever she thought about Karen carrying all those feelings inside her and never able to talk, she felt so sorry for her and all feelings of judgment subsided. This however was not helping her relationship with Richard who she could see was not feeling as supported as he felt he should be. Eva was worried about him and knew that Richard was struggling with the thought of the new baby being a part of Grace and Amelia's lives, which was why he wanted the girls the girls living with him. *How would all this work out long term?* Eva pondered.

Chapter 44

'Goodnight daddy, love you,' Grace said.

'Goodnight poppet, love you too,' Richard replied as he kissed her forehead. He reached across to Amelia who flung her arms around his neck, 'goodnight sweet pea, love you.'

'Love you daddy,' Amelia said with a contented smile. He put the night light on and left them both lying contentedly in their single beds separated only by a bedside unit. They weren't sleeping but he knew it wouldn't be long before they both nodded off. Sometimes he would hear conversations between them before sleep came. He loved the fact they were so close and regularly hugged each other during the day. Grace was so patient with Amelia. *What a gift that was?* Richard loved having the girls with him. He loved them so much and wished they were with him all the time. He knew he could make them happy. They were very content when they were him, he could see that. As far as he was concerned, they didn't miss their mum when they were with him. However the conversation earlier with Eva had disturbed him. He was hurt by her words and felt a little let down by her empathy for Karen who had recklessly broken down their family. *Had he driven Karen back into the arms of her ex-lover?* He asked himself. The conversation with his mum had played over and over in his mind. *Was he controlling?* He never thought of himself in that way. Proactive and organised would be how he would describe himself. *What was so wrong in wanting things to run smoothly? It made life easier didn't it?* He could never understand people who seemed to just let things happen without a plan. *And as for having to talk continually about how you were feeling, what was the point? It didn't change anything. You just had to get on with life.* However, his marriage breaking down had made him reflect on how he had dealt with problems or situations in the past. He was a practical person and didn't operate on emotion. *Was it conceivable that he had played a part in Karen's mental health deteriorating?* He recalled the times when she just seemed unable to cope and how the simplest of tasks for others were too much for her to complete. She never really had much confidence and always seemed happy for him to organise everything. He liked the fact that she relied on him and always asked his opinion about things. He knew what was best for her and she had said countless times how much she appreciated his input. *So when did things change?* He didn't have a clue. He hadn't spotted the signs. He had to admit that the constant talk of Robin and the desire to tell his mum had baffled him. He didn't understand the continual need to question a decision that had been made previously for all the right reasons. Karen had given up Robin at a point in her life when she felt she couldn't manage. He had gone to new adoptive parents who wanted and loved him. She now had two beautiful daughters and he just couldn't comprehend why they didn't or couldn't fill the hole that Robin had left. Whenever the subject of Robin arose, he hadn't encouraged her to talk because he was simply trying to help her. He didn't want her to indulge in painful memories. *What was wrong with that?* And if she had told his mum, that would have been a reason for never putting it behind her. *Surely to keep dwelling on something that you couldn't change wasn't healthy? Wasn't it far better to bury it and move on? Clearly not!*

Now there were questions he wanted answers for. *Had she gone back into the arms of Pete simply because he was Robin's dad? Had she cheated on him with Pete because they had the loss of Robin in common? Someone she could talk to because she couldn't talk to him? Or did she still have feelings for Pete?* He never saw Karen as someone that would cheat. She seemed to be a loyal person. *He had got that wrong!* The more he thought about what had happened, the more he realised that Karen for whatever reason had needed to talk about her feelings. Although he didn't understand it, he began to acknowledge how different everyone was in how they dealt with things. *If he had allowed her to talk about Robin and how she felt about giving him up, maybe they would still have a marriage?*

Richard didn't like these kinds of conversations with himself. *Was he actually starting to blame himself for her cheating? No! He was not going to take the blame for it. Damn it!* Yes, he loved her still and wished that he had done things differently but the last thing he was going to do was to blame himself. *Okay so he got it wrong, but he didn't deserve this. She knew exactly what she was doing when she slept with her ex-boyfriend. You can dress it up all you like with emotions, but she committed adultery!* It was something that had never ever entered his head, even when she had distanced herself from him at times with excuses whenever he wanted to make love. He had understood that she was tired and he never wanted to make too many demands. *So it was unforgiveable and she would jolly well suffer as a consequence! Why should she get the girls?* He loved them just as much.

Chapter 45

Karen found the last month of her pregnancy really difficult. She looked at herself in the mirror turning left then right and observed her frame, which was huge. She smiled as she cradled her stomach and felt happy and sad at the same time. She thought about her first pregnancy and the parallel with this one, pregnant for the same man in her parents' home with an uncertain future ahead. She remembered how hard it had been emotionally the first time. Ironically, she was coping this time. She wasn't sure why but she didn't feel broken like she did the first time. She tried to assess her feelings and emotions. *Why was she so accepting of her current situation?* As she contemplated she realised so much had happened but losing Robin had trumped every other hurt and disappointment in her life. The deep pain she felt the first time had come from the shock and distress she experienced by Pete's cowardice and rejection. He had completely let her down. She had sunk to the depths of despair and never thought she would ever feel whole again. It had not been a good place to be and it had taken her years to overcome. She now felt strangely untouched by pain. She was never ever going to allow herself to depend on anyone emotionally or be wounded like that again. But she didn't have to face that this time as Pete was so attentive. He rang regularly, sometimes three or four times a day. He reassured her that she was not alone and reminded her that he was there with her in spirit if not in body. He wanted to visit her and pleaded on many occasions if she would allow him to pop by and see her to make sure she was okay, rather than them always having to meet in the impersonal space of a coffee shop but she hadn't wanted that. She didn't want the girls confused. They were still too young to have explanations about the fact that their new brother or sister would only be their half sibling and that Pete was the new baby's father. All of these things would have to be addressed at some point in the future but she wanted it done one step at a time. There was also her mum and dad to consider who had had their lives disrupted. It was their home and she wasn't sure that they were ready to meet Pete. There was still so much for him to sort out with Vanessa and his marriage. And of course there was Richard, she had hurt him deeply. She had no wish to deepen his wound. The custody battle was still ongoing and she was not going to jeopardise her chances of keeping her girls just so that Pete could feel he was being supportive. She knew he was there for her this time. He would have to manage his own guilt about not being there for her when she had Robin. She was aware that it had affected him but she couldn't fix that for him, nor was she going to try. The confident self assured happy person of his youth had gone and was replaced with a guilt ridden man who seemed unable to know how to deal with his own emotions let alone help anyone else. She loved him and genuinely dreamed about them being together as a family even after two wrecked marriages between them and four children. Although Robin wasn't with them physically and never would be, he would always be a big part of their story and the reason why another life was created. *Had it not been for Robin, this little one would not be nearly here.* She thought, as she stroked her belly. She was pleased that Robin had been at the heart of it, because then in a way, he was still with them too. *But what did the future really hold for her and Pete?* He wasn't sure first time around when she was pregnant with Robin and now it was she who wasn't sure this time. He felt absolutely certain that once Vanessa got used to the idea and became stronger he would be able to persuade her to separate and sell their house. He would then be able to buy a house for Karen, himself and all the children to live in. He had some savings and taking everything into account, he felt that financially they would be okay.

'This is what I want Karen, I want to be with you. Of course I feel incredibly guilty about Vanessa but I know she will come around soon, I'm sure of it.' He had said in one of the many conversations they had.

'Pete, she tried to take her own life,' Karen said with emphasis, 'this is not something that will change overnight. She's mentally unstable and anything could tip her over the edge again.'

'Yes, I know but you need me, the baby's going to need me. How many directions can I be pulled in? You and the baby have to be my primary concern. She's going to have to get over it,' Pete said wearily. Bizarrely Karen felt guilty because she knew that Pete's dilemma was bound up in the fact that he had let her down before and was determined not to do it again; but she didn't want Vanessa's deteriorating mental health on her conscience. She wasn't convinced they could be happy knowing that Vanessa wasn't coping. But he was adamant their future lie together and he refused to accept any other ending. The irony of it all was he really wanted it this time even at the cost of his marriage, the demise of Vanessa's mental health, the gaining of two stepchildren which would bring inevitable contact with Richard and all the potential challenges that would bring. It was huge and he still wanted it. *The rose coloured glasses were definitely on for him!* Karen thought. She however was totally realistic about the future and what lay ahead having had many nights alone to think and ponder. She definitely had her reservations but Pete had been persuasive with his points and there were moments when she started to believe that maybe they could make it work this time until she remembered how she had thought the same thing all those years ago with Robin. That dream had been shattered and with so many broken dreams behind her, Karen was afraid to hope.

Chapter 46

That night as Karen lay in bed in the early hours of Saturday morning, she felt a searing pain in her back, she turned and tried to get comfortable but there was more pain. She knew the signs, her baby was coming. She looked at her mobile phone... it was 2.23am. She got out of bed and bent forward holding onto the chair in front of the dressing table hoping that it would ease. It didn't. This pain was intense. She walked slowly alongside the bed back and forth thinking that it would distract her from the pain but it almost disabled her. She gasped as the pain in her back gripped her trying not to cry out.

Karen felt so alone although she knew she wasn't. Her mum and dad were sleeping in the room along the landing. She was however grateful that Grace and Amelia were with Richard. She wouldn't have wanted them to see her in pain. He had collected them as usual early Friday evening to have them for the weekend. When the door bell rang, she opened the door wide enough to send the children out to him without him seeing too much of her. She had deliberately wrapped herself in an oversized cardigan to try and disguise her stomach but he barely looked at her. She knew her pregnant state was hard enough for him to bear and she did not want to hurt him further by openly displaying her form. Fortunately there was no packing of overnight items to send. Richard had decided that the girls would have whatever they needed at his house so that there would be no need to send clothes and toys back and forth. They had two sets of everything at both houses. Richard had made it very clear that they were *at home*' when they were with him. Whatever they needed while they were with him, he would provide but it would stay in his house. Karen wasn't surprised at this decision. This was Richard to a tee he had to have control in whatever area he could. *Fine, she didn't have the energy to argue about it and in many ways it benefitted her.* It meant she didn't have to get anything ready for their weekly departure. Thankfully, the children skipped out to their dad without a backward glance. They were always ready on a Friday night to go with their dad. They really did look forward to seeing him and of course their grandmother Eva. Karen thought about Eva, and how difficult it had been to maintain their relationship. Karen was incredibly grateful for Eva's impartially even though it was costing Eva dearly in terms of her loyalty to Richard. It had been a few weeks since she had spoken to her because their last conversation had been so emotional.

Richard knew that his mum had contact with Karen because there were occasions when Eva collected the children from school during the week and she would take them out for a meal then return them to Karen ready for bath time. What he didn't know, was that they still had a sort of friendship. On the occasions Eva would drop the girls back, she and Karen would exchange a few words on the doorstep about the girls and the usual catch up about how the other was coping. But on one particular evening, Eva looked troubled and distracted so Karen asked if she wanted to come in for a few minutes. Marina was sitting in the lounge as the girls ran in and she stood up to greet Eva. The two mothers hugged one another and Marina offered her a seat. Marina and Eva had always had a warm and amicable relationship. They didn't know each other particularly well because they didn't see that much of one another apart from family celebrations that threw them together, however conversation flowed easily whenever they saw each other. Marina said she would get the children bathed and ready for bed and would leave Karen and Eva to talk. Grace and Amelia both threw their arms around Eva at the same time and planted big kisses on both sides of her cheeks before going for their baths. Tears started to well up in Eva's eyes as she squeezed them tightly and then let them go.

No sooner had the children left the room with Marina; Eva broke down. Karen immediately sat next to her and put her arm around her. Eva sobbed uncontrollably. Karen had never seen her like this before and it really affected and disturbed her. She passed her a tissue and offered her a cup of tea. Eva nodded in acceptance. While Karen was in the kitchen making them both a cup of tea, she wondered what had bought Eva to this state. It was so unlike her. She was always so calm and composed. Nothing really seemed to faze her. Even when the children were being boisterous or difficult, she always remained even tempered. Karen admired her greatly. *The nicest person I have ever met.* She thought. Her children were truly blessed to have such a beautiful person in their lives to call their grandmother. Although the children now enjoyed a very close relationship with Marina, who was wonderful with the children, it had grown due to the fact that Grace and Amelia were now living with her. Marina had always worked and Karen understood that. She knew her mum loved her grandchildren dearly so she didn't resent her mum for not being available. However a lot of the children's time had been spent with Eva and their bond with her was undeniable.

Karen brought their drinks in and handed a mug to Eva. She slowly sipped the hot liquid without saying a word. They sat in silence for a few minutes both drinking their tea. 'Eva, I'm so sorry for all the hurt I've caused you and Richard,' Karen paused for a minute before adding, 'I never meant or planned for any of this to happen, you do believe me, don't you?'

'I know you didn't,' Eva blew her nose into the tissue.

'I've never seen you cry like this and it breaks my heart. I know I've done an unforgiveable thing to you. Can you ever truly forgive me?' Karen said pleadingly.

Eva sighed, 'This is so hard probably the hardest thing I've had to deal with since Greg died. To see your marriage break up was bad enough but this custody fight that's happening is worrying me so much. I'm not sure he's doing it for the right reasons. He doesn't want the girls to live with you and the new baby. I've tried to tell him that the baby will be their sibling and they will share the same mother and nothing can change that, but he doesn't want to listen.' Karen sat quietly as she continued, 'I know that the toughest part for him is the new baby, he's taken it really hard Karen. He hasn't said it because he doesn't talk about how he's feeling, but I know him,' Eva took another sip of her tea, 'whenever he's hurting, he always angry and then goes about trying to solve things. It's so painful to watch him going through it. If I'm honest, it's hard for me too. I'm beginning to feel resentful towards the baby and I shouldn't. I feel so ashamed. The baby's a victim, an innocent child that deserves to be loved and to be a part of a loving family like any other child, but how is it going to work out in practice Karen?'

'I do understand Eva how you and Richard must be feeling and how hard it is for both of you. Both Grace and Amelia are my children and so of course I want them to have a relationship with the baby.'

'This is not an easy situation,' Eva shook her head slowly from side to side, 'I'm worried about Richard, he's angry with you Karen, but I don't think he's trying to punish you. He loves the children and they're all he's got right now. The way he sees it, is that you'll have the baby. He won't stop you from the seeing the girls, he just wants them living with him.'

'But he works full time Eva. He's relying on you to pick them up from school. I know that he'll try his best to get off work early some days to get them but it's not fair on you or the girls,' Karen replied.

'I know,' Eva shrugged her shoulders in resignation. The conversation had been long and difficult and left both of them emotionally spent. There were no easy answers. Eva was really torn between loyalty to Richard and the best interests of the girls. *She knew he loved them deeply and could look after them practically* but *how happy would they be on a daily basis without their mum?* Eva wasn't sure about the answer to that question. She knew that was not what Richard wanted to hear. He felt disappointed and let down by Eva for not backing him on this but she just wanted what was best for the girls. Eva had to stay neutral. In the long run that's what would benefit the girls. Karen and Eva talked about so many scenarios and situations that could arise in the future and how it could be handled and Eva had many concerns. She knew how strongly Richard felt about the new baby. He was adamant that the girls should be with him.

Karen groaned. The pain in her stomach interrupted her thoughts and brought her back to reality. She really should go and tell her mum that she was in labour and then of course there was still Pete to contact too but a part of her wanted to delay the birth as long as possible. She knew that as soon as this baby was born, all their lives would change. Forever! *Was she ready? No!* But she really didn't have a choice right now. This baby was ready to come into the world. *Poor little mite!* She thought. She picked up her mobile and rang the hospital.

Karen and Marina were at the hospital after being dropped off by Cecil. She had finally knocked her parents' door to alert Marina that the baby was coming. The hospital had told her to make her way there and they would monitor the situation. The problem was Pete; he had said that he wanted to be there to see his baby born and Karen understood that but her thoughts were about Vanessa. The poor woman was struggling with anguish over the ever evolving circumstances in her marriage. *Could she deal with Pete leaving the house in the middle of the night to watch the birth of his baby? She doubted that!* But as the labour progressed, she knew that she had to ring Pete so she asked her mum to make the call. Karen handed her phone to Marina who reluctantly took the handset. Marina had never met Pete but all that he represented for her was trouble and suffering for Karen. He was the last person she wanted to speak to but this was not about her.

Pete's phone rang. It was 4.40am. He was in the lounge. He hadn't gone to bed. It had become something of a habit. He was drinking more alcohol than usual in the evenings and so tended to flake out on the sofa in the lounge most nights. With all that was happening around him; a shot of rum, a couple bottles of beer or a few glasses of wine, whatever was to hand, just seemed to help numb the all consuming feelings and emotions. It was comforting. He knew he was spiralling slightly but he couldn't stop. Vanessa was trying so hard to be normal as if nothing was happening. It was freaking him out. He just couldn't handle it. And then of course, there was Karen who was trying to keep him at arm's length. He wanted to be a part of his baby's life. He just felt so helpless and nothing seemed to be in his control.

'Karen, are you okay?' Pete answered the phone.

'It's not Karen, it's her mum. She's in hospital and the baby is coming. She asked me to call you.' Marina ended the call before he had a chance to reply.

He needed to get there. He went upstairs and looked towards their bedroom door where Vanessa was sleeping. He didn't know what to do. *Did he tell her? Or just go and tell her later?* He looked at himself in the bathroom mirror noting his dishevelled appearance and wondered whether he should get a shower or just go as he was. *Why was he struggling to make even the simplest of decisions?* Everything was such a dilemma! He decided to skip the shower and just wash his face. He tucked his shirt into his jeans, threw on a jacket and ran a comb through his hair. He sat pondering what to do about Vanessa. He knew he wouldn't be able to drive as he had been drinking, so he called a taxi. While he was waiting for the taxi to arrive, he kept on deliberating whether to tell Vanessa. He looked at his watch. It had been ten minutes since making the call. The taxi was due any minute. He made the snap decision to tell Vanessa where he was going. It wasn't fair to just disappear on her. He could be gone for hours. He walked into the bedroom to find Vanessa lying awake in the dark.

'Where are you going?' she asked flatly.

'I'm so sorry Ness, its Karen she's gone into labour I need to go to her,' Pete said apologetically.

She reached across and put the bedside lamp on and raised herself up into a sitting position. She'd been crying. Her eyes looked red and sore. 'I'm sorry I couldn't give you a baby,' Vanessa said quietly.

'Ness, please don't do this to yourself. You have nothing to apologise for. I'm the one that's let you down, it not your fault.'

'I'm useless, totally useless, no use to you.' Her body racked with sobs. It was heartbreaking. A text message came through on his mobile phone that the taxi was waiting outside.

'I've got to go now, will you be okay?' There was no answer just sobbing. *How could he leave her like this?* Knowing what she had tried to do previously, he couldn't take the risk that she wouldn't do something to harm herself again. She needed him. He would stay for a while at least until she was calmer. Then he would go. He went outside and told a very disgruntled taxi driver that he no longer needed him. He came back into the bedroom and sat next to her on the bed and held her close. He could feel her frame through her flimsy nightdress. She had lost so much weight recently. She let herself lean into him and he could feel her heartbreaking sobs from deep within her body. He wasn't sure how long he held her for but gradually the crying stopped but she was still clinging to him. He needed to let Karen know he was still coming but he was afraid to even loosen his hold now that she was calmer. He knew she still needed him to hold her close. She was totally broken. While he was holding Vanessa, he thought about Karen. My poor sweet Karen who had risked everything for their baby was alone again when he should be there with her. He felt so incredibly sad and torn as he looked down at the crushed weak woman in his arms and thought of the immensely brave and strong woman who was about to have his second child. He needed to be with Karen so he tried to ease Vanessa from him. She clung tighter. *What's happening to my life? How have I managed to make such an almighty mess of everything? What did you expect?* He chided as he asked himself those difficult questions. *That everything would go according to plan. You fool, you idiot. Life isn't that simple!*

He stroked Vanessa's hair as she relaxed against him once more. He had absolutely no idea how much time had passed but it seemed interminable and he was beginning to feel anxious. He tried once more to extricate himself from Vanessa's hold and heard the words, 'please don't leave me.'

'I have to. I know I'm not being fair to you but I can't let Karen down either,' Vanessa was crying again, 'okay, I won't go yet but I need to make a call. I owe her that.' He got up off the bed and left the bedroom. Marina took the call from Pete. It had been brief. He was delayed but still coming and wanted Karen to know. He went into the kitchen and made them both a cup of coffee and took them upstairs. He went back into the bedroom to find Vanessa sitting perfectly still. He handed her the cup. 'Ness, you know I have to go, don't you?'

She nodded, 'I do and I know you need to be there for her. I also know I said I could cope with the situation, but it's much harder than I thought.'

'I knew it would be, I don't see how we can stay married and you accept my baby. This baby is going to grow up. This will never go away. If there's one thing I've learnt, pretending something hasn't happened doesn't work.'

Again, she nodded in agreement, 'I love you Pete, I want to be a part of this. I know my family and friends think I'm crazy and that I should get you out of my life quick but you're not a bad person. They don't know you like I do. We can make this work, I know we can.' Vanessa took a sip of her coffee.

'It's one thing to accept the baby, but you're forgetting Karen, she will always be a part of our lives too. We need to understand the enormity of it all. Don't make any decisions now. It's too soon,' Pete replied.

'Go! That little baby needs his dad, I'm fine now.'

'Are you sure? You're not going to do anything are you? I need to know that!'

'I won't, I promise. Don't worry. Just go. Ring for another taxi,' Vanessa smiled as she said it to give him reassurance.

'I'd better ring another taxi company,' he grinned as he said it. The taxi arrived and Pete shut the front door behind him. Vanessa was still in bed. She lied back down and put the covers over her head and sobbed.

Chapter 47

It had been a few hours since Marina rang and the taxi driver was now starting to hit the busy Saturday morning traffic. Pete sat anxiously observing. He rang Karen's phone but had not received a reply. It went straight to voicemail. He left a brief message, 'I'm on my way.' He watched as the taxi driver weaved his way through the traffic and was glad he wasn't driving as he knew he would have lost his temper by now and he would still have had to find parking when he got there. *Why is it when you're in a rush, everything seems to happen to delay you?* He thought.

He reflected on the conversation earlier with Vanessa and how much better she seemed when he left her. He knew that he still needed to tell her that although she wanted him to stay and make a go of their marriage he wanted to be with Karen. But that could wait for now.

As the taxi pulled into the hospital drop off point, Pete put a twenty pound note on the passenger seat next to the taxi driver and said, 'keep the change,' and he was out of the taxi before the driver could even say thanks for the very generous tip.

Pete raced around the hospital corridors following the signs for the maternity section almost knocking people down in the process. As he approached the woman behind the desk, she smiled and asked if she could help him.

'Karen Chapman, she came in a few hours ago, I've been delayed, where is she?' Pete was rambling.

'And you are?' the lady asked.

'I'm the baby's father,' he said timidly, 'where is she? I need to be with her.'

'What's your name sir?'

'Peter Barton.'

'I'll take you to her, she's been expecting you, follow me.' She led him through a double door and along a short corridor with small single rooms leading of it. She opened the door of the end room and waved him in. Pete walked in to see Karen sitting up in bed with the baby lying in the cot next to her. Marina was sitting in an armchair on the other side of the bed. Karen smiled as he walked in and said, 'You've got another son Pete.'

'I'm sorry Karen I really tried to get here to be with you. I wanted to see him born,' the expression on his face was pained as he bent over the cot and peaked at the sleeping baby, 'he's absolutely beautiful.' He became visibly relaxed as he looked at him.

'Do you want to hold him? Just wash your hands over there,' she pointed to a small sink in the corner of the room.

Pete did as he was told and all the time Marina sat silently observing him. She rose from her chair and gestured that he could have it. Marina spoke only to Karen and said that she was going to get herself a coffee and possibly some breakfast in the hospital cafeteria. She didn't even look in Pete's direction. She was gone.

'She hates me, doesn't she? I don't blame her,' Pete said as Marina left the room.

'How can she hate you? She doesn't know you. She's just worried about me.'

'Of course she is. I just wish things could be different,' he replied. Pete bent and took the sleeping baby out of the cot and sat and held him, he couldn't take his eyes off him. He felt Karen watching him and he took her hand, 'thank you my darling, I'm sorry I didn't get here to be with you to see him born. It was Vanessa...' He trailed off.

'Don't worry, I understand,' Karen said.

'Really, you do?' Pete asked with genuine bewilderment on his face, 'I truly don't deserve you Karen.' He said with humility. His eyes became watery with tears that threatened to spill. There was silence while he composed himself.

'We need to think of a name,' Karen said smiling, quickly changing the subject from herself to their new baby.

'Well, Jacob's my middle name,' Pete paused as he continued looking in wonder at the perfectly formed baby in his arms, 'would you mind if we named him that? We could call him Jake for short. What'd you think?'

'That's a lovely name. He's your son so of course you can give him your name,' she squeezed his arm with reassurance, 'it's a Bible name too so my grandma will love it.'

'Thank you Karen, it means so much to me for him to have my middle name, I love you so very much. I feel honoured that you're the mother of my children. You're incredibly special. I can't find the words to describe. I can't think of any adjectives that adequately express just how much you mean to me and how happy I feel right now.' He said it all without taking a breath.

'Wow adjectives eh? Okay teacher,' she said jokingly.

'Seriously Karen, I want you to know that I'm here for you and always will be. I know I didn't make it for his birth, but please believe me, I tried. I really tried.' He shook his head in disappointment and looked at the sleeping baby in his arms, 'daddy is sorry little man,' he knew Jacob couldn't hear a word he said but he didn't care, he needed to tell him, 'I promise to never let you down ever again.'

'How is Vanessa, Pete?' Karen enquired.

'Not good,' he bent his head, 'I'm not even going to burden you with my troubles it's not fair. You've got this little one to take care of so leave Vanessa for me to worry about.' Karen smiled weakly knowing how hard this was for Pete and aware how strong he was trying to be. They were both silent for a while. Shortly after that a couple of medics came in and checked that Karen was recovering well. She had been told she would be discharged later in the day so Marina went home to prepare for Karen and the baby, leaving Pete with her. Pete spent several hours just being with them both savouring every single minute wishing this precious time could last forever but of course he knew it couldn't because Karen would be taking baby Jake home with her. He would have to go home to Vanessa.

Chapter 48

'Nanny, we've got a brother,' Grace said and ran towards Eva as she walked in the room. Eva glanced across at Richard. His face remained even and unchanged.

'I know,' Eva replied smiling as she bent down and hugged both the girls. Amelia had run towards her too, 'have you been cuddling him?'

'Yes,' said Grace excitedly, 'mummy made me sit on the sofa so I could hold him. Are you coming to see him Nanny?'

This is difficult. Eva thought. *Trying to support Richard and yet remain normal for the girls who were excited, and rightly so, about their new brother. How she loved the innocence of children. Why did adults have to complicate life?* She hesitated, 'yes, one day.'

'When, Nanny when? Come soon. I want you to see him.'

'Right, that's enough now Grace,' Richard said as gently as his tone could muster, 'let Nanny get her coat off.' Inside he was seething. *Damn you Karen!*

'You and Amelia play for a while and then Nanny will come and read the next chapter of the story.' Eva had been reading a new book to them that had them both captivated. It was about a little girl of five who went on all sorts of adventures. As Eva read the story they felt that they were on the adventure too. Her storytelling was mesmerizing and immersive and they were always completed gripped.

Eva followed Richard into the kitchen where he had made her a cup of tea. She sat on the kitchen stool alongside the breakfast bar. 'This is what it's been like since I picked them up last night. They've been with Karen all week from last Sunday when she came home with him,' Richard rolled his eyes, 'in fact they didn't really want to come. I had to bribe them with all sorts of things. They just wanted to stay with the baby.'

'It's understandable. They know nothing of the pain behind all of this Richard, only the joy of the new baby. This is what I have been worried about with you trying to get custody. It won't work.' Richard sighed, 'I know it's not what you want to hear,' Eva said.

'It's not fair mum. I was a good husband, okay so I probably handled the whole Robin thing wrongly, but it wasn't intentional, I thought I was helping.' He raised his hands in exasperation and hopelessness.

'I know that, but...'

'But nothing,' Richard interrupted, 'I provided a home and security for her and the girls, she wanted for nothing. How could she be so ungrateful?' Eva nodded. She understood it from both sides and that was the problem. She didn't condone what Karen had done but she didn't judge her either. If she was honest, she couldn't fully understand why she didn't feel more animosity towards her and wished in some ways that she did. It would certainly have made life easier for her if she had 'picked a side' so to speak and given that Richard was her son, she knew it should be his. But it really wasn't as simple as that. She had invested in Karen and had really grown to love her. It was hard to turn off her emotions especially knowing Karen's 'back story'. *Her head must have been all over the place, poor girl.* Eva thought. *How she wished she'd known earlier about Robin! Maybe, just maybe their marriage would still be going. Richard had unwittingly made things worse for a broken woman.* As she looked back, Eva began to put the pieces together. Karen lacked the confidence that was so often present in young people. On reflection she could now see that there was a sensitivity and sadness about her which was usually only present in someone who had been through a trauma. This was a young girl that needed careful handling emotionally and Richard had not been equipped to deal with it. He had developed his own strategies for coping with painful situations and it worked for him but he didn't seem to have the ability to understand that everyone was different. He lived by routine and discipline and it seemed to help him function and avoid feelings of melancholy. Eva knew that it had not been deliberate but he had possibly contributed to Karen's mental health declining, as hard as that would be for him to admit. And then there were the children, she was still their grandmother and Karen would always be their mother. She hoped that in the end it would work out in everyone's best interest. *Was that even conceivable or just an unrealistic dream?* Eva was totally torn. *How could she ensure that the best would be achieved for everyone?* A part of her felt that she should go and see the new baby for the girls' sake; not really for Karen. But after the chat with Richard, she was left in no doubt that he did not see any need for her to see the baby, not even for the girls' sake. 'They should not be indulged in that way. They'll know soon enough that I'm NOT the baby's father and therefore you're NOT the baby's grandmother,' Richard glared, 'reality has to kick in for all of us. It certainly has for me!' His words had rang in her head ever since. *He was right. Reality would kick in eventually but these things had to be managed slowly. A sledgehammer approach wouldn't work.*

Chapter 49

It had been a juggling act for Pete to try and see the baby while Karen was actively trying for him not to see Grace and Amelia. Karen had made it clear that she didn't want the girls' lives disrupted and confused anymore than was necessary. So much had happened already and although they appeared to have taken everything in their stride, she knew that it had to be 'one step at a time' where Grace and Amelia were concerned. She was so pleased with the way they had accepted and loved Jake. She had been concerned that there would be jealousies and tantrums, but no, so far so good. She figured maybe it was yet to come. But for now she was happy that all was going okay. They were as good as gold both wanting to play with him and hold him. There had been some magical times especially during the first week of bringing Jake home. She and the girls would be on the settee, all of them together while she breastfed Jake. She felt so happy with her children flanked either side of her as they sat in complete absorption, fascination and curiosity as they watched their little brother being fed from mummy. It was pure joy and she enjoyed sharing this experience with them. Karen was happy to live in her 'bubble' with her children. The only one missing was Robin but he was always in her heart and remembering him gave her the strength to continue to be strong for the children she had with her. She owed it to them, to herself and to Robin. Never again would she allow anyone to distract her from her children. They were her number one priority. It was clear in her mind that it was too soon for Pete to be a 'stepfather' to Grace and Amelia. Pete's situation was far too unstable for him to be introduced into her children's lives. He was still married and living with his wife who had no intention of letting him go, that was evident. Even though he kept telling Karen that he was trying to sort things out and that they would be together soon, Karen knew that was wishful thinking on his part. There was still so much to sort out. It would take time for him to sell his house and they wouldn't be able to start looking for a suitable property together until then. Their plans to be together were still a long way off. She loved Pete but she didn't want to rely on him or need him. She had pledged to herself that she would never depend on anyone ever again, even if that meant being alone in the short term. She now understood that love wasn't enough, you had to keep a clear head at all times because people weren't necessarily going to behave in the way you wanted or expected them too. They inevitably would let you down. That much she had learnt from both Pete and Richard. She understood so much more about the complexities of people and herself; as she too had let people down. In the last few months she uncovered a hidden strength that she never knew she had and she liked it. The custody hearing was looming and she wasn't looking forward to it but she knew that it was a battle she had to fight and she was going to do it with every bit of strength she could find within her. No one was going to break her or make her feel that she was inadequate. She was going to prove to herself that she could do it.

She was so grateful to her parents for allowing her to move back in with them. They had reassured her that there was no urgency for her to leave and that she could stay as long as it took for her and Pete to sort out their finances to enable them to get a place together. Her mum and dad had been so generous not just with their money but with their love and support. *How could she ever repay them for their kindness? Without them, where would she have gone?* They had provided a safe haven for her and the children which had given her the time she needed to work out what she wanted for the future. They had allowed her the peace she needed throughout the pregnancy and a new normality for the girls. In the many conversations she had with her mum she had repeated time and again how grateful she was to them both. It was on one of those occasions that Marina started crying. Surprised at this sudden and unexpected flow of tears Karen asked her mum what was wrong? 'Karen, we let you down, we should never have let Robin go,' Marina sat very still and licked the salty tears that ran freely down her face and onto her lips, 'I was so obsessed with my job and the fact that I had reached my goal of being a manager. And if I'm honest, I don't think I was ready to be a grandmother back then either. Does that sound awful? I'm so sorry Karen. We should never have left the decision of whether Robin stayed or went with a young frightened girl who had been abandoned. What other decision would anyone make in those circumstances?' Karen started to cry too.

'Oh mum, please don't be too hard on yourself. I didn't even tell you I had a boyfriend, it must have been an enormous shock for you.'

Marina continued, 'it's no excuse. Your father and I have talked about it so much, we do have to take some responsibility for the effect it had on you and the fact that it bought you to this point. It's not just Richard who contributed to your mental health problems we did too by also sweeping it under the carpet and not talking about it.' Karen listened as her mum talked, 'it's strange all the things you think are important, and then you realise that they're not important at all. My job made me feel important and validated. I don't know why I needed to prove it to myself so much,' Marina's tears continued to flow, 'maybe I do know but never wanted to admit it to anyone. Perhaps it was to prove to my dad that I could still progress and make something of myself despite marrying a black man.' It was then that Karen realised that her mum had her own issues and she was as vulnerable and insecure as the next person. Yes, Marina was her mum but she too had a story and was on her own journey. Karen reflected on the huge cost to her mum being estranged from her own father after losing her mother at a very early age. Marina had been really close to her dad and sacrificed a lot to be with Cecil. Apart from her Auntie Marjorie, her mum had given up her entire family. She had a lot to prove to herself that she had made the right decision when she married Cecil and her story had been the loss of her relationship with her dad and her brothers. So Marina understood Karen's loss and what it felt like. However, as painful as it had been,

Marina had learned to live without her dad until just before he died. She had also seen and felt racism from those whom she loved and that had been a massive deal for her and not to be understated. Plus she had never reunited with her brothers. Karen suddenly saw her mum with fresh eyes and had enormous admiration for her. She didn't blame her mum for Robin going and she didn't blame her dad either. They had done what they believed to be right at that time. *Was it right or was it wrong?* Karen didn't believe there was a right or a wrong anymore. It was what it was! 'I believed wrongly or rightly at the time, that we all have to make our own decisions and learn to live with them, as I did, but I now know that that wasn't right for you. You were still a child with no life experience. It was different for me. When I met your dad I was an adult and knew what the consequences were. I made an informed decision and I've never regretted it. I've felt sad at times yes, but no regrets.' She said with emphasis. Karen understood so much more. Her parents' guilt in believing that they had let her down had led them to decide that they would always be there for her now and their home was hers and the children's home for as long as she wanted. They just wanted her to be happy. Marina also confessed that she and Cecil struggled with Pete. Their impression of him was not good. They saw him as weak and cowardly for deserting Karen first time around and now for the hurt he was inflicting on his wife, but he was Robin and Jake's father so they were prepared to accept him for Karen's sake.

It had been an emotional conversation that day between mother and daughter but it had definitely drawn them closer together and given them both a deeper understanding of the other. Karen no longer felt grateful to her parents in quite the same way understanding that it was their way of 'putting right' what they believed they had handled wrongly all those years ago. Marina in particular had felt enormous guilt and Cecil knew just how much it had weighed on her. In their private discussions, Marina had even said that she was no better than her own dad. She felt that she had let Karen down in the same way her dad had let her down. Cecil had tried to reassure her that there was no comparison, but Marina wouldn't listen. She bitterly regretted that Robin had been adopted. He then began to realise just how deep Marina's sadness was for her to compare herself in that way. He had spent enough years with Marina and had known and seen the impact her estrangement from her dad had had on her. It was then he began to realise that Marina likened Karen's loss of Robin to her own loss of her father. It all started to make sense to Cecil. The memories of the time that they met and the personal battles for Marina flooded back and he thought about the great sacrifice she had made to be with him. Whenever Cecil recalled Marina's separation from her father with the aching pain she endured alongside it for his sake; it made it even more important for him to support her completely in her desire to do all she could to help their troubled middle child to find some peace in her life. Grandma Rose had been saying to him for many years how concerned she was for Karen and if he was really honest with himself, Cecil hadn't fully understood why his mum felt that way. He was surprised that Karen had been so damaged by it all. He thought that the support they had given her at the time had been enough, considering the circumstances and the shock of it all; but as the years rolled by it had become evident to him also that Karen was more than a little broken because of that period in her life. Ever since Robin had gone, she had been directionless, just drifting. She lacked confidence. The only comparison he could use were his other two daughters Susan and Fiona. They were so much more self assured in a way that Karen wasn't. It had become crystal clear.

Chapter 50

She had been dreading see Richard but of course she didn't really need to see him apart from opening the door for Grace and Amelia to go to him.

Coming home with Jake had been emotional and magical all at the same time. At last she had her new baby boy that she could love and keep forever. His conception had caused so much disruption to so many lives and Karen felt incredibly guilty about that but he was here now and he was worth it. She loved him so much, her beautiful baby boy. There was still so much turmoil but somehow just having him in her life knowing he was hers to love and enjoy and treasure no matter what was going on externally gave her so much joy. She was determined that Grace and Amelia would be as much a part of this journey as possible with their new brother Jake, despite the fact that Richard was trying to take them from her. When the girls arrived back late Sunday afternoon after being with Richard and walked in and saw Jake, they were so excited. She had been preparing them for weeks beforehand and had told them that a new baby was coming but she didn't know if it was a boy or girl. It was as if Christmas had come early when they walked in and saw the new baby. Karen had wondered how they would be once the baby came. She had worried that with all the changes in their lives that it would be another overwhelming event that they would have to 'wrap their heads around' that could have caused problems. But she could never have dreamt in her wildest dreams that it would go so well. They didn't want to leave him to go to school each day and every evening was spent coaxing them to go to bed. They loved him. Even when Jake was sleeping they would be peering into his Moses basket. When she was feeding him, changing him, bathing him she had two little shadows following her. She knew the novelty would soon wear off but for now she was content to see that they were happy and wanted to be involved. It meant everything to her. So when the following

Friday evening came and they had to go to Richard as usual, Amelia said for the first time ever that she didn't want to go. Now Karen knew it wasn't that she didn't want to see her dad, it was about not wanting to leave Jake, but she knew Richard would not see it that way.

'Mummy, can we stay with you?' Amelia asked when Karen mentioned that their dad was coming shortly.

'Why?' Karen asked, 'don't you want to see daddy?'

'Yes,' but I don't want to leave Jake,' Amelia looked crestfallen.

'I know my darling, but you'll see Jake when you get back. Daddy's looking forward to seeing you.' Amelia pouted in the most endearing way, it made Karen smile. When Richard arrived within half an hour of the conversation, Amelia still did not want to go. She wanted to stay with Jake. She kept insisting, even when Richard was at the door.

'C'mon poppet, daddy's got your favourite sweets in the car,' Richard coaxed.

'But daddy, I don't want to leave the baby. I love him,' Amelia replied. Richard completely ignored mention of the baby.

'Daddy's also got you a present.'

'What is it daddy?' Amelia asked with interest.

'Well, you'll have to come with me to get it,' Richard said.

Karen could hear the irritation in Richard's voice. She knew it only too well. She couldn't see his face as he was bending down to speak to Amelia. As she observed this exchange between father and daughter, she felt uncomfortable. Fortunately because of his positioning, Karen couldn't make eye contact with him and neither did she want to. The mere presence of him made her feel slightly ashamed. He still had that effect of making her feel as though she wasn't good enough. She couldn't really blame Richard for that. She had recklessly given him permission to claim that position of power. She had often said how much she admired his decisiveness and would watch him glow with pride as he received the compliment. The arena that had been created during their marriage which gave him validation had only added to her feelings of inadequacy. No wonder she hadn't thrived while they were together. There had been no room for her own personal growth while she always had self doubt and relied on him. He always seemed so sensible, so calm and collected, whereas she hadn't been any of those things. She determined in her mind that had to change, she was away from him now. She had her own life to live now, no matter what he thought of her, she must not let it bring her down. It didn't matter what he thought anymore. So *why did it still feel like an uphill struggle?* She knew she needed to build her confidence and show strength of character and determination if she was to keep her girls.

'Bye mummy,' Karen bent down as Amelia turned around and reached up throwing her arms around Karen's neck tightly. Finally, Karen thought. She heaved an internal sigh of relief. She wasn't sure how long Richard would have continued to try and win over his youngest child. She felt a little bit sad for Richard because she knew that Amelia adored him and always looked forward to seeing him and there was normally never any hesitation. Jake was very much the reason for her unwillingness on this occasion. Amelia was his baby and Karen was only too aware how much Richard needed to feel wanted by his children. He knew Amelia loved him but Karen also knew that this would be hard for Richard; competing with a baby that he wished had never been born. Karen closed the door and leant back against it for a moment reflecting how much her life had changed. Jake started to stir and let out a little cry. She was back in the moment. No time for reflection.

Chapter 51

Pete felt like he was trying to please too many people or maybe he was trying not to upset too many people. He wasn't sure which. All he knew was that he was struggling to manage everything in his life that needed managing. Vanessa was a major issue. He needed to make her understand that what she was proposing wouldn't work. But somehow she seemed in denial so desperate was she for him to stay, but he didn't want to stay. *Why couldn't she just accept it?* She seemed on the surface to be coping. Whenever he said he was going to see Karen and the baby, she would wave him off and say she was fine but whenever he returned home, she clearly hadn't been fine. Very often, her eyes were red raw from crying. The thing that concerned him the most was how much weight she had lost. Her clothes hung from her as if from a coat hanger. Gone was the shapely woman replaced by a gaunt frame he no longer recognised. She was a shadow of her former self. He felt like he was destroying his wife and watching it unfold before his eyes. He was so incredibly sad and very torn.

He loved his time with Karen and Jake. It was a beautiful bubble that he could enjoy for a few hours. Karen had said that she didn't want him to visit during the week because she didn't want to introduce the girls to him yet. She didn't want to add confusion to an already complicated situation; which he completely understood. So he lived for the weekends. It was the only time he could go and see Karen and Jake. He would get up early on Saturday mornings and leave before Vanessa would have any chance to stop him. He couldn't wait for the time to hold and cuddle Jake. It meant everything to him. He felt happy and relaxed while he held him and it fostered feelings within him that he couldn't fully describe but it gave rise to an appreciation of deep fulfilment. Life seemed to have more meaning. All the anxiety that he felt most of the time seemed to just disappear when he was with Jake. It was a feeling he wished he could keep and preserve forever. The love he felt for his son as he held him in his arms was overwhelming. He wanted to protect him and make him happy. He could never have imagined how he would feel before Jake arrived. He knew he wanted him and that he would love him but this feeling was mind-blowing, so much more than he expected to feel. He had to resist the urge to not think too much about Robin or he would be so overcome with guilt that he would not then be able to enjoy his precious time with Jake. But he did ask himself many times why he had been such a coward all those years ago or had it just been pure selfishness. He despised the old Pete and wanted to be a better person. He made a promise to Karen and to Jake that he would be the best dad he could. He would not let him down the way he had with Robin. His thoughts went to Robin. It was hard not to; no matter how hard he shook his head to try and get rid of his thoughts, it just wasn't possible. *Why couldn't I have just taken responsibility back then? Why had I been so mean? I was young!* He told himself. *No excuse!* He told himself again. *Countless people have faced that position and stepped up!* If he had done the right thing, he wouldn't have hurt Karen then and he wouldn't be hurting Vanessa now. He would have his first son with him calling him dad, playing football and board games with him. He truly hoped that Robin was happy.

He watched Karen and admired the way she was with Jake. She was so good with him and so calm while she was around him despite the circumstances and how she was feeling. They had many long conversations about their plans for the future and whenever they spent time together with Jake, their love grew and their bond deepened. Reality however was always around the corner because he had to go home and deal with Vanessa and Karen was worried about the upcoming custody hearing for her girls. They both knew there was a long way to go but they had to remain hopeful. Somehow Karen kept both their feet on the ground. She reminded him that the 'happy ever after' would not be their real world. Too much had happened and still a lot to sort out and resolve before their lives could be entwined. The most that they could hope for were the moments of happiness in any day that they were fortunate to have together. To look too far ahead would be foolhardy and disheartening for both of them. The custody of the children was her priority and no decisions about their future as a family could be made until that was settled and he would have to make the break with Vanessa before he could even be a part of their lives and ultimately their future. Her parents had helped them to come this far but they had had their lives disrupted because of her and Pete's affair. She wanted him to really understand that they needed to plan their future and make their life together work once the hurdles had been overcome and to stand together and face whatever obstacles may come. This was the second time that their actions had impacted others; first it was with Robin and now it was with Jake, but with an even more far reaching effect this time. They weren't teenagers anymore. They couldn't keep messing up. It would be a journey of maturity. Pete sat and listened to the wisdom that Karen imparted. He admired her so much. *When did she become so wise?* He thought? *Where did she get her strength from?* He felt weak in comparison. He had so much to learn from her. He knew what he had to do. He was determined not to let her down.

Work was getting more and more difficult, he just wasn't coping. The job of Head Teacher required application and focus that he no longer had. He was just so distracted and he knew he wasn't performing well at work. One particular day, he just felt he had to escape, so he grabbed his jacket and decided to go for a walk during his lunch break. Not far from the school was a large woodland area so he decided to head there. He really needed to clear his head of everything that was going round and round. As he made his way down an alleyway which was a shortcut to the woodland his thoughts went to Karen and Jake. He needed to be with them but Vanessa was making it really hard. As he walked, he was so deep in his own thoughts that he almost bumped into a middle aged woman who wasn't pleased that she had to sidestep him to save herself from being knocked down.

'So sorry,' he said waving by as he continued on his way.

As he entered the woodland area he stopped for a minute and admired the large Silver Birch tree that towered elegantly above him. He felt immediately calmer. He noticed a seat carved out of a tree stump a little further on so he decided to sit and listen to the birds and he watched the scurrying of the squirrels around him. He wished that his life was as simple as theirs. There was a gentle breeze and he could see the clouds forming in view through the tops of the trees. *It's going to rain. I'd better get back before I get caught in a downpour.* He thought. But somehow he felt rooted to the seat of that tree stump. He didn't want to leave the comfort and peace of the woodland. He felt safe and far away from his reality in that moment. He closed his eyes and allowed the soft breeze to kiss his face and remind him that he was still alive. I *don't feel alive anymore?* He said to himself. He was just about surviving when he was at home with Vanessa and at work. His head felt like it was going to explode most of the time but as he sat on that tree stump, a peace seemed to envelope him. He opened his eyes and saw a robin perched on the branch of a tree opposite. He remembered the story that Karen had told him about how she had named their son Robin. He sat and watched the robin and he seemed perfectly happy sitting on the branch. Pete knew if he remained absolutely still and didn't make any sudden moves that the robin would probably stay on that branch until it was ready to go. They only tended to fly off when you made a noise or got too close so he sat quietly and watched this beautiful little bird with its red breast sitting happily resting for a while on the branch of the tree.

All of sudden the tears came. Where did his tears come from? He had no idea but they literally flowed and flowed. He just couldn't stop. He cried and cried until he felt emptied. He was crying for Robin, his first child that he abandoned, refused to even meet. *What kind of person does that? How callous had he been? No wonder he was suffering now. He deserved everything that was happening to him. What right did he have to be happy and have his life the way he wanted it when he had altered the path of Robin's life. Was Robin happy?* He really hoped so. One day he hoped to meet him and say sorry to him man to man. He had to believe that Robin would want to meet him and give him the opportunity to apologise for his spinelessness. Then there was Karen. He had let her down once before and now he was in danger of letting her down again. He had caused her untold heartache when he left her pregnant and alone the first time. He didn't like thinking about it too much as it gave him an ache in his heart. It was hard to describe but he sometimes felt like he was going to have a heart attack because it was so painful. He also had to add Vanessa to the list of people he had hurt and let down, who he had lied to and cheated on. She never knew the man she had married had had a child that he never even wanted to meet. She never knew the man she married was a liar and a cheat. She never knew that the man she married was weak and pathetic. In that moment as he sat amongst the trees observing all the beautiful wildlife, he hated himself. *What use was he to anyone?* He really didn't feel effective at anything anymore. He was incapable of making sound decisions at work so his job was suffering. He felt constantly unsure of himself. He knew that some members of his staff had noticed that he wasn't his usual enthusiastic self as they had enquired with looks of concern on their faces about his wellbeing. Some thought he was worried about Vanessa as she had confided to a couple of the teachers about her infertility problems. But no one knew the real reason that Vanessa was off work. *How could he tell anyone?* He was deeply ashamed of the person he was. He had always been a cheerful self assured person. The lack of confidence that he had started to experience was new to him and he didn't like it. As he sat and thought about everything, he realised that the disappointment month after month when they had been trying for a baby had started to take its toll some time ago and especially dealing with her incredible lows alongside it. Added to all of that was his intense feelings of guilt for so many reasons. It had become an enormous weight too heavy to bear. He had noticed a while ago that all sight of the old Pete had gradually slipped from view and a new person had inhabited his body. Jake's birth had brought everything to a head and efforts to stay focused and composed had become almost impossible. *What did the future really hold? What would it look like? There was just too much to contemplate and so much that needed fixing. How? When?* He felt trapped. Nothing was straightforward. Every time he made a decision and felt settled with that thought, a conflicting thought came and snatched away the peace that he had temporarily felt. It was a dilemma that was hard to resolve without causing further pain to some or all concerned. He contemplated the last time he had felt happy. It was undoubtedly when he saw Jake for the first time. But it had been momentary.

Suddenly there was loud sobbing. He was wailing. The noise he could hear coming from within himself was powerful and overwhelming. He was bawling and he felt like he couldn't stop. His head felt like it was literally going to erupt. *Make it go away! It's all too much!* As he held his head in his hands and looked around with tear filled eyes, he noticed that the robin had gone, like Robin had gone. At that moment, he realised that he couldn't cope with life as it was. The pain was too much to bear and his weeping went on.

'Hello, can we help?' he could hear a voice.

'Can we help?' he heard the question again but it seemed so far away. Whoever it was, he thought, wasn't talking to me, it seemed like it was in the distance. If only this pain in my head would go away. It was hurting to even think. He wasn't okay and he didn't have the strength to move either. Then he heard another voice and the two voices were conversing. *Who were they? What did they want?* He couldn't stop crying. It was all too much. He felt broken.

Chapter 52

He woke feeling restful and calm. *Where am I?* He looked around and he was in a room that he didn't recognise. It was a pleasant room with white walls. A curtain with bluebells on a white background hung stiffly either side of a small window with venetian blinds angled just enough to enable the sunlight to flood the room making it bright and uplifting. *Where am I?* He thought again.

Just at that moment a very petite nurse walked in. She gave the warmest smile he had ever seen, 'Ah, you're wake? How are you feeling?' She stood still and waited for his reply.

'I'm okay,' he replied tentatively, 'where am I?'

'You're in hospital, you've been here overnight,' she answered.

Pete looked blankly at the pretty nurse who he thought was possibly from the Philippines, 'why?'

'You were very distressed when you came in and we had to sedate you,' she paused and continued, 'you'll be going home shortly and the doctor will come and see you about 11am to discharge you but I'll arrange for you to have a cup of tea and some breakfast first.' She helped him to sit up and plumped up his pillows and arranged them comfortably around him. Then she was gone!

He sat in bed looking out of the window which had a well tended garden directly outside which extended far enough for him to admire the carpet of peonies, roses and rhododendrons within a large flowerbed. He looked further into the distance where he could see a car park with cars driving in and out and people walking to and fro. He felt unusually calm as he watched from his hospital bed; a feeling he had not had for as long as he could remember. *This is nice.* He thought. *I wish I could feel like this forever.* His thoughts returned to the nurse that had just left his room. Her smile had never left her face and he wondered about her life and how she was able to have such a lovely smile. *Was she married? Did she have children? How long had she been in this country? How long had she been a nurse?* He envied her easy smile and wished that he could smile more. Smiles didn't come easy anymore. Then he realised what made the nurse's smile different; her smile reached her eyes.

The doctor came to see him as promised and discharged him giving him a prescription for sleeping pills and a sick note for a fortnight off work, plus details of a therapist that would be contacting him in the next couple of weeks to make an appointment. He told him that he had had what seemed to be a 'meltdown' in the woods. Two women who had been walking their dogs heard him crying and went over to see if they could help him. Apparently he had not been able to stop crying so they called an ambulance for him and he had been given a sedative when he arrived at hospital. Fortunately because he had plenty of ID on him; it provided enough information for the hospital to make contact with Vanessa who came to fetch him.

For the first two days when he returned home, he slept most of the time. Vanessa fussed over him making cups of tea and holding his hands asking continually if he was okay. He had lost his appetite and she kept saying that he needed to eat something. He could tell that she was concerned for him. *How strange that their roles had suddenly switched! She was looking after him instead of the other way around.* He felt slightly drowsy and detached most of the time. He slept a lot. *Maybe it's the medication.* He thought. Karen and Jake came into his mind. He missed them so much and he knew he should contact Karen but even contemplating that was overwhelming. He didn't have the energy. It was all too much. As he laid his head back against the pillows, he closed his eyes and tried to forget if only for a while.

Chapter 53

Karen woke early with a feeling of dread; the forthcoming custody hearing resting heavily on her mind. She never thought that Richard would take it this far. *Why couldn't he just leave things as they were? It was pure spite!* She was feeling nervous, she couldn't deny that. *How could she possibly compete with Richard in terms of his means and ability to provide?* He had a well paid job, an established home that the children knew well along with his mum a loving grandmother that the children adored who would help him. *In contrast what exactly did she have to offer the girls?* She was living in her parents' home with no income and a new born baby that was the result of her adultery with her lover. Her mum had a full time job and her dad worked away from home frequently. *It was not looking good!* Her solicitor had tried to keep her optimistic but at the same time he had kept her feet firmly on the ground with the possibility that she could lose the girls to Richard and then she would be the one seeing them weekly. She wouldn't have the privilege of waking up to her beautiful girls every morning with their sleepy faces and warm embraces. She would be denied the pleasure of preparing them for school each day too. Her heart was breaking even at that thought. Yes, things had changed for the girls but they were still happy and settled. In the short space of time, that Jake had been with them, Grace and Amelia had grown close to him. They kissed him constantly. Thinking of it made her smile. It was hard to imagine life without Jake now. And even though her mum worked full time and would never be able to compete with Eva's availability, she helped every single day with the children's care. Marina was fully involved in the evening routine helping with bath time, engaging in conversations with the girls about their day and what they would need in preparation for the following day. In the mornings Marina, while herself getting ready for work still prepared breakfast for them. It was always laid out, coffee for Karen, orange juice and cereal for the girls.

She would even get their school bags ready. *But was all of that enough to retain custody?* She just wasn't sure. Karen then felt intensely sad about the uncertainty of her life and future with her girls. As Jake started to stir, she watched while his little body stretched as he yawned. *How beautiful and innocent he is? My little boy who has come into this complicated and complex situation!* He fell back to sleep again.

Her thoughts turned to Pete. She hadn't heard anything from him in three days. Not a phone call. Not even a text message. This was simply not like him. She wondered if all was well. He normally rang her every day to see how Jake was even if it was just for a minute. It wasn't always convenient to take his calls if she was in the middle of bathing or feeding Jake but she always replied by text later if she couldn't phone him and he would give a thumbs up in response. She knew that he was still trying to find a solution with Vanessa but their situation was tangled and was not going to be easily resolved. She was only too aware that there was not going to be quick resolution for her and Pete to be together as a couple. There were just too many variables. *So why am I so overly concerned that I haven't heard from Pete?* She thought. She deliberated whether to ring or maybe send a text. Then she reminded herself that she was not going to rely on Pete. He wasn't available, he was still married and living with Vanessa even though he kept insisting that he didn't want to be with her anymore and it was only the house that tied them together. Karen was conscious that she had to be strong for her children and understand that the plans and dreams she and Pete had may not materialise. As well as the custody of her children which was hanging in the balance, Pete needed to split with Vanessa before they could even start their journey together. She also didn't want to show any insecurity by constantly checking that he was still onboard with everything. She shouldn't have to. *She should have more faith in him than that otherwise what would be the point of them starting a life together?* She also wanted to prove to herself that she could do it on her own if she had to. Her children were her main love and priority. She was determined that she didn't want to need anyone again. Her emotional and mental health depended on it. No one could break her again if she kept her expectations low and realistic.

However, her instincts told her that there had to be a justifiable reason that he had not been in touch. Pride however stopped her from contacting him. He had let her down before when she really needed him. She had been so sad all those years ago that she thought her heart would literally break in two. She believed in him and thought that he would stand by her decision to have their baby. She knew he wasn't ready but neither was she. None of them were prepared for a baby but she had at least been willing to believe that their love for each other would have been able to help them stay as a couple and raise their child together. *How wrong had she been! He had been too self-centred. But how could she judge him when she too had given Robin up? Why didn't I just keep him?* She had asked herself that question so many times and she always gave herself the answers that she wanted to hear. *It had been for Robin's sake. She had given him up for adoption so he could have a better life than a sixteen year girl could offer. A childless couple now had the child they had dreamt of.* *She had been noble. She had been generous.* But then she would tell herself that it was all excuses. *She had been selfish just like Pete. She didn't want to be a single mum. She wanted to get rid of the embarrassment she felt that she had bought on herself and her family. She wanted to go back to normal. Whatever 'normal' was?* Now she had learnt that you can never go back to who you were after a life changing event because you are changed forever. You have to accept where you are and somehow find a way to live with yourself because regret destroys your mental health. Uncover inner strength and ask yourself what you've learnt and decide what you want for yourself going forward and remember that no matter how much you beat yourself up, it won't change the past. Her many deep and profound conversations with her mum had really helped her to understand herself more. She began to grasp the gravity of what she had been through and that she had not been in a good place at that time in her life. Her decision to give up Robin had been in the shadow of shame, sadness and pain.

She had been grateful for the many conversations that she had had with her grandma Rose too. She had been amazing. She had said that Karen shouldn't be so hard on herself and to forgive herself as God forgives us. *How comforting that was to know that God forgave her!* It really did help. Karen knew her faith wasn't strong like her grandma's but she believed in God and it brought her a lot of peace. She was determined to move on and not be critical of herself or Pete's past actions nor judge his present behaviour either. He was under a tremendous strain with Vanessa.

Chapter 54

Karen's phone was ringing and she had just put Jake down for a nap. Her phone was in the kitchen and she rushed to answer it thinking it might Pete. She looked and saw Lynda's name on the screen.

'Hi Lynda, how are you? It's lovely to hear from you.'

'I'm good,' Lynda replied.

Karen immediately felt guilty that she never rang Lynda as often as Lynda rang her. Lynda had become a good friend over the years and had never made any demands on their friendship. She was easygoing and a genuine friend that Karen valued. They tried to meet every few months for a drink or meal whenever she could arrange with Richard to babysit. Invariably it would get postponed for one reason or another so sometimes it would be six months or more before they saw one another but they were always in touch by text and phone calls. She always enjoyed her time with Lynda who would bring amusing anecdotes of life in the chemist as well as updates of her own life. Lynda loved working at the chemist and had now moved to a supervisory position. Her knowledge was great and she was highly valued. She worked hard and was recognised for it and was content to stay at the chemist. Lynda was now married but didn't have any children yet. Her husband Dave seemed to be the perfect fit for her. Karen had met him a couple times. She and Richard had had a night out with Lynda and Dave once and it hadn't gone particularly well. There wasn't much common ground between Richard and Dave. They were incredibly polite to each other and both made an effort throughout the evening but when they came home Richard admitted to Karen that he had little interest in going out again as couples. They had also gone to Lynda and Dave's wedding party but Richard barely got through the evening. He couldn't wait to leave. He just didn't seem to fit in with Dave and his friends so after that Lynda and Karen decided that it would just be the two of them in future with no husbands in tow. They had an honest discussion and there were no hard feelings. Their husbands were very different people and just because they were friends, it didn't mean the men had to be friends too.

With the demands of Richard and the children, she had allowed their friendship to flag. She regretted that now as Lynda had proved a faithful friend. She recognised that during her marriage she didn't have a mind of her own and had constantly looked to Richard for guidance and direction. She looked back now and wondered why she had allowed herself to be so manipulated, unwittingly of course. She didn't want to blame Richard anymore she should have had a mind of her own. Lynda somehow seemed to accept the way Karen was and their friendship grew despite them not seeing each other as often as they would have both liked. Whenever they did see each other, they just seemed to pick up where they left off. They had a real connection and trusted one another. Karen had previously shared with Lynda about Robin so she always felt safe to talk to her about anything. Lynda would simply listen without interruption and allow Karen to offload. Karen had found it hard to show her vulnerability to anyone as she had always been aware that her feelings could be abused, but she didn't feel like that with Lynda. She was a true friend and as the years went by she treasured her more. Lynda had been invaluable when her affair with Pete and the pregnancy was out in the open. She had simply been there with no judgement at all. She had been really supportive too.

'Lynda, I'm so sorry I haven't been in touch lately.'

'Whoa! Stop! No apologies right, that's not how we operate you know that.' Lynda replied with a smile that although Karen couldn't see, she could feel. She immediately relaxed.

'I know, but you're always there for me and I feel bad that I can't be there for you more. Every time we speak, it's always about me and my problems. It must be so boring for you,' she said with a forced laugh.

'Not boring at all, you know that. Karen what's up? I'm sensing something's bothering you. It's my day off today do you want me to come over?'

'Oh Lynda, would you? I really need a good chat right now.'

'I'll be there in an hour,' Lynda replied.

'See you in a bit, bye,' Karen responded.

Karen opened the door to Lynda an hour later and was presented with flowers for her, colouring book and crayons for each of the girls and a teddy bear for Jake. Karen's eyes filled with tears as she hugged her friend.

'Oh Karen, what's up my darling?' Lynda asked as she walked into the lounge with Karen, 'I could tell over the phone that you were not yourself.' Jake was sleeping in his Moses basket at the end of the sofa and Lynda took a peek at him. 'He's gorgeous Karen, I mean seriously gorgeous.' She said with emphasis and looked up at Karen and then back at Jake staring at his sleeping frame that was swathed in a brilliantly white shawl.

'I know,' Karen agreed with a smile, 'and he's so good too. He doesn't seem affected by the noise from the girls when they're playing at all. Even when I'm getting him in and out of the car to fetch the girls he just goes with the flow. He's wonderful. I love him so much. I'm so glad I got my driving license all those years ago and have my own car, at least I have a degree of independence without having to bother mum too much. She already does so much to help me.' Karen then sighed unexpectedly, 'I haven't heard from Pete in days,' she said changing the subject without warning, 'and I'm worried. I think something's happened. He normally rings every day. It's just not like him,' a frown appeared on Karen's forehead.

'Have you tried ringing him?' Lynda asked enquiringly.

'No,' she sighed again.

'Why is that my love?' Lynda asked softly.

She shrugged her shoulders, 'I can't afford to depend on Pete again Lynda, he let me down once before. He's still got Vanessa to deal with. She's not coping by all accounts. He keeps telling me that he's trying to sort things out so that we can be together but I suppose it's a pride thing too I don't want him to know that I need him. I don't want to depend on any man. I feel sad that I hurt Richard but I needed to find me and I feel like I have. I feel stronger too, truly I do. So the last thing I want to do is go back to that old me who's always relying on someone else.'

'Do you want me to ring him?' Lynda asked.

Karen thought about Lynda's suggestion before answering her, 'what would you say though? He might think it's a bit random,' she moved her shoulders upwards and slowly raised her arms at the same time before gradually lowering them back down again, 'I'm not sure.'

'You're assuming that he's just abandoned you again, aren't you? But he's been attentive throughout this pregnancy so something must be wrong if he normally rings every day,' Lynda said.

'I guess so...' Karen trailed off.

Lynda listened and understood her friend's desire to remain strong and focussed. They chatted and Lynda cuddled Jake when he eventually woke up. Before they realised it, time had flown and it was time to get Amelia from school. She had recently started Reception class and was doing mornings only for the time being. Karen was looking forward to when Amelia was doing full days so that she could pick her up at the same time as Grace at the end of the day. Karen suddenly felt weary as she said goodbye to her dear friend. All this talk of Pete and wondering how he was had affected her mood. This was exactly what she didn't want! She didn't want to be affected by anyone. If she had to do this alone, then she was prepared. *Damn you Pete!* She swore under her breath.

Chapter 55

The pre-trial hearing was just six days away. Karen looked at the calendar hanging on the back of the kitchen door. Her mum always bought a calendar for the back of the kitchen door Karen noticed. It was something her mum did as far back as Karen could remember. She always said that with all the activities they did as children, parents' evenings to attend, birthday parties to take them to, family occasions to put in an appearance at, social and important events to patronise; without a calendar she would never remember anything. When Karen came back to live with her parents, it was strangely comforting to look at the calendar to see what was happening as Marina always kept it up to date and of course as soon as the solicitor gave her the pre-trial date, Marina immediately put it on the calendar. It had been months away when she had received the letter, she was about eight months into her pregnancy and it seemed way in the distance then and she had been glad at the time, she needed to prepare for the birth of Jake. It had been good knowing that at least for the next few months her girls would be with her. But now looking at the calendar with only four days to go, she was beginning to feel nervous and not confident about her case for keeping the girls.

How could she compete with Richard? On paper, he was the model husband and father who worked hard and provided for his family. Whereas she had been a teenage mum who gave her baby up for adoption and then she became the cheating lying wife who had an affair and had gotten pregnant by her ex lover and was now living in her parent's house without a job and no real prospects. Her solicitor had said that if she could manage to persuade Richard to drop the custody battle it would be better for everyone. *If only he would agree to at least talk to her, would have been a starting point but she was always met with a wall of silence.* He made it clear that any communication he would have with her was via text only. He simply refused any conversation. There had been occasions when she had tried to make conversation when he had come to collect or drop the girls back. Admittedly it had been a feeble attempt on her part, but she had tried. But no, he would not engage. She still felt awkward and unsure of herself around him. She had been married to him and had two children with him and had had a life with him but she still felt slightly inadequate around him. She tried to work why out she felt that way and even though she hated to admit it to herself, she felt judged by him. She sighed with her hands on her hips as she recalled the last time she had mustered up the courage to speak. She cringed as she remembered it. He completely ignored her as if she didn't exist.

She hadn't spoken to Eva for a while either, she thought. It had been a few weeks. She realised that Eva hadn't seen Jake even though she had promised the girls that she would. It was not surprising and completely understandable that she hadn't been to see him. Eva was caught right in the middle of a difficult situation. *Poor woman!* The girls would come back after a weekend with their dad and grandmother full of tales of their time with them. They were always happy and spoke freely. Karen was pleased to see that the break up with Richard hadn't affected them too much. It was too soon to tell how it may impact them in the future but she was glad that for now they seemed content wherever they were. *How she wished that adults were as adaptable as children.* It had been a real comfort to witness their capacity to adjust to change. Eva had been a large part of their life when she was with Richard and she was so glad that Eva had remained a constant in the girls' lives throughout the break up. *How she loved Eva and how she missed Eva too!* But she knew that she had placed Eva in an impossible position. Grace had come home two weekends running saying that Nanny Eva was going to come and see Jake. But it hadn't materialised. Knowing Eva, as she did, Karen knew that it would have been hard for her to not fulfil her promise. She knew that loyalty and possibly not wanting to hurt Richard would be the reason. Karen couldn't be sure but she guessed that maybe Eva would promise the girls and then maybe check with Richard or maybe she just made the decision not to come because she didn't want to hurt or upset him. Richard didn't talk about his feelings but Eva was always sensitive enough to pick up how he was feeling from his mood and behaviour. She was his mum and understood him more than anyone else.

The last few weeks had been difficult for so many reasons. Richard's behaviour, although expected still bothered and disturbed her. With very little contact from Eva and no contact from Pete, her mind had been extremely troubled. If only she could speak to Eva and get her to speak to Richard to just drop the custody battle. 'Hi Eva, how are you?' Karen had plucked up the courage to phone Eva. She didn't want Eva to compromise her relationship with Richard but she had to try and get her to reason with him. She was her only hope.

'Hi Karen, I'm fine thank you. It's lovely to hear from you, is everything okay? I'm sorry I haven't had an opportunity to come and see the baby yet, but I've been so busy lately,' she said in a rush. *Poor Eva, she doesn't need this kind of guilt trip.* Karen thought.

'Oh Eva, I'm so sorry for what I've put you through. I genuinely miss you and feel so incredibly sad.' All the bottled up emotions of the last few weeks came flooding out in uncontrollable tears.

'Karen, sweetheart what's wrong?' Eva asked soothingly, 'I miss you too,' she concluded. The sobbing she could hear was heartbreaking. How Eva wished they could all just turn the clock back and do things differently but that wasn't possible and we are where we are she thought. She waited for Karen to compose herself.

'I'm so sorry Eva,' she said again.

'I know you are,' Eva replied softly.

'I'm going to lose the girls unless he agrees to mediation but he won't even talk to me Eva. I know why and I don't blame him, but I just don't want to lose my children. I can't lose them. I've let them down like I let Robin down. What kind of mother am I?' The question was rhetorical as she answered it before Eva could reply, 'useless, that's what!' She stated.

'Believe me Karen, I have tried to talk to him so many times hoping I could stop him taking it this far. The current arrangement you've both got with Grace and Amelia is working well and it's a waste of money in my opinion but his pride is getting in the way. I'll try again my love, after all I've got nothing to lose other than him getting cross with me. I'll do my best but don't get your hopes too high, I can't promise anything,' Eva said with a sigh.

Chapter 56

After the conversation with Karen, Eva sat reflecting on everything that had happened and tried to think of the best way to approach Richard. It was one last roll of the dice.

'Hi mum,' Richard said with surprise as he opened the front door, 'you normally ring to let me know when you're coming. Is everything okay? I'm just finishing off some work on the laptop. Give me five minutes and I'll be with you.' He went back into the lounge while Eva headed for the kitchen. She filled the kettle and sat at the kitchen table while she waited for it to boil. She felt nervous knowing that Richard didn't really like spontaneity. He liked prior warning about everything but she knew that had she rang him first he would have wheedled it out of her and taken his usual stance. She knew that she almost needed to catch him off guard to gain any kind of advantage.

The conversation that followed over the next hour had not been easy. Eva left feeling drained but it had been worth it. She had finally managed to get through to him. There had been home truths which had resulted in hurt on both sides but it had been necessary.

She had pointed out that Karen had wronged him and she was never going to defend that but it was time for him to learn to talk about things and not bottle his feelings up. He also needed to listen when other people needed to talk and not just try and bring a solution or dismiss it. That's what had been the problem in his marriage to Karen and things needed to change or the pain and hurt would go on for years. No matter what Karen had done, she was still their mother and the girls loved her. He owed it to them to at least talk to Karen.

Richard sat staring into space ruminating on everything that he and Eva had talked about. It had been painful, extremely painful in fact. He didn't want to hear about the things that he had done and the part he had played in the breakdown of his marriage and the 'breaking' of Karen. But he was faced with the stark reality and the truth of the situation. His mum had suggested that maybe he needed therapy. *Why did he need therapy?* There was nothing wrong with him. He was perfectly fine. He was organised and logical. *Therapy was for people who constantly looked inward at their emotions, people who lived in the past constantly asking themselves questions. What if? What if? What was the point?* He reasoned to himself. *You can't change what's happened.* Yes, of course he had days when his emotions were a little nearer to the surface, he was human after all, but when he felt like that he would ignore it and do something practical to distract himself. *What use was it to analyse every feeling and every emotion?* But now Eva had persuaded him to consider that sometimes we have to look inward and do an honest appraisal of ourselves. She had said so many things that gave him a lot to think about. He didn't know where to start. *Could he ever consider forgiving Karen?* When Eva asked him, his first reaction and emotion was no but now he pondered and dared to ask himself if he could. The strange thing was that he had only ever thought about forgiveness as an option in relation to possibly taking her back. He hadn't considered forgiveness in terms of their relationship as parents and even friends. Eva had planted a seed about understanding and accepting that although Karen had done wrong by him, it did not make her a bad mother. She was human like everyone else. The children loved him and they loved Karen too. Hurting her would ultimately hurt them. He hadn't been able to see it before because his pride had got in the way. He had focused upon the infidelity and the pregnancy and judged Karen on that. He had taken the moral high ground as though she had done all the wrong and he had done nothing. What he was slowly beginning to realise was that it was easy to judge her one big final act of betrayal and be the victim without looking at what drove her to that in the first place. She had been so sweet and unchallenging, easy going and kind. He loved that about her. She had been a wonderful girlfriend and that was why he had wanted to marry her. He remembered from the countless conversations that they had that she wanted to be married to him and have a family and truly treasure it. She had said on so many occasions throughout their marriage how blessed she felt to have him and the girls. So he knew how important their life, their relationship, their children and marriage was to her. *So why would she sacrifice that? Why hadn't he listened to her unspoken words?* He knew of her sadness about Robin and now he was 'kicking himself' for being so insensitive about how that part of her life had shaped her and ultimately changed her. And that it wasn't negative for her to cry or remember her son or feel sadness about what had happened. If only he had realised it back then. His lack of validation of her feelings and emotions had been a gradual wearing down of her love for him. Meeting Pete again was a plaster that covered a wound that hadn't healed. And of course they both had Robin in common. He could see it now. *Why couldn't he see it before?* While it was easy to judge her because of her behaviour and the outcome of a pregnancy that had broken the family, he had to admit he played his part. He had bit by bit unknowingly drained all of her energy and spirit. For the first time he felt more sorry for Karen than for himself.

The conversation with Eva had definitely challenged him in a way that he didn't like but he needed it. He was forced to think about things that he had never previously considered or entertained. *Was he selfish? Did he like everything his own way? Was he controlling?* Ouch! *That one he did not like!* He didn't recognise that about himself. He prided himself on knowing his own mind and what he believed was right for others too. *He was helping, not hindering. He was caring, not controlling. Surely not! This was not what he was! How could his own mum suggest that he had these traits?* He sat shaking his head. This is exactly why he didn't like to ponder and analyse. It was all too much.

Chapter 57

Karen heard her phone ringing. It was after 9pm. *Who was ringing her at this time?* The girls were in bed sleeping soundly and Jake too! She was sitting watching a drama on the television that had caught her interest and had temporarily distracted her from her own worrying thoughts. She didn't usually have time to watch the TV. There was always something to do, especially once all the children were in bed. She would catch up on chores but not tonight, she had become engrossed. This was an interruption she could do without. She picked up the phone slightly irritated and saw that it was Richard. *What did he want?* He never ever rang. He had only communicated via texts since the breakup. He had made it perfectly clear that he wanted no conversation with her. This was surprising and unsettling at the same time.

'Hello,' she said tentatively and guardedly. She couldn't even say his name.

'Karen, it's me, Richard.'

'I know, what's wrong?' Karen's heart was beating hard and fast as she waited for a response.

'Karen, can we meet?' Richard asked.

'What now?' Karen replied puzzled. Knowing Richard as she did, she knew that he liked to plan everything. Spontaneity was not his way.

'No, I want to arrange it in the next couple days.'

'Oh, okay,' Karen's heartbeat had started to return to normal.

'Let me know the best day and time that suits you. I know you will need to arrange it with your mum. I'll wait to hear from you. Bye,' then he was gone.

Karen held her phone in her hand and continued to look at it for long time. She was stunned! This was a bolt out of the blue. *What could he possibly want to talk about?* He had always made his position clear, that there was nothing to discuss or say to her. *So what had changed?* Her mind was completely preoccupied and all interest in the television drama had gone. She really wanted to tell her mum what had just happened and to talk her fears through but Marina had gone to bed early as she had been nursing a migraine all evening. Karen felt so disturbed within but she would have to wait until the morning to talk to her mum. There was a lot to think about and it was laying heavy on her; the impending court case and Pete's lack of contact recently had been top of the list and now the call from Richard added to it. She felt restless and the knot in her stomach was getting worse. She had no idea whether she would actually get any sleep that night.

Chapter 58

Pete sat on the sofa staring at the television but not really watching it. He knew he had to contact Karen but he didn't have the strength to do anything. *What was wrong with him?* Vanessa was in the kitchen preparing a salad for their lunch. He started to think about Karen, how he loved her. His beautiful strong Karen who had bore him two children. She had been all alone throughout her pregnancy with Robin. He reassured himself that he had at least been there for her in the pregnancy with Jake. *But where was he now? Why did he always let her down?* He didn't mean too. *What was wrong with him?* He needed to be there for her and Jake. *So why was he not doing anything to make it happen?* He asked himself. Instead he was with Vanessa who seemed so much happier since he had what he himself described as a 'mini breakdown'. He still felt fragile to some extent more aware than ever of his own mental health. Never before had he fully understood how emotions could overwhelm and disturb the balance of your mind. The medication definitely helped. It made him feel calmer and helped him to sleep. He had gradually felt better but whenever he started to think about the situation and the obligations he had to so many people who needed him, he would start to sink back into what felt like a black hole. It was impossible to be there for one person without hurting another. He felt personally responsible for disturbing and causing disruption to so many lives and that was hard to deal with. The problem was that he knew that he had to face reality. He was aware that he had to go back to work at some point and also talk to Vanessa and let her know that he had not changed his plan about selling their house and for them to separate so that he and Karen could then look for a house and start their life together. Then there was Grace and Amelia, they would be his stepchildren which was another big responsibility; living and caring and protecting another man's children for the biggest part of every week. *Was he capable? Could he do it?* There was so much to think about. There were a lot of hurdles to jump.

'Pete, lunch is ready. Do you want it on a tray?' Vanessa asked as she stood at the doorway to the lounge.

'No, I'll eat in the kitchen. I'll be there in a bit,' Pete replied.

'Okay,' she said as she walked back to the kitchen.

His eyes followed her as she made her way into the kitchen. He considered how lovely she had been when he came out of hospital. She had really cared for him. He appreciated that she had not judged him at all throughout this whole situation. In fact, he had seen something of the old Vanessa since they had both been at home cocooned from the world and all its problems. They had walked and talked, ate and slept and watched films together. It felt like the old days again.

'Karen, I'm sorry I haven't been in touch but a lot has happened,' Pete said apologetically. His words rushed out quickly. He had finally plucked up the courage to ring. He had felt nervous and didn't know why. His heart felt like it was beating out of his chest and his stomach was doing somersaults as he spoke. He had decided to take the opportunity to ring Karen while Vanessa was out. She had gone food shopping with her mum after preparing lunch.

'Pete, what's happened? I did wonder why I hadn't heard from you,' she paused, 'I missed you,' Karen said quietly.

The tears flowed down his cheek as he said, 'I missed you too, how's Jake?'

Karen looked over into the Moses basket at a sleeping Jake, 'he's beautiful Pete. I love him so much.'

'I don't deserve you Karen, you would be better off without me.' Loud sobs came down the phone and Karen became alarmed.

'Pete, what's wrong? Please tell me. I can take it. There's not a lot that could break me now. I have no expectations from anyone,' Karen said kindly but firmly.

'I'm on sick leave. I think I'm getting better now but I had 'an episode', I guess you would call it,' he paused, 'long story short, I ended up in hospital and now I'm on medication for anxiety and depression. I really don't know how it happened. I thought I was on top of everything but it turns out I wasn't. I didn't realise how far along the road I had gone...' Pete trailed off feeling overwhelmingly sad. He continued before she could answer, 'I kept telling Vanessa that I wanted to be with you and Jake and that we needed to sell the house but she wouldn't listen. I couldn't seem to get through to her. I felt like I was hitting my head against a brick wall. I couldn't seem to make anything happen or move things forward,' Karen listened, 'I'm a mess Karen, what good am I to you? How are we ever going to make a life together when there's so much to overcome? Vanessa is just burying her head in the sand. She doesn't want to talk about the situation. It's like she wants to pretend it's not happening. I guess that's her way of dealing with it but it's playing with my head.'

Wow! Karen thought. This is much worse than she could ever have imagined. So Pete was ill now too. It wasn't just Vanessa. This was too much. She had her three children to care for. She couldn't afford to take this on. She needed to remain strong for the kids. Yes, she loved Pete but she needed someone to help her not hinder her. *Was that cruel?* She thought. She didn't mean it that way but she had to be pragmatic and think about herself too. She had come a long way on her journey from giving up Robin and it had not been an easy road. The last thing she needed right now was to take a step back emotionally and mentally. She owed it to herself and her children. Whatever decisions she made had to be in the best interests of the children and she needed to keep a clear head to do that. Their needs came first. Karen fell silent as she contemplated.

'Karen, are you still there?' Pete asked.

'Yes, I am,' she replied, suddenly aware of the silence that had fallen between them. As the conversation continued, Karen realised just how affected he was. He had so much angst and she had felt his burden as he spoke. She could sense his anxiety, it was palpable. She knew that he wanted to be there for her and Jake. He was trying to set everything in motion and it was in trying to do this that he had crumbled. His mountains were huge and he was struggling. Poor Pete! *This is serious, he doesn't need any extra pressure put on him, it could send him right 'over the edge'.* She thought. 'Listen, you concentrate on getting yourself better Pete. We're doing just fine. Please don't worry about letting me down okay.'

'Okay,' he said quietly submissively.

'Pete, take care and we'll speak soon.'

Pete sat perfectly still for a while staring into space and felt marginally better for speaking to Karen and letting her know what had been happening to him. He didn't want her to think that he had let her down again. That had been his biggest worry.

Karen however came off the phone with her thoughts deeply troubled wondering just how her future was going to look. It seemed to be one thing after another to deal with. She speculated on the call from Richard the night before wanting to meet and talk not knowing what that would bring and now this call from Pete who was clearly ill. His mental health had diminished without her even being aware of it. *What is going on? Is there ever going to be an end? Will life ever be normal? Whatever normal is? I need a voice of reason.* She thought.

Chapter 59

'Hi Gran, how are you?' Karen said.

'Hello child, lovely to hear your voice, how are you?'

That's what's so wonderful about Gran, she thought, she always calls me 'child'. It was such a term of endearment that meant a lot to Karen and gave her a warm comforting feeling whenever she heard the familiar greeting throughout her life. And it wasn't that she was the only one that Granny Rose used the term with. She had the same greeting for Susan and Fiona too but she wondered if it meant as much to them as it did to her. She had never discussed it with them but it dawned on her that she had never needed to hear it as much as she did today. *Why was her life so problematic? There was always something to throw her into turmoil.* She rolled her eyes in disgust at herself as she replayed quick flashes of events in her mind and then quickly shook her head to get rid of them.

'Gran, I'm going to pop over with Jake in about hour, is that okay with you?'

'Of course child, come when you're ready. I'm not going anywhere.'

Granny Rose only lived five minutes away by car but as Karen picked up the car keys and opened the front door and saw the glorious sunshine she decided to walk for a change. She was looking forward to chatting to Gran she mused as she pushed a contented Jake in his buggy with his eyes wide open. It really was a beautiful day she thought with a completely blue sky and the right amount of warmth on her skin. She looked at the houses and front gardens as she strolled by and dared to dream that one day she would have her own house with a safe and secluded garden for the children. One day, she thought, one day it will all come good. It has to. She really needed to believe that.

Fifteen minutes after leaving her parents home, she arrived at the small terraced house that her grandmother had lived in for nearly fifty years. Jake was fast asleep. The fresh air had done him good. She rang the door bell and Granny's face appeared in the front window from behind the net curtain with a warm smile. She gestured for Karen to go to the Entry door that was unlocked which opened into a short corridor that ran along the side of the house. Karen decided that Jake would be fine sleeping in his buggy which she could alter into a lying down position with the parasol shielding him from the sun's direct rays. As she walked out of the shared Entry and turned right into the garden, she was hit by the beautiful smells of Rosemary and Thyme, Lavender and Honeysuckle. Gran was a keen gardener and loved growing herbs and vegetables as well as beautiful flowers in borders and pots. The garden was narrow and long with views of the neighbours' gardens to the left and right over low fences on both sides. Just outside the kitchen door was a little private courtyard which housed a table and two chairs as well as a comfortable lounger that had seen better days with a little table next to it. This was where Gran sat and read her Bible on sunny days like this one with a cup of tea. She was so active for her age and lived by herself without any assistance apart from Cecil mowing the lawn when necessary and Marina taking her shopping. She loved tending to her plants and pottering in the garden. It was clearly therapy for her as she was one of the calmest people that Karen knew.

After hugging one another, Granny Rose poured Karen a drink from the jug of juice that was full of ice that she had prepared while Karen was on her way. She sat in her comfy lounger while Karen sat on one of the chairs by the table as she gently pushed Jake back and forth in his buggy.

'What's troubling you child?'

'Gran, I don't even know where to start,' she threw her hands up in exasperation.

'I know your life is upside down at the moment but it won't last forever,' Granny Rose said reassuringly.

'That's definitely good to know,' she smiled.

Karen told Granny Rose everything that had happened recently, the call from Richard wanting to meet up and the call from Pete, and how bad his mental health currently was.

'Gran, I've caused such a lot of pain and heartache through my stupid mistakes. I can't go on like this. I need to make sensible 'head' decisions not 'heart' ones.'

'Yes, you do,' Granny Rose said truthfully, 'but you're human and you're young.'

'Not that young, I'm in my thirties now,' Karen interrupted with a roll of her eyes.

'Now child you still have plenty of life left,' Granny Rose said with a smile, 'listen to me, no one goes through life without making mistakes, that's how we grow and mature and become better people. You are no worse than anyone else. You have to stop beating yourself up and looking back at what's happened or what you've done. You can't change that now. So just look to the future and decide what you want to do. What do you want to do?'

'I feel like there's so much to repair before I can move forward. That's the problem,' Karen threw her hands up in exasperation.

'You are not responsible for anybody's actions, only your own. And even we can't do anything in our own strength. We need God's help.'

'How can God help me Gran?' she asked earnestly, 'I've seriously messed up. God isn't going to want to help me. I've known right from wrong all my life so why would God want to help me?'

'Because God doesn't judge, He knows we're human and we will fail that's why he sent His Son Jesus into the world to save us, not judge us. Don't condemn yourself child because Jesus doesn't. Allow yourself time to connect with God and seek His peace for your life and ask for His guidance. I've been praying for you and I will continue and I truly believe God will make a way. Sometimes good can come from the hard trials of life.' Karen sat and listened carefully to every word. Granny Rose continued, 'when you meet Richard keep an open mind. You don't know why he wants to meet you. Yes, it's been a battle between you and him and there may well be more to come but ask God for strength and wisdom and He will grant it.'

'Yes, I will. I feel so bad about Richard and how much I've hurt him but on the other hand, I feel anger that he didn't validate my feelings when I was sad about Robin. I don't think I'll ever be able to forgive him for that,' Karen said wistfully.

'You will in time,' Granny Rose responded.

'I think I've made a decision now about what I want to do. Talking to you has made me feel calmer and my mind is clearer too.' At that moment Jake stirred and woke up with a cry. Karen gently lifted him out of his buggy and held him close to her. She put him to her chest and started to breastfeed him. 'Yep, I think I know what I want and what I need to do. I can't keep being at the mercy of Richard and Pete. I need to take some control,' Karen said.

'I know that the thought of Richard gaining custody of the girls is unthinkable and I pray it doesn't happen,' Granny Rose held her hands in front of her in the prayer position, 'and if it did, I know it would break your heart but you would survive.' This time, she moved her hands and crossed them as she laid them on her chest and held them there.

Tears fell from Karen's eyes, 'oh Gran, I couldn't bear it,' she wiped her eyes with a tissue from her handbag.

'Don't cry child remember that you would still see the girls regularly so they wouldn't forget you. You would still be in their life, it would just be differently,' Karen sniffed and blew her nose and looked intently at her Gran, 'you would still be a part of their lives and have influence and be able to have happy times and create memories on the days when you have them. All will not be lost my child. Believe me when I say, I speak from experience that we have to accept what we can't change. In a strange way, acceptance is control. Do the best you can with what you have and try to be content and satisfied. With regard to Pete, I don't have any answers,' Granny

Rose said thoughtfully. 'He's clearly got a lot of sorting out to do in his life. But let me put you straight child you are not to blame for his mental health. He knows in his own heart that he has let people down; you, his wife, Robin, and possibly now Jake. That's why he's struggling. He will work it out. I know you love him but you can't do anything to help him. The only thing you can do which will help him is not make any demands on him. He's clearly not strong right now so you don't want to break him. But that's all you can do.' Granny Rose said with emphasis and kept her gaze firmly on Karen as if to ensure she fully understood what she was saying. 'Do not even attempt to do anymore than that. I know it sounds harsh but you don't owe him anything more than that. You're already paying a price for your own actions. Pete has to carry his own burdens and be accountable for his own actions. There are always consequences and he can't escape his,' she paused,' 'think carefully about the future and how it may look. Pray about what is best going forward, not what you want, because we know that what we want isn't necessarily what's best for us, don't we? My advice right now is to take it one step at a time and don't make too many decisions at this stage,' Karen nodded in agreement, 'enjoy that little one in your arms while you can too. They don't stay babies for long.' Granny Rose ended.

Karen kissed the top of Jake's head as she held him tightly and looked up at the unbroken blue sky. For the first time in a long time she felt at peace. As Karen strolled back, she felt lighter, calmer somehow. *Maybe I do need to pray more.* She thought. Talking to Granny Rose and seeing how her faith really helped her had given Karen positivity. Granny had not had it easy herself. Life had been hard for her Gran but she had dealt with the tough seasons of life which sometimes had been long and painful but she always kept her faith and the belief that better days would come. And if the good times didn't come as quickly as she expected, she asked for God's strength but she never gave up hope. She had always lived a quiet life without too much expectation and was always grateful no matter what her circumstances. *Maybe that's the key.* Karen thought. She had so much admiration for her Gran.

Chapter 60

The day started like any ordinary day but it wasn't.... so much had happened, so much had been lost. *Could she ever repair the damage she had caused to so many lives? Was it even possible?*

As Karen sat staring out of the cafe window in the early evening watching people walk by going about their business, dealing with their own lives and issues, she realised after a long journey and search that she was no different to anyone else really. *Why had it taken her so long to grasp? Everyone had their demons, why did she make hers so big?*

Richard had asked to meet her. She had to remain hopeful that she had not completely destroyed everything...

The door opened, he walked in. Her stomach flipped over and over. It was time to face the future.

Richard strode across to the table that she was sitting at and sat down opposite her and smiled. She hadn't seen him smile in a long time. She tentatively smiled back. He had been cold and distant for so long that this warmth from him was unnerving.

'Hi Karen, are you okay?'

'Yes, not bad. How are you?' Karen asked. *This is polite.* Karen thought.

'Thanks for meeting me. I know I haven't been very agreeable recently. I wouldn't have blamed you if you'd said no,' Richard said with his head slightly bent with guilt.

'That's okay,' Karen replied.

'No it's not okay, you're too nice, too accommodating of me. I can understand now why you were unhappy. I couldn't see it before. I pushed you too far. I'm sorry for everything. For not understanding about Robin and now this custody battle. Mum made me realise it.'

Karen sat stunned into silence. She was not expecting this at all. She had been dreading it thinking it would be more of the same nastiness and attitude. This was more than even she thought she deserved. In her mind, no matter what he had done, she had been unfaithful and had a baby that wasn't his. *He had a right to be angry, hateful and hurt. She got it!*

'What are you trying to say to me Richard? I'm confused. I'm grateful for your apology but you're still going to take my girls from me. I'm sorry for cheating on you and hurting you, I truly am, but I will never apologise for my beautiful son. He's here now,' Richard sat quietly as she spoke, 'in fact, I will never ever apologise for loving and wanting my children. I'm tired of fighting to just love and keep my children. I wasn't even allowed to mourn the loss of my first son. I was made to feel ashamed for missing him. It didn't make the love I have for Grace and Amelia any less. If anything, it made me love them more. Having Robin and losing him was life changing and rocked my world.'

Karen looked away as her eyes welled up with tears that didn't spill out and her voice wobbled, 'so although I appreciate your "sorry", forgive me if I don't do a dance but I'm about to potentially lose my girls as well,' then the tears fell.

Richard reached across and wiped the tears from her cheeks with one hand, first the left cheek then the right and then he took both her hands and looked straight into her eyes, 'I'm so sorry Karen,' the tears flowed unchecked from Karen.

'I'm going to drop the case. The girls can stay with you.'

'What?' Karen stared at him as though she didn't understand what he had said or misheard him.

'I said the girls can stay with you. I won't fight for custody,' Karen stared at him open mouthed as he continued. She was lost for words, 'I don't think I realised until mum explained just how hard it must have been. I've been a fool. What I thought and my opinion was irrelevant. I should have listened to how you felt.' He paused before continuing, 'I've asked myself a thousand times over the last few days why I was fighting for full custody of the girls. If I'm honest I don't know the answer. All I know is that I wasn't thinking enough of Grace and Amelia, I was thinking about myself. I suppose I wanted to hurt you for the pain and embarrassment you caused me. I wasn't thinking about the reasons that led to it. All I could feel was my own despair. I was angry and I literally couldn't see any other point of view. What was I thinking? I feel ashamed. I almost allowed innocent children, my own children to be used as pawns to exact revenge on you. What does that make me? Mum made me see the ugly side of myself and I didn't like it.' He paused and took a deep breath while Karen looked at him, 'when I thought about it, I realised that I was going to let my own children lose out on the loving caring mother that you are just to punish you. I expected you to just forget Robin, when I know I could never forget Grace and Amelia. How unfair have I been?' More tears flowed from Karen at the mention of Robin's name, her sweet first child that she didn't get a chance to love. It was almost too painful. 'And then I wanted to hurt Jake, an innocent baby, what kind of man am I? A baby is no threat to me. It's Pete that I should hate for so many reasons,' he shook his head as if in disgust, 'Pete let you down when you had Robin and then he stole you from me because I wasn't looking and noticing what was happening to us. I was a fool.' He kept shaking his head at the thought of his own behaviour, 'instead I try to keep an innocent child from knowing his beautiful big sisters who love him. What was I thinking? I've seriously questioned myself as a father. I've put my own feelings above the needs and consideration of all the children involved. You're far more worthy to be a parent than I am. I wanted to hurt you but I would have hurt the children too, they would be the losers. I can't deny it, I didn't want the girls to be close to Jake, and it's something that I'm struggling to deal with,' he paused again, 'but I'm big enough and ugly enough to understand that I can't get everything my way. Jake's here now and I can't change that as painful as that maybe.'

Karen sat in silence, dried her eyes and took a sip of her cold latte and suddenly realised that Richard hadn't even ordered his drink.

'Richard, thank you,' Karen said incredulously, 'you have no idea just how much this means to me!'

'I think I do,' Richard said quietly and got up to order his coffee. Karen sat and watched as Richard joined the short queue to order his coffee and she felt such love and warmth towards him that she hadn't felt in a long time. She had of course felt incredibly guilty about cheating on him and causing him pain but he had been so cold and distant towards her that she had lost affection for him. She even wondered if she had ever really loved him because the only emotion she had was a compassion that she would have felt for anyone that was hurting. Suddenly however she felt differently, some of the old feelings for him began to resurface while he was talking. She still couldn't believe he was going to let Grace and Amelia stay with her. His kindness had touched her soul more deeply than he would ever know. She now knew that he cared about how she felt and demonstrated it with sacrifice for himself. That was something that she hadn't really seen him do before and she would never forget it. Richard had always been especially sweet and protective in so many ways but more for her physical welfare rather than for her emotional wellbeing. *Boy had he come a long way!* She pinched herself to make sure she wasn't dreaming. This was an answer to prayer. She immediately thought about Granny Rose and knew that she was going to be the first person she would ring. She also knew that she owed a lot to Eva. Beautiful caring Eva who had always been there for her and had never judged her and yet she had every reason to. She knew that she had to go and thank her personally.

Richard strolled back with a tray carrying two cups, a fresh latte for Karen and a coffee for him. *This feels surreal!* She thought. *We're sitting here as though nothing has changed, as if we we're still married. What is happening?*

They talked about the practicalities of the arrangements for their individual time with the girls going forward. He acknowledged that he had been unreasonable not allowing her to come to the house but he wanted to change that now. He wanted the girls to see them interacting as parents and getting along. Karen couldn't believe the change in Richard. He was just so reasonable. The time flew! They were about an hour and a half into their time together when Karen said she had to go as she needed to be with Jake.

'Thanks Richard. It means everything to me and I will never forget this,' Karen smiled as she looked into his eyes.

Richard smiled, 'it's okay, now go and be with... Jake.'

'Goodbye Richard,' she rose from her chair, touched his shoulder and left. He'd mentioned Jake's name so many times during their conversation. He had told her how he felt so she knew that must have been so difficult for him. That showed a level of acceptance that was surprising to say the least.

Richard sat for a while after Karen left. He felt better for telling Karen what he had decided and recalled the joy that seemed to radiate from her and then seeing visible relief in her face when she realised that she could keep the girls. She looked truly happy. *She just wants the freedom to be who she wants to be. She just wants to care for her children and be a good mum.* He thought. It felt good knowing that he had brightened up her day. It meant a lot to him. He sat staring into space rooted to his chair unaware of how long he'd been sitting there when tears rolled down his cheeks. He had no idea where this emotion that had been buried for so long came from. He bent his head and sobbed quietly. It was such a release. He couldn't remember the last time he had cried.

Karen returned home on a high. What a day? She spoke to Granny Rose as she walked to her car after leaving Richard. She could feel the happiness and elation that her Gran had for her even down the phone. It was truly an answer to prayer she said. Karen completely agreed and promised to go to church with her the following Sunday. Granny Rose had said to her that she mustn't make a promise unless she knew she was going to keep it. She had said it with a smile on her face that Karen obviously couldn't see but could feel.

'I will Gran, I will come, you'll see, I promise,' she said.

It had been an emotional couple of hours. As she walked in the house, it was quiet. Both the girls were in bed but Marina was sat holding Jake who was wide awake. She swept him up out of her mums' arms and hugged him so closely.

When she told her mum about the meeting with Richard and how well it went, Marina could scarcely believe what she heard. She breathed a sigh of relief. This was indeed good news. Mother, daughter and baby Jake hugged for the longest time.

Chapter 61

Karen put her hand on the knocker of the familiar door. She raised it and knocked it a couple times. As she stood waiting for the door to open, she remembered the many happy times she and Richard had spent here. There had been many contented evenings enjoyed before they got married and even after they were married before the children came along. Eva opened the door to a beaming Karen.

'I think I know why you're here,' Eva didn't finish her sentence before Karen flung herself at her and gave her the tightest hug she had ever had. They stood on the front doorstep locked in an embrace as they rocked back and forth.

'I will never forget what you've done for me Eva, never!' Karen said.

'Come in and sit down Karen,' Eva gestured towards the lounge.

'I mean it you have done something for me that is worth so much more than anything in this world. You've not only been the best mother-in-law I could have ever wished for, but you have been a friend too. You never judged me and you were always honest and fair. I don't deserve you and I will spend the rest of my life doing whatever I can for you.'

'Steady on Karen, you might live to regret that,' she said with a wry smile on her face.

'I don't mind, you've been like a second mum to me. I'll do anything for you. I don't know many mothers-in-law that would have be as gracious as you. I hope that I can be that kind of mother-in-law to my kids' partners,' Karen's face grew serious, 'I'm truly sorry Eva for hurting Richard. I never intended to. It wasn't planned. I was in a bad place and it's no excuse I know. And I know you don't need to know, but it only happened once. I regretted it immediately. Then of course Jake happened but I don't regret Jake, Eva. I never want to feel regret about my children. I want to feel pride. I'm not proud of the circumstances into which he was born but I'm proud of him, I'm not ashamed. I felt ashamed and guilty about Robin for so many reasons. It was years of those kinds of feelings that caused me to spiral downwards. I can't live like that again and I don't want to either.' Karen said quite soberly and quietly. Eva nodded like she really understood. Then Karen's mood changed and her face lit up. 'Richard was amazing, I couldn't believe it. He said that he owes it all to you. It seems we all owe everything to you. You've saved our family Eva. I know Richard and I won't be a family again in the traditional way but we'll be a new "type of family" and that's good enough for me,' Karen said.

'It's not been easy believe me,' Eva paused, 'we've had so many disagreements. I was worried that I would lose Richard. I knew I had to go easy but in the end it was the girls that swung it. He loves them so much Karen, they mean everything to him.'

'I know they do and I will make sure that he sees them as often as he wants. He can have unlimited access,' she said with arms wide open to endorse her words and a smile on her face, 'they love and need him too.'

'I'm happy with that. Children need to be with their mother, especially girls. As much as I know Grace and Amelia love their dad and I would have helped as much as I could, it wouldn't have been a satisfactory life for them away from you. They would miss you and no amount of cinema trips, days out and restaurant meals would ever satisfy their longing for you. He would have been fighting a losing battle and he knew it deep down,' Eva concluded with a sigh. Karen had listened intently to Eva and now understood why Richard had had a change of heart. Everything she said made absolute sense. 'Well, I still haven't met Jake have I?' Eva said lightening the atmosphere.

'No, you haven't, you must come soon,' Karen agreed.

'I do want to see him so yes I will definitely come soon.'

Karen smiled at Eva and just felt incredibly blessed and happy. Eva wanted to meet Jake. It meant so much to her. 'Thank you Eva,' she said sincerely. Karen then stood up, 'Eva, I must go.'

'But you haven't had anything to drink or even a piece of cake. Do you want to take some with you?'

'Yes please,' Karen said. Eva made terrific cakes and she could never resist.

Eva went into the kitchen and cut a large slice of a beautifully moist lemon drizzle cake and wrapped it in foil before handing it to Karen.

'Bye Eva, I love you and see you soon.'

'Take care of yourself Karen, see you very soon,' Eva closed the front door after Karen left and leant back on it briefly and thought I must phone Richard.

As Karen drove home, she reflected and was greatly humbled that Eva chose to believe in her and who she was. She hadn't judged her. She looked at both sides and more importantly she relied on what she knew about Karen. She wasn't influenced by others but trusted her own instincts and acknowledged that most people would let someone down at some point in their lives as she had failed with Richard when his dad died. Eva never hid the fact that she didn't handle things well and through her own experience she had a real understanding of human failings. Karen felt privileged to have her in her life.

Chapter 62

In the weeks after their chat a wonderful period followed for Karen and Richard which found them communicating and working together for the first time since their split. Richard allowed Karen to drop the girls off at the house and even invited her in and encouraged her to stay a while and sit and play with Grace and Amelia, maybe watch a bit of TV or play a game with them. He said he wanted the children to see them both together acting normally. Karen kept pinching herself. She couldn't quite believe if this was a dream that she was going to wake up from. She would watch his face whenever the girls mentioned Jake, which was often, and inside she would cringe because she could see that it was difficult for him to handle but she was grateful that he was trying to put his own feelings aside for the sake of the girls. This was certainly a side to Richard that she had not seen before. He was changing right before her eyes. He seemed to have put everything behind him. He was different, she could feel it. She knew that he was still dealing with the pain of everything that had happened but he didn't just blame her, like before, he accepted that he had played a part in the demise of their relationship.

What Karen didn't know was what Richard truly felt. What she saw was kindness and she was immensely thankful for it but she didn't know how much he mourned the loss of their marriage. He had truly loved Karen, still did and the thought of her loving Pete hurt him to the core. He loved Karen and missed her deeply. He wanted his family back together. It was when she had gone that he realised just what an authentic sensitive person she was. They had been a unit along with their two beautiful daughters. He didn't have his dad growing up and he didn't want that for his children. His own dad had tragically died but he wasn't dead. He was still very much alive and wanted his children with him every day. *Why had he not realised just how unhappy Karen was?* He was annoyed with himself for trying to heap even more pain trying to gain full custody of the girls. It wouldn't have been fair to the girls and his mum had really made him realise just how selfish he had been. He now knew he had to come to terms with life as it had become and make the most of it. His beautiful family that he had created would never be the same and he knew deep down that he had contributed to losing it. It hadn't been easy to admit that. How he wished that Karen and the girls were with him again and that they could go back to how they were. Then he thought about Jake and felt slightly guilty for wishing an innocent baby away. Even though Jake could never replace Robin, he realised that Jake had filled a space in Karen's heart. She seemed whole. This new Karen was stronger and self assured and he liked and admired her. *If he forgave Karen and asked her back would he be able to treat Jake like his own? Would he ever be able to accept Jake?* He wasn't sure of the answer. He seesawed back and forth on that one.

He remembered reading a book many years ago about feeling the fear and doing it anyway. He did not like feeling unsure of anything. He always prided himself on knowing exactly what to do. Feelings never ever came into any decision as far as he was concerned. You looked at the problem and came up with the solution. If there was more than one way to tackle something, you looked at the pros and cons. How you felt never came into it. *What did feelings have to do with anything?* A logical conclusion was all that was needed but now he had to face this 'new person' that he had become. One who listened and analysed how he felt and realised that he needed to do that. He had spent most of his life ignoring how he felt. He had learnt very effectively all those years ago not to take any notice of feelings. Now he was listening to his feelings. He was trying to picture every possible scenario about the future if he and Karen were to get back together.

Chapter 63

Pete was becoming a constant source of concern for Karen. He had been a couple times recently to see Jake but he just hadn't been his usual self. In fact, he was a shadow of his former self. The self confident, carefree person she knew had been replaced by an indecisive individual she didn't recognise who now not only lacked confidence but his spirit seemed broken too. Karen felt sad about that. Even Jake seemed to sense it. Every time Pete picked him up he cried which seemed to affect Pete even more which just created a cycle of no confidence for both of them. The bond that had been forming before Pete had his breakdown now seemed non-existent. Karen became increasingly apprehensive about a future with Pete and wondered whether it was a realistic or even sensible proposition. Pete however seemed to think that it was still going to happen and that all he needed to do was to convince Vanessa. That however was the problem he still needed to persuade Vanessa. Nonetheless from what Karen could see, he needed more than persuasion because she did not want to let him go. Or maybe she couldn't let him go. Karen wasn't sure which. From the many conversations with Pete, she concluded that they were two people who were hugely co-dependent upon each other. She analysed that Pete and Vanessa's relationship was not a particularly healthy one, it seemed to be that they needed each other as much as they loved one another. Pete had let Vanessa down badly in so many ways yet she still wanted to be with him. She didn't seem to have the strength to go it alone and more importantly she didn't seem to value herself. She had had to deal with the shock and the knowledge of finding out that her husband had a son before he had even met her and had kept the knowledge of it from her for all those years and then accept another son that he had fathered within their marriage while she was mourning her own inability to produce a child. From Karen's viewpoint that was a lot to deal with and was puzzled that Vanessa still seemed to want to hang on to their marriage but the more she thought about it, it became increasingly evident to Karen that any split would be extremely traumatic for both of them. Vanessa was hard on herself about her infertility and seemed to allow it to overshadow everything. It had brought on deep sadness which seemed to have stripped her self esteem. Low self esteem was something Karen identified with only too well. *Poor Vanessa!* She thought. Karen started to feel guilty that she had played a part in causing her so much pain. If Pete left her now it could really break her. *How could she and Pete cause her more agony?* It would be heartless.

Karen knew she was 'in the middle' of a marriage that she had no right to be in. Here was a couple that had been together a decade through good times and bad. *Could Pete ever truly commit to her?* She knew he loved Jake and yes she knew he loved her too. *But how much of him would she really have?* As hard as it was to admit, she knew that Pete loved Vanessa too. Karen didn't blame him. She understood that it was easy to love two people even though she believed that there was usually only ever one person in life that 'truly stole your heart', but of course it was possible to love two people at the same time. Karen reasoned that hearts are full of love to give to our family and friends and romantic love was no different with varying degrees and depths of emotion. The question was whether you were prepared to sacrifice everything for true love and risk the happiness of others to do it? *Would his guilt of hurting Vanessa tarnish their happiness in the future?* Karen feared that it would. There really had been a lot of 'water under the bridge' for her and Pete. It was clear to Karen that his own guilt about the pain he had caused to her first time around, and to Vanessa, not to mention how he had let Robin down and now potentially Jake, had contributed to his failure to even forgive himself and was at the centre of his struggles with his own mental health. It would take a long time for him to heal. *Do people ever really heal or recover when they have so many regrets? Yes it's possible!* She answered her own question but she knew from her own life that it took time. *While all the children were so young and would need so much care and attention, was it fair for them to grow up possibly witnessing so much anguish from having Pete around them?* The formative years for children were so important and for them to suffer, to be a part of such a deep healing process, albeit unintentionally, would surely affect them for the rest of their lives. She knew only too well how hard it was when you blamed yourself. It was something she had struggled with throughout her own marriage to Richard. Her own lack of confidence and low self esteem could have affected Grace and Amelia. She was grateful that she saw it so clearly now. She didn't want them to be like her. She wanted them to be confident individuals who didn't struggle with self doubt all the time like she had. Living with regrets was hard but after talking to Grandma Rose, she realised that you can't change the past but you can make the right decisions for the future. Sensible choices did mean fewer regrets. She knew that life would always throw the unexpected but when it was glaringly obvious that something was a mistake, 'decide to listen to your head and not your heart' were Grandma's words. Karen knew that for the future her heart must not rule her head. She was determined not to let romantic notions lead the way like she had in the past. It was always short lived and was wrought with heartache. It was time to make a logical decision in this instance rather than being led by emotion.

Pete was mentally unstable right now. *Was it even possible to build a life on such a weak foundation? What kind of father could he be to Jake? What kind of stepfather could he be to the girls?* He would be with them full time if they all lived together as a family. The children needed stability. She needed security. Yes, the girls had Richard who she knew would be a solid permanence for them but if they were dealing with a stepfather whose emotions were unpredictable that wouldn't be good for them. Pete knew that Vanessa needed him and Karen recognised that in a strange way Pete needed Vanessa too. They were broken together and were strangely patient with each other because of it. None of them knew how to be strong because their relationship wasn't based on strength. They held each other up and were a crutch for each other. He felt an obligation to Vanessa and yes, even though, he didn't want to admit it, she knew he loved Vanessa.

Pete was definitely in a dilemma, Karen had observed it correctly. *How could he leave sweet Vanessa who had never done anything other than love him? How could you not love someone who had only ever been kind and totally forgiving?* One thing he did know was that it wasn't the same love that he had for Karen. Karen was incredibly special to him and he despised the person that he had been all those years ago. The arrogance he possessed thinking that it should have been easy for Karen to have a termination and believing that everything could have carried on as before. *How incredibly stupid and naive had he been? He had destroyed something so important and life changing.* Now faced with another life changing dilemma, he was torn between what he wanted to do and what he should do.

The more Karen thought about it the more she realised that Pete would probably be a better father to Jake from a distance. He could build his own bond in his own way. He could come and take Jake and spend time alone with him or he and Vanessa could spend time with him as a couple. He had mentioned that Vanessa had expressed a desire to be a part of Jake's life which convinced Karen even more that Vanessa was ready to forgive him and wanted to stay with him. In some ways Jake would have the very best of both parents with the addition of a step mother to love him too. *We were never meant to be together. We never stayed together when we got pregnant with Robin and we both belonged to other people when we became pregnant with Jake. It was an unrealistic dream.* She could see it clearly now. It had been sadness over Robin and their belief and hope of seeing him again that kept him alive in their hearts and made them think that they should be together but that was not the case anymore. They were trying to capture something that had long gone. Robin was no longer theirs he belonged to his new parents. Robin would be able to look for them when he was ready. They had found temporary solace in each other because of their shared history. Their love for each other was strong and always would be but what they had was for the past not the future. That was the mistake they had made and were in danger of continuing to make. The situation right now for three young children required commonsense decisions. Love on its own wasn't enough when raising children. She wanted her children to have the best of her and the best of their fathers.

Karen thought long and hard about what the future could hold and what it would potentially look like with Pete. There was a feeling inside that just didn't sit comfortably with that prospect. She knew then that she had reached a decision. She wanted to go it alone. Strangely having made her decision she felt happier, lighter even. She just needed to tell Pete now. Karen picked up her phone from the sofa and pondered for a minute and put it back down. She picked it back up again and found Pete's number.

'Hi Pete, how are you? How are you feeling today?'

'Karen,' she could hear the delight in his voice, 'I'm okay, not bad.'

'Are you still at home?'

'Yes.'

'When are you going back to work?'

'I've got another two weeks off and then I've got to go back and see the doc so he can assess me.'

'Pete, I'm so worried about you, can we talk? Let's meet. I'll ask my mum to keep Jake while we go for a coffee.'

'Okay,' Pete said.

'Let's meet on Saturday about 11ish. Does that suit you?' Karen asked.

'Yes it does. Don't worry about me Karen, I'll be fine. It won't be long before we'll be together. I love you.'

'I love you too. See you Saturday at the usual place.'

After the call ended, Karen let out a deep sigh of sadness with the recognition that the dream was over. *That's a good thing, isn't it?* She thought. *You have to wake up and 'smell the coffee' as they say.* She smiled to herself. Then her smile quickly turned to a frown as she pondered how she was going to tell him. She wasn't looking forward to having that conversation with Pete but she knew it had to be done. She couldn't put it off any longer. *Maybe Pete's mental health might improve if the pressure is off. We can't go on like this, something needs to change. It's unsettling for everyone. Even me!* She thought.

Chapter 64

The irony of the situation was that while things were breaking down with her and Pete, it was improving with her and Richard. Eva had been to see Jake and he loved her. *Who wouldn't love Eva?* She was the gentlest soul and Jake knew it too. It had been wonderful to see Eva and she looked really relaxed as she held him. It was evidence of Richard's acceptance of Jake.

Since Karen's meeting with Richard he had continued to encourage her to drop the girls off at their house on a Friday evening and stay awhile instead of him coming to collect them from her parent's front door and leaving with them. It had been working really well for the last few weeks. She had gone in and sat with the girls and Richard. It felt like she had never left. It felt a little strange but not particularly awkward, which surprised her. Richard was a changed man. One Friday evening when Marina was working late and she couldn't mind Jake, Richard came to collect Grace and Amelia instead. He knocked the door and Karen opened it. She ran back into the lounge as she was in the process of changing Jake and he was lying on the changing mat. Richard stood outside as usual but this time Karen beckoned him into the hallway. Richard stepped inside and the girls ran to him shouting, 'daddy daddy.' They threw their arms around his legs. Just at that minute, Jake started to cry and Karen picked him up to comfort him. Richard stood transfixed as Karen soothed Jake. It was as if time had stood still, he couldn't hear the girls talking to him or even feel the tugs to his hands.

'Is he okay?' Richard asked.

'Yeah, of course he is, he just doesn't like his nappy being changed. He'll be okay,' Karen said as she held him close to her chest. Richard watched her and admired Jake who had a mop of black hair. He looked like a handsome little chap. He observed how gentle she was with him and how confident she seemed too. That confidence had been missing when she was with him. He suddenly felt regret about how much he had lost. He had been robbed of the real Karen with his demands for a structure that suited him but no one else. *Why hadn't he just let her be 'her'? Why did he try to change this beautiful caring woman? It was utter madness.* He could see it so very clearly now but it was too late. So much had happened. Karen put Jake into the playpen and came back into the hall to hug and kiss the girls.

'Be good for daddy and I'll see you on Sunday,' Karen said.

'Can we kiss Jake mummy before we go?' Amelia asked.

Karen glanced quickly at Richard and he smiled and nodded in reassurance. Karen went and picked Jake up and held him down to the girls' level to kiss him and he gurgled happily from all the attention.

'He's a happy bunny now with all those kisses,' Richard commented, 'c'mon girls, let's go.'

'Bye mummy,' they said in unison. Richard opened the front door and they all left.

What the heck just happened there? Karen thought. She shook her head in disbelief. She was in complete shock. She felt like she was on another planet. *I need to get back to earth!* She smiled and reflected. She had so much respect for Richard. 'Right buster,' she said to Jake. 'Let's get you something to eat.' Karen had a contented beam on her face.

Saturday morning came and Karen woke up feeling confident. She gave Jake his breakfast and spent time preparing his bottles and food for his lunch so that Marina could just enjoy her time with Jake while she was out with Pete.

Karen and Pete hugged as they both arrived outside of the coffee house at the same time. Karen knew that she had to be strong in this situation, 'shall we walk before we have a coffee?' Pete suggested, 'I love being outside, maybe it's being cooped up these last few weeks.'

'Sure,' Karen replied, do you want to walk anywhere in particular?'

'Can we walk to the fountain?' He grabbed her hand and headed in that direction.

'Pete, we're not a couple yet, you've still got to consider Vanessa.'

Pete gently and slowly let go of her hand, 'I'm sorry, you're right. Sometimes I just want to forget.'

'You can't forget Pete,' she said softly, 'we've already hurt so many people. We can't twist the knife.' She looked at him as they walked. Pete's head slightly bowed. Karen knew she had to go carefully with Pete right now. He was still fragile and on the road to recovery but he had to know what she had decided. Maybe outside in the open without the confines of the coffee house was the best place to tell him. All around the fountain were iron benches strategically positioned to watch the mesmerising flow of water. There were a couple of empty benches. They wouldn't be empty for long once people came with their food and drink from the fast food restaurants nearby. They sat on the first empty bench they arrived at with some space between them as they both angled their bodies towards each other.

'Karen, why do I keep messing up and getting things wrong?' The pain on his face and the sadness in his eyes was so evident.

'Oh Pete, please don't do this to yourself. Believe me I've spent the whole of my adult life beating myself up. I understand so much more now. Things happen in life and we think we should have had more control or been strong enough to do things differently but sometimes it's not about that.'

'What do you mean?' Pete looked puzzled as he asked.

'Things happen in life for a reason and we don't always know why but they enable us to learn and grow as people. My grandma Rose has helped me so much. I'm not saying that mum and dad haven't helped me. They have done so much for me practically. I know that I will never be able to repay them and they have given me so much love and support but my Gran has helped me understand so much more about myself. She has a strong faith in God that mum and dad don't have. She's taught me that no one loves me like God does and that He doesn't judge me. He made me and knows my weaknesses. Through the trials and tests of life, I've become stronger. It's taught me humility and to have a greater understanding and compassion for others. We all make mistakes. We're human,' Karen smiled and let out a small laugh, 'I sound like a preacher don't I?'

'I hate myself right now Karen, how can God possibly love me?'

'That's exactly how I've felt over the years but Granny Rose has helped me put everything into perspective. She's been through a lot in her life and she's shared some deeply personal things that she has had to overcome and has come out of it so much stronger and better because of it. God doesn't hate us. The problem is that we hate ourselves and we're judging ourselves and so we think God is too but He isn't.' Pete sat perfectly still listening and looking into Karen's eyes as she spoke. 'Pete, listen to me it's time to release ourselves from this pain. I have my girls and Jake. You now have Jake. We can't raise children with guilt and self loathing, it will ultimately affect them. She took both his shoulders with her hands and held him firmly for a minute, 'are you hearing me Pete? Really hearing me?' He slowly nodded his head. She released her hands from his shoulders and heaved a sigh of relief, 'Pete, the burden of guilt and shame is too heavy for any of us to carry and it's time to put it down. We can Pete, we really can. We were young and frightened and we both made mistakes. None of us had the maturity to deal with an unplanned pregnancy. No one's to blame. More importantly I want you to know that I don't blame you. Not anymore anyway and I really mean that.'

'You don't?' Pete questioned with his eyes filling with tears.

'No, I don't,' Karen said with emphasis.

The tears flowed from both of them and they reached across to each other and hugged for what seemed forever and it didn't matter who saw them. It was a time of healing that they both needed at that moment. Eventually they released their hold from each other naturally and both felt calmer for it.

'I feel better,' Pete said with a smile.

'Good, so do I as it goes,' she replied with a smile too.

They both sat silently soaking up the peace that they both were experiencing.

'Pete, there's just one more thing I need to say.'

'Okay.'

'What we had and what we have is incredibly special and no one can ever take it away. We had Robin and now we have Jake. I know that Robin isn't with us physically but we hold him in our hearts, don't we?' Pete nodded again with watery eyes, 'we've been blessed to have Jake, he's ours and no one can take him away from us as long as we both remain strong and be good parents to him, he's ours for life,' Karen smiled brightly.

Pete smiled back, 'you're right, he's ours.'

Karen's face became serious, 'but his birth has caused pain to Vanessa and Richard and we must never forget that.'

'No, we mustn't,' he nodded in agreement.

'I've made a decision that I believe will be in everyone's best interests. We need to sacrifice ourselves for the sake of others and the most important ones being the children,' Karen paused, 'I don't think you leaving Vanessa to come and live with me and the children will work. I fear that it may not even work in the long term,' Pete started to open his mouth to speak, 'just hear me out before you say anything. I've given this a lot of thought,' she touched his arm gently in reassurance. Karen then went on to explain to Pete that it wasn't fair on Vanessa. He had put her through enough and her mental health was not good, not to mention his own mental health that would possibly continue to be affected with the guilt of what he had done to her. This in turn would not be good for Jake or the girls. Plus she still had to consider Richard's feelings. All of that aside, she didn't think that they were getting together for the right reasons. She had not been in a good place when they had met secretly and conceived Jake. But now she felt better since leaving Richard. The time spent with her parents had given her the arena she needed to find out more about who she was and what she wanted and for the first time in her life, she had been able to think clearly. She would be forever grateful to Richard for dropping the custody case and he deserved something back from her. She reminded him that Vanessa had forgiven him for all the hurt he had inflicted and despite all that she wanted to share in Jake's life. The pain of the past for all concerned can't be changed she explained but she had no desire to continue to hurt people. Pete wouldn't have the pressure of living with stepchildren and Richard wouldn't have to deal with seeing Pete or trying to avoid Pete whenever he wanted to see Grace and Amelia. Vanessa would have Pete and get to keep her marriage, which she was clinging onto for dear life anyway. She also pointed out that her relationship with Eva was special not just because she was the girls' grandmother, but she was also a friend who had stood by her and never judged her. She didn't want to compromise every other relationship that was precious to her so that she and Pete could make a life together that was fraught with problems and hurdles from the start. It simply wasn't worth it. 'I know that sounds hard but that's the reality.' She said gently. She then went on to expound how she felt and why this decision had to be made. More than anything she wanted time alone to get to know more of who she was and become the kind of mother to Grace, Amelia and Jake that she regretted not being to Robin. Plus the girls and Jake would have the love of all the adults in their lives without angst and trauma. She knew that she would never have the chance again with Robin and she had reconciled that now and she was determined not to beat herself up anymore. As grandma Rose said everything happens for a reason and we could possibly live our whole lives and never know why so looking for answers was futile. We just have to get on with life and make the most of and appreciate the good bits. She had been blessed to have had her children and she was truly satisfied with where she was right now. And although they loved each other, love really wasn't enough in these circumstances.

Pete had sat and listened quietly without interruption as she had requested, 'you really have thought this whole thing through, haven't you?'

'Pete, I don't expect you to say anything right now. I've thrown a lot at you. You need time to take it all in and process your own emotions; whatever you're feeling be it anger, sadness, whatever?' Karen raised her hands to reinforce her words, 'I'll understand. You don't need to say anything here and now but please do let me know how you feel about my decision once you've had time to mull it over. It will affect you so don't be afraid to tell me what you're feeling or thinking. If it's one thing I've learnt, we have to be honest with the people we love. We need to know how the other feels even if we don't want to hear it.'

'I need to go now,' he leaned forward and his lips brushed her cheek. He stood up and left. Karen sat completely still and watched as he walked away with his head bent low and his hands in his pockets. She felt sad for Pete. *He had been through a lot but hadn't they all?* She was determined not to put Pete's feelings above her own. She couldn't carry anybody else's burden. It had taken a long time for her to realise that you couldn't please everyone. From past experience her efforts to please had pleased no one anyway. It was time to do what was right for Karen. This was not selfishness it was self care and although their lives at crossed and had created two beautiful boys, their journeys were different and it was the end of the road for them. She felt relieved.

'Pete,' Vanessa said as he walked in the door, 'I've been worried about you,' she ran to him and cradled him warmly.

Pete stroked her head and said 'I'm fine love.' They both stood perfectly still in the hallway just holding each other.

'I'm staying Ness, let's do this together.' They walked into the lounge locked in each other's arms.

The walk back home had given him plenty of time to think and although he didn't want to admit it, he felt relieved and released. Karen had done it again! She had set him free. And Vanessa was there for him too. He didn't deserve the love of these two very different but both incredibly special women.

Chapter 65

Richard and Eva sat talking in her sitting room. Eva had been surprised by the unexpected knock at the door. It was early evening and she had not been expecting anyone. She opened the door in anticipation of who it might be. It was Richard. He never ever just turned up. He always rang ahead. She made them both a cup of tea.

'What's wrong son?' Eva asked as she sat down.

'Do you think it could ever work between me and Karen again?' Richard asked.

Well she had not seen that coming that's for sure. 'What about Jake?' Eva questioned with a furrowed brow.

'I know, I've been thinking about it so much. Had I not rejected Robin, then possibly she wouldn't have had Jake.'

'Okay, not sure I understand where you're going with this,' Eva said with a slightly mystified look.

'It was my fault that things went the way they did. I can see that now,' Richard stated simply.

'Richard please don't take all the blame, I'm not sure that's particularly healthy because we know that it's never just one person to blame in any relationship breakdown. Maybe blame can be apportioned but it will always be both parties,' Eva responded.

Richard was silent for while. Eva watched and waited for him to reply. 'I hear you and you're right. Jake's an innocent child and so was Robin. I just don't want to reject him,' Richard said.

Eva was so proud of Richard for coming to her and talking about how he was feeling and what he wanted, 'Jake is not Robin. Their births are two different periods in time. Don't confuse or compare them. Richard, listen to me, I would support you all the way if you want to get back with Karen, but don't make any assumptions. You don't know what her plans are. I know she's with her parents right now and Jake's dad is still with his wife but you need to be sure that they haven't made plans for the future.'

'He can't offer her what she needs. I know this is going to sound arrogant mum but I'm not sure she loves him. I think it was all about Robin. I could be wrong,' he shrugged, 'I love her mum. I've tried to hate her. I wish I could but I can't. If I hadn't been so demanding, I know I would still have her and the girls. She loved me mum, I know she did. I don't know how much anymore but how can we ever know how much anyone loves? All I know is I've lost someone I love and a good woman.'

'I know, but she has Jake now. If you couldn't deal with the knowledge of Robin from her past, how are you going to deal with the physical presence of Jake for the future every day? Jake will be a daily reminder of what happened. Could you handle that without feeling resentful towards Karen? It could even affect how you may treat Jake!' Eva presented so many scenarios and potential drawbacks. Richard and Eva talked for the longest time that Eva could remember. Richard never talked. This was definitely a new Richard and the breakup of his marriage and not having his children with him daily had really affected and changed him. She would not have wished this on him ever but she was now starting to see a more humble Richard. One that was willing to consider someone else's point of view and opinion.

When he stood up to leave and she walked him into the hallway and watched him get into his car from her doorway, she was a little worried about him. Nothing she had said had changed his mind. He just wanted Karen and the girls back, even if that meant having Jake. He said he was prepared and thought he could handle it. He wanted to give it a go.

Chapter 66

Richard rang Karen and said he was coming to see her. *He needed to strike while the iron was hot!* He needed to do it while he had the courage while he was optimistic without any fears or doubts to assuage him.

All the children were sleeping and this was normally her time to relax and unwind. She wondered what Richard wanted to see her about. Obviously it would be about the girls. She was just so pleased that their relationship was now amicable. She really liked him now and felt like the love she had lost was coming back. *How fickle was she?* She thought. *Do you love only when things are going good?* No, it was more than that, she knew that deep down. With everything that had happened she realised that she did love Richard because love is about understanding, care and respect. The door bell rang and her dad who was home having some time off opened the door and greeted Richard. She heard exchanges between them which were convivial. Cecil had not always found Richard easy to converse with but tonight the mood seemed different. Her mum and dad left them alone.

Karen offered him a drink and he refused. He wanted to get straight to the point. He apologised for not fully understanding her pain at losing Robin. He now had an understanding of that loss since he and Karen had split and he was no longer seeing the girls on a daily basis. She had had to deal with complete amputation and he now was able to empathise and see it from her perspective. *How cruel had he been?* Her heart had been breaking and he didn't know that he was breaking her. Karen listened without interruption. *This was what she had wanted back then. Why did it take for everything that had happened to happen for him to realise? Why had he not been able to see someone else's point of view? She was glad to hear it now, of course she was but it was too late! Why hadn't he been able to understand? It wasn't fair! It had been an incredibly hard experience that had shaped her for life.* As she sat listening to

Richard finally saying that he understood how she must have felt made her feel a little bit of anger towards him but it then very quickly went to pity for herself. Her feelings had been legitimate after all. *She hadn't just been on a self pitying road trip all these years.* Hearing it was almost too much to bear. She had worked hard over the last year to gain strength and self belief and she was in danger of losing it in a split second. *Stay strong! Stay strong! Stay strong?* She kept telling herself over and over as he talked. Richard could see that she was visibly affected. His words had given her the validation she needed. She started to cry uncontrollably. He went across to her and comforted her.

'Karen, I love you. Please forgive me for all the pain I caused you. I just piled it on. No wonder you were broken. I'm so sorry my darling. Can I ever make it up to you?'

'You have made it up to me Richard. You let me keep the girls. I have the greatest respect and love for you. After losing Robin, if I had lost the girls that would have broken me completely.'

'I'm so sorry Karen,' Richard said.

'It's okay, you don't need to keep saying sorry. I know how hard it was for you. Thank you. I will never forget it.'

'Are you still with Pete?' Richard asked out of the blue.

Stunned, Karen answered, 'no, why?'

'Karen is it too late for me and you?'

Without hesitation, she answered him, 'yes Richard, I think it is. I've got Jake now. Things can never go back to how they were. Too much has happened. Too much has changed,' Karen said simply.

'Couldn't we try? I think I could love Jake. He seems like a lovely boy. He's a cute little thing.'

'What happens when Pete comes to see him or collect him? What happens when he gets older and becomes a naughty boy and a sullen teenager? He's not going to stay a cuddly baby who doesn't answer back.'

'Karen, we could make it work. I know we could. We could at least try.'

'There lies the problem Richard. We could try and what happens if you can't handle it, then it's another split all over again and more disruption for the girls. No I can't take that risk not for the girls or for me,' Richard sighed, 'listen Richard, there's way too much water under the bridge, too many hurdles to jump and a very high mountain to climb. I'm not sure I've got the strength for it. I want to give the children all of me, not just some of me. And not only that, I need to finish this journey alone. I know it sounds corny but I need to find me. I've been searching for Karen for a long time now and I think I've finally found a bit of her. There's still more of her to find and that's going to take time and being in a relationship wouldn't be fair on you. At first my search was about Robin but he's not mine anymore and I accept that now. Now I know my search is about me. I don't want to rely on anyone. Self preservation is crucial right now. I've told Pete the same thing if that makes you feel any better. I hope we can carry on as we are co-parenting the girls and giving them the best of ourselves even if we're not together.'

'Of course we can, you've taught me so much about parenting, and about me. We can do it. I know what it's like to not have a dad and I want my girls to have as much of me as possible. I'll never let them down.'

As Richard opened the front door to leave, he turned and said, 'be happy special lady, you deserve it.'

The next day Karen picked up the phone and made a call.

'Gran, guess what?'

'What is it child?' Granny Rose replied.

'I'm happy Gran for the first time in a long time,' Karen said.

'I think I know who we've got to thank for that. God has answered my prayers,' Granny Rose looked upwards with a smile as she responded.

Karen sat still for a while after the call ended and reflected on everything that had happened in her life. She had been through a lot and parts of the journey had been tough but through the challenges, she had learnt so much. And there was still more of life to live and she was determined to realise her value. No more comparisons with anyone. She was good enough. This was a new day and a new start. She had finally found the courage to be Karen. She would continue on her journey to freedom.